THE CULT

THE DEIFORM FELLOWSHIP TWO

SARAH ETTRITCH

NORN PUBLISHING
TORONTO, CANADA

Copyright © 2013 Sarah Ettritch

All rights reserved. No part of this book may be reproduced,
except for brief quotations in articles or reviews,
without written permission from the author.

This is a work of fiction. Names, characters, places, and incidents are the
product of the author's imagination or are used fictitiously, and any resem-
blance to actual persons, living or dead, business establishments, events, or
locales is entirely coincidental.

Library and Archives Canada Cataloguing in Publication

Ettritch, Sarah, 1963–, author
The cult : the deiform fellowship two / Sarah Ettritch.

ISBN 978-1-927369-13-5 (pbk.)

I. Title.

PS8609.T87C84 2013   C813'.6   C2013-906372-2

v1

Published by Norn Publishing
www.NornPublishing.com

For Kath and Jim

Acknowledgements

My thanks to Debbie Stevens (my good friend and fantastic beta reader) and Marg Gilks (my fabulous editor).

Chapter One

WITH A SATCHEL slung over her shoulder, Jillian strode along the sidewalk toward the courthouse, her skin crawling. She scanned her surroundings, searching for a Beguiler, even though she knew it was nerves. With a gaggle of reporters standing on the courthouse steps, smiling into cameras as they breathlessly delivered live reports to their newsrooms, she wasn't about to be kidnapped or killed. If they came for her, it would be on a quiet country road, in a dark alley, or someplace to which they'd lured her. Not here, though she wouldn't be surprised if they were watching her. For the past three weeks, she'd spent her weekdays at the same location.

One of the newspaper columnists waiting on the steps smiled at Jillian. "It's going to seem weird, not showing up here tomorrow." She grimaced. "Unfortunately, I think the bastard's going to walk."

"You think the jury will return the verdict today?" Jillian asked, resisting the urge to duck her head so she wouldn't be caught on camera. Wearing a blonde wig because she'd only been "dead" for four months, and being over a thousand kilometres away from the city she'd called home, it was unlikely she'd be recognized. *Over a thousand kilometres away from Mom and Danny.* She was suddenly aware of the phone on her belt. Would the compulsion to call subside, or would she still be fighting it in twenty years?

"They've been at it for two days. Damn, I wish that cop had done his job correctly. You'd think they—" The columnist's phone rang. She peered at it. "Sorry, I have to take this."

Jillian nodded, pulled out her own phone, and pretended to read while she listened to the reporters chattering around her.

"... tried for the rape and murder of five girls. The jury is entering its third day of deliberations ..."

". . . maintained his innocence from the moment of his arrest, and legal experts are predicting that the jury will agree with him. What the jury doesn't know, Carol, is that journals, photographs, and video were ruled inadmissible by the judge due to an improperly executed warrant."

"The city's Catholic community was relieved and gratified when police arrested Taylor, but now it might be plunged into terror again. If Taylor is acquitted, students, parents, and teachers will once again live in fear. They'll know for sure that the psychopath who's raped and killed five Catholic schoolchildren is still out there . . ."

". . . psychiatrists say that Taylor will likely offend again . . . Yes, Don, that's true. Some *are* speculating that Taylor will leave the city . . ."

"We can go in," someone shouted.

Jillian lowered her phone and joined the line shuffling into the courthouse. At the security checkpoint, she flashed her Press ID that identified her as a reporter for an online Catholic publication. As her satchel passed through the x-ray machine, she walked through the metal detector, then lifted her arms when a guard approached to swipe her with a handheld detector. Yep, they were checking everyone twice. Too many people were out for Taylor's blood.

She claimed a seat in the press room and settled in for what could potentially be a long day. Within ten minutes, every chair was occupied. Any reporter who missed the verdict would probably be fired. Only the TV reporters who had to deliver live updates to their newsrooms remained outside. They'd have arranged to have seats in the gallery reserved for them.

Jillian pulled a tablet from her satchel and killed time by watching a whodunit movie, aware of two reporters peering over her shoulder, and not minding at all. Fortunately for them, the movie finished before the jury reached a verdict. Jillian checked her watch and inwardly sighed. Another hour before lunch, when she'd take her chances and visit the washroom. Should she start another movie? Maybe an hour-long documentary?

"The jury is coming back!" someone yelled from the doorway, to electrifying effect. Everyone was on their feet and hastily gathering their things. Jillian grabbed her satchel and joined the queue to leave the room. "When?" a reporter barked to the guard in the corridor.

"Half an hour," the guard growled.

His answer didn't discourage anyone from grabbing a seat in the press gallery. "Finally," the TV reporter who plunked down next to Jillian murmured. Spectators from the general public streamed into the courtroom. Several women set her teeth on edge. Taylor's fan club. She'd never understand women who were attracted to monsters. Everyone—except the freaking jury—knew beyond a shadow of a doubt that Taylor had raped and murdered those children. Jesus, were they that desperate?

The first of the families arrived. To strengthen her resolve, Jillian made a point of watching them as they shambled down the aisle and went to the places they'd occupied for the entire horrific trial. The pale parents, so fragile and exhausted, still bewildered and lost, as if they couldn't believe it had actually happened. The older brother, who always sat with his head down and rocked. The single mother who'd lost her only child entered the courtroom next; she'd often wept while listening to the testimonies. On her heels was the grandmother. The judge had cautioned her twice not to shout during the trial. How would she react if Taylor was found not guilty? How would the rest of the families now entering the courtroom react?

The lawyers took their positions. The jury filed in. Everyone looked to where Taylor would make his entrance. The door swung open. A frisson of excitement competed with an undercurrent of disgust and loathing. The arrogant bastard swaggered in and nodded to his defence team. The psychiatrists were right. If the prick got off, he'd leave town, lie low for a while, then begin a new reign of terror. And the families here in the courtroom? No justice. No closure. Just relentless pain.

"All rise."

Judge Connelly entered, probably wishing that, just this once, he could have thrown the law book out the window and allowed Taylor's meticulous chronicles of his crimes to stand. What had run through his mind when he'd instructed the jury that they must acquit if they had a reasonable doubt about Taylor's guilt?

Connelly rapped his gavel. "This court is in session. I remind those present to refrain from using your phones within the courtroom." He turned to the jury. "Have you reached your verdicts?"

"Yes, your honour," the jury forewoman said.

"For the charge of the first degree murder of Elizabeth Mary Clark, how do you find the defendant? Guilty or not guilty?"

"Not guilty."

A collective gasp rose from the courtroom. "You animal!" the grandmother shouted. From the other side of the courtroom rose a heart-wrenching sob. Jillian's stomach knotted.

"I would remind those present that outbursts will not be tolerated." Connelly said, gazing in the direction of the grandmother. "For the charge of the first degree murder of Cynthia Rose Matthews, how do you find the defendant? Guilty or not guilty?"

"Not guilty," the forewoman said, over the sounds of weeping.

The grandmother leaped to her feet. "This isn't justice! This is a travesty! That animal shouldn't be allowed to live."

Connelly nodded to two guards. As they approached the grandmother, she marched into the aisle and pointed at Taylor. "Hell isn't good enough for you, you piece of shit! You're a goddamned waste of space!" The guards grasped her arms. Having said her piece, she didn't protest when they escorted her from the courtroom.

Connelly waited for the whispers to die, then asked the forewoman for the verdict on the next first degree murder charge. Not guilty. The same verdict was delivered for every first degree murder, sexual assault, and lesser charge.

The moment the judge said to Taylor, "You're free to go," guards formed a protective barrier around him and everyone in the press gallery practically climbed over each other to get outside and deliver the news. Jillian followed the crowd, and wasn't surprised to see that a podium had already been set up on the courthouse steps. Taylor wouldn't pass up the chance to rub everyone's noses in it.

At the base of the steps, she sucked down a deep breath, then pulled out her phone and dialed a number.

"Yes," a voice barked.

"Not guilty, on all charges," Jillian said.

"Repeat."

"Not guilty. It's a go."

"Understood." The line went dead.

She slipped the phone back into its holder and waited for the triumphant defence team and its client to emerge.

". . . found Taylor not guilty of all charges. One has to wonder, Carol, how the jury will feel when they find out about what they weren't allowed to see."

". . . will probably lie low for a while. Police can try to keep an eye on him, but they could be accused of harassment if they crowd him too much, and many are questioning whether the police can do anything at all. With overstretched budgets . . ."

". . . spoke to a mother earlier today who said she'll consider home-schooling her children if Taylor is exonerated. But two of the victims were snatched from the mall. Nowhere is safe. The principal of Holy—here come Taylor and his defence team."

Cameras swung in the direction of the podium; reporters crowded around it and held out their microphones and recorders. Jillian hung back, not so far that she'd draw attention to herself, but enough that she wouldn't have to elbow through too many people to make it to the sidewalk. She pulled out her phone. The defence team and Taylor clustered behind the podium. As the lead defence attorney said the usual—great day for justice; Mr. Taylor, who'd always proclaimed his innocence, vindicated—Jillian watched Taylor, who couldn't contain his smirk. She pretended to tap notes into her phone and focused on breathing evenly.

When the attorney finished speaking, a few reporters asked questions, but most called for Taylor to say a few words. Jillian's muscles were so tight, she could hardly breathe. Any moment now . . .

"That monster shouldn't be allowed to speak," a heckler shouted.

But Taylor was determined to grab the spotlight. The attorney stepped back. Taylor moved to the podium and nodded. "Ladies and gentlemen, I—"

A shot rang out. Taylor crumpled to the ground. A moment of stunned, confused silence, then a scream pierced the air. "Shooter!" a guard shouted. "Get down!"

Chaos erupted. Shrieks rose from every direction. Jillian whirled and joined the others racing to the sidewalk. A horn blared when someone ran into the street, anxious to reach another building, any building. When a reporter stumbled in her high heels, another one grabbed her elbow and dragged her along. "Holy shit," someone blurted as he passed Jillian.

Jogging down the street, she glanced over her shoulder. The podium area had cleared. Not one person was with Taylor, neither protecting him nor performing CPR. The defence team's support of their inno-cent client apparently ended at risking their own lives. If it was anyone else, perhaps the guards or the police would have dragged him out of the line of fire, but nope. One reaped what one sowed.

She rounded the corner and headed for the gray sedan parked halfway down the block. Two men ran past her. Focused on saving themselves, they wouldn't notice the reporter from the online Catholic publication climbing into a sedan and disappearing. Jillian yanked the door open, dropped into the passenger seat, and pulled the door shut. Sam hit the accelerator and merged into traffic. Two blocks away, she slowed and pulled to the right at the sound of an approaching siren. A police car sped past, its lights flashing.

As they resumed their journey, Jillian slowly exhaled. "Roberta was right, he couldn't resist talking to the press. He's down. Warren took his time, though."

"He needed a clear shot. The last thing he wanted to do was hit someone else." Sam turned on the radio and tuned in to a news station.

". . . clearing the area. Again, John Taylor has been shot. That's all we know at this time. We'll keep you up to date with this developing story. Now, over to Todd for the latest traffic report . . ."

"I hope Warren will be okay," Jillian said when another police car raced by.

"He'll be fine." Sam drove onto the on-ramp for the highway and headed away from the safe house, reminding Jillian that they were returning to the island.

Mission accomplished. Time to go home.

AS SOON AS Jillian entered the conference room, her eyes went to the newscast on the large monitor.

"Good work," Roberta murmured from the table before calmly sipping her coffee.

Sam pulled out a chair across from Roberta. "Is Warren away?"

"Yes. By the time they figured out where the shooter must have been, he was long gone." Roberta shifted her attention to Jillian. "You did well."

Sitting next to Sam, Jillian snorted. "I didn't do anything. I sat in court for three weeks and called Warren." While Sam had played babysitter. She'd probably hated every minute of it, but Jillian wasn't fully trained.

"You left the island, which I know can be nerve-wracking the first few times. You confirmed the verdict."

"That was all over the TV and radio news stations thirty seconds after we left the courtroom."

"We wanted to hear it from one of us. We had to be sure. You made the call."

Yeah, she'd essentially sealed the man's fate, not that she felt guilty. They were certain that Taylor had committed the crimes of which he'd stood accused—and more. There was no way she could have stood by and watched that monster leave the courthouse, free to prey on more young victims. "I'm glad Warren's safe. Maybe we shouldn't have practically shot Taylor on live TV, though."

"We didn't want to lose him." Roberta jutted her chin toward the monitor. "Now nobody will have to lie awake at night wondering if he changed his name, where he is, if their daughter is safe."

"I didn't use any of the gifts," Jillian said, still regarding her contribution as meagre.

"You don't always need to. But Taylor is no longer our problem." Roberta pressed a button on the control panel in front of her. The monitor went black.

"What's next?" Sam asked.

"For now, focus on continuing Jillian's training."

"I'll meet you in the library in fifteen minutes." Sam pushed back her chair.

"Sure," Jillian mumbled, not surprised at Sam's eagerness. The sooner she was trained, the sooner Sam would be rid of her.

Chapter Two

Two weeks later, Jillian hopped from one foot to the other and shook out her hands and arms. Anyone watching her would think she was warming up for a marathon. She wished she was; running one had to be easier than whatever Sam had in store for her. Why the basement? So far, she'd trained in the library. "It's physical," Sam had muttered when Jillian asked. She eyed the large mat on the floor and wished Sam would come down, already. Every passing minute increased Jillian's apprehension. Loosening up wasn't helping, and considering that she had no idea what she was about to learn, it could be unnecessary.

Sam and the other Deiforms she'd met described using the gifts as surrendering oneself and connecting to Him. Since Jillian didn't believe in God, she'd taken the view that the gifts were within her; it was simply—ha!—a matter of learning how to draw on them. Rather than "connecting to Him," she'd "find her centre." Instead of constantly butting heads over phrasing, regarding this and other concepts, Sam and the others had accepted her chosen terms and she accepted theirs, though what they really thought about her atheism, she didn't know. Perhaps they'd snickered behind her back when she'd turned out to be a slow student.

When she'd begun her training, her skepticism had worked against her. It wasn't that she hadn't believed in the gifts—her time with Sam had shown her that Deiforms possessed powers that science couldn't explain. Accepting that *she*—Jillian Campbell—had been chosen by God to use the gifts as she worked on His behalf: different story. But after leaving behind her life and parents to join the Fellowship, she'd been determined to master the gifts, come hell or high water. Oh, how quickly that determination had faltered!

They'd started with telepathy. Day after day, Jillian had tried to speak telepathically to Sam, only to fail over and over and over again. After weeks of discussions, shouting, temper tantrums, and fantasies of murdering Sam, she wondered if she'd ever find her freaking centre. She was sick and tired of Sam telling her that all she had to do was accept that she was a Deiform. Couldn't she drink some type of psychedelic tea and have the Fellowship beat her with sticks until she entered a delirious state and achieved nirvana? It would be easier.

She'd never forget the afternoon she'd finally experienced her breakthrough. As she waited for Sam, she relived that glorious moment. They'd been in the library, Sam seated opposite her.

"You must believe first," Sam had said. "See it, then experience it."

Jillian nodded, then promptly discarded the information and fought the urge to punch Sam in the face. She'd never believed in visualization. Sit around in your dinky apartment imagining yourself driving a Porsche with money bags in the back seat, and voila! You're soon rolling in dough and have three Porsches sitting in your mansion's eight-car garage. Yeah, right.

"Relinquishing one's will, handing over control, isn't a weakness. It takes great strength." Sam paused. "I trust that it will happen, and it does."

Something clicked. Jillian had been trying to communicate telepathically with Sam through sheer force of will. Rather than trying to push out her thoughts, direct them at Sam's head, imagine a telephone wire between them, and all the other mental tricks she'd tried playing on herself to make it work, damn it, she'd assume that the gifts were only reachable at a subconscious level. Those gifts inside her had to be buried pretty deep; they'd gone unnoticed for 36 years. But not anymore. Awareness of the existence of her centre was the game changer. All she had to do was desire to communicate telepathically, and that deeper part of her would take care of the rest.

Desperate, mentally exhausted, and angry at herself, at Sam, at the freaking chair she was sitting in, she blew out a long, heartfelt sigh. *Okay, you damn, idiotic, moronic, pathetic excuse for a centre. I'm a freaking Deiform. I didn't leave Mom and Danny behind to play mind games with myself. I am freaking-well going to speak telepathically to Sam, and you're going to damn-well help me.* She closed her eyes, stilled her thoughts, and said, *"If you don't hear this, I think I'm going to kill myself."*

"It's a good thing I heard it, then."

Jillian's eyes flew open. An ice cube burning a hole through her hand would have shocked her less. "You heard that?"

Sam's mouth twitched. "I heard it."

Jillian didn't quite believe her. *"What's my name?"*

"Jillian."

"What colour is my t-shirt?"

"Blue."

"Where are we?"

"The library."

Jillian blinked at her. She wanted to laugh, she wanted to cry, she wanted to throw herself at Sam's feet and apologize for all the terrible names she'd silently called her, and the less offensive ones she'd said out loud.

After that, they'd continued with other gifts she'd seen Sam use: time shifting, rudimentary communication with animals, astral projection . . . she'd known those gifts were real before she'd tried to perform them. She'd worried that her skepticism would rear its ugly head again when she tried to learn gifts she hadn't witnessed, but that hadn't happened. So there was no need to be nervous.

She eyed the mat on the basement floor again. Whatever was coming would be a piece of cake, right?

Footsteps thumped down the stairs. Jillian took a deep breath and managed a small smile when Sam strode up to the mat. As usual, Sam was all business. "Let's get started. Stand in the middle of the mat."

"What are we doing?" Jillian asked as she did as Sam had instructed.

"I'm going to stop your heart."

"What?" As if protesting along with her, Jillian's heart raced. She raised her hands. "Wait a minute, wait a minute. What do you mean, you're going to stop my heart?"

"Exactly what I said."

Her throat tightened. She cleared it and swallowed. "You'd better explain exactly what you mean."

"I will. Calm down, okay?"

Feeling the shakes coming on, Jillian shoved her hands into her pockets.

"I'll stop your heart," Sam said. "You'll collapse onto the mat. In about fifteen to thirty seconds, your heart will beat again. There won't be any damage to it."

"Oh, well, now that you've explained it, sure!" Jillian shook her head. "No."

Sam heaved a sigh. "You need to learn gifts that will help you to defend yourself."

What about healing? She hadn't learned that one yet. Sam must be chomping at the bit to be rid of her student. Yep, teach Jillian what she'd need to fend off Beguilers, and then Sam could go back to working on her own. Jillian clenched her jaw, then consciously tried to relax, recognizing that fear was fueling her unjustified anger. She wanted to learn all the gifts, but this one . . . "You're asking me to stare death in the face. Maybe that wouldn't be a big deal for you. You believe you'll live on. For me, I'm facing the end. Curtains. Game over."

"You won't die."

Sam sounded so confident of that. Jillian pulled her hands from her pockets and paced the length of the mat, her apprehension crushing her chest. She forced down a couple of deep breaths, then stopped and whirled toward Sam. "Why do you have to do it to me? Shouldn't I be doing it?"

"To receive this gift, you have to experience it. You have to trust that He'll restart your heart."

"That's a problem for me."

Sam chewed her lip. "Trust like a child. Accept that you'll survive it, without understanding how. Don't question, just accept."

Just accept? Sure. She folded her arms. "Tell me again what will happen."

"I'll stop your heart," Sam said calmly. "Fifteen to thirty seconds later, it'll start again."

Jesus. That trust exercise of closing one's eyes and falling back into someone's arms had nothing on this. What if her heart didn't start? Okay, worst-case scenario, she *did* die, right here, today. Hadn't she already cheated death once? If not for Sam's gift of healing, she would have died the night they'd run into Lilibeth. So, did that mean she'd already had more life than she deserved, and so she shouldn't be upset at the prospect of dying in five minutes, or that she should trust that this heart-stopping gift would restart her heart, because a gift had already saved her life? "I suppose I trust in a lot of things without understanding how they work. I trust a lot of strangers too, no questions asked. For all I know, the guy at the pharmacy could be filling my prescription with cyanide pills. Every time you get on a plane . . . or even into a cab. Hell, crossing the street on a green light is an act of trust." *Stop babbling.* She could time shift and astral project. She believed Sam could stop her heart. If Sam said her heart would start again, she'd trust her. "Okay, let's do this," she said, ignoring the part of her that was screaming not to do it, that wanted to curl up into a fetal position and admit that joining the Fellowship had been a terrible mistake.

"Stand in the middle of the mat," Sam said, pointing. "I can't predict which way you'll fall."

Jillian tramped to the middle and faced Sam. Her heart thumped. Oh, god. "I'm trusting you," she said, not surprised by her quavering voice.

Sam met her eyes. "*I'm* trusting Him."

A surge of panic—Jillian opened her eyes and blinked in confusion at Sam's feet.

"Welcome back," Sam said.

She rolled over and pushed herself to a sitting position. "You did it?"

Sam nodded.

"Let me stand up," Jillian said, wanting a minute to collect herself. She felt fine, as if she'd awakened from a nap. "How long was I out?"

"About twenty seconds. You came around pretty quickly."

"Is it always like that?"

"Assuming the person doesn't land funny, yes. It'll give you an opportunity to run, nothing more. Now, think about your heart."

Jillian drew a deep breath and exhaled slowly, then focused on her heart—and sucked in her breath. It wasn't the heightened sense of her beating heart that frightened her. It was the knowledge, the certainty, that crippling that heart would be as easy as flicking a light switch to stop the electrical current. She didn't have to tell Sam that she now possessed the gift that could stop hearts; her reaction had made that clear.

"My turn on the mat," Sam said, shooing Jillian off. She stood where Jillian had stood. "Go ahead."

"What?"

"Stop my heart."

Terror strangled her. "No," Jillian whispered. *I'm trusting Him.* She couldn't do that! What if Sam fell and never got up again? Shit! She clenched her clammy hands together. "I don't think I can do this."

Sam frowned. "You received the gift."

"Okay, I won't do it. I can't. What if you heart doesn't start again? I can't. I just can't."

"You need to do it once, just to know for sure that you can."

Jillian gulped. "How can you be so calm about it, especially when it's me? How can you trust *me?*"

"I'm not trusting you, I'm trusting Him," Sam snapped. "I know He'll restart my heart. You'll have *nothing* to do with it."

"Sorry," Jillian mumbled, dismayed by Sam's angry tone. Sam had sometimes grown impatient with her during training, but she'd never lost her temper.

"Come on, Jillian. This gift could be a life-saver for you."

And could potentially kill its target. Not for the first time, she figured that if there was a God, He had a wicked sense of irony. Jillian squared her shoulders, gazed at Sam, and . . . "I can't do this."

"Come on, Jillian, you left everything, remember? Your mother, Danny, your life. For what? To die the first time you run into a Beguiler by yourself? That's what you want?"

"What's the problem?" a voice asked from the direction of the stairs. They both turned as Roberta strolled up to the mat and stopped next to Jillian.

Sam met Jillian's eyes. "Now that Roberta's here, do you think you can do it?"

Why, because she wouldn't be alone when Sam died? Shit. Shit, shit, shit!

"She's worried about stopping my heart," Sam said to Roberta, who merely nodded as if they were discussing the weather.

Roberta turned to Jillian and smiled reassuringly. "Don't worry, Sam will be all right." She moved away and clasped her hands behind her back. Jillian wondered if Roberta didn't want her white knuckles to show.

"Let's do it, Jillian," Sam said. "Come on. Don't wimp out."

Okay. Okay. Deep breath. She squared her shoulders and gazed at Sam. *God, Sam, how can you trust me to do this?* Not wanting to prolong the agony—hers or Sam's—Jillian shifted her focus to Sam's chest, thought about the heart beating inside it, and simply desired that heart to stop.

Sam toppled onto her side and lay still.

Jillian rounded the mat until she could see Sam's face. Sam's lips were bluish. Her chest was motionless. Shit. Shit, shit, shit! If Sam didn't survive, Jillian would never forgive herself. Her own heart raced; she dug her fingernails into her palms. She wanted to run to Sam and administer CPR.

How long had it been? It felt like a freaking hour. Jesus! Jillian glanced at Roberta, who hadn't moved. Was it because she was paralyzed with fear, as Jillian was? At least fifteen seconds must have gone by, right? Would Roberta think less of her if she went over and felt for a pulse? Her own heart felt as if it were leaping from her chest. *Come on, Sam. Please. Please, please, please.*

Sam groaned.

Jillian's knees almost gave out. Being the target of the gift didn't damage one's heart, but using it probably did!

Sam sat up and scratched her head. "Good. Another gift mastered."

"You're doing well," Roberta said.

Jillian marvelled at how casual they sounded. How was it that only the atheist in the room felt as if she'd just witnessed something mind-bogglingly phenomenal? Maybe they were holding back *because* there was an atheist in the room.

Sam was on her feet, looking as bright as a daisy. "I think that's enough for today. You did good. From what others have told me, it takes some Deiforms several days to try that one."

What? A minute ago she'd despaired that Sam wouldn't live; now she wanted to kill her.

Sam's eyes glinted. "I knew you'd have the guts to go for it today, though."

Jillian couldn't help but grin. "Sure you did," she said, forgiving her. "How long did it take you?"

"She didn't hesitate." Roberta stepped to Jillian's side and looked at Sam. "I'm glad you're finished for the day, because we have a situation we need to discuss." She turned to Jillian. "Both of you. We'll meet in the conference room in fifteen minutes."

Sam nodded at Roberta's receding back. "Let's roll up the mat."

Jillian went to one end and crouched. "Can't I stop someone's heart multiple times in a row, to keep them down?" she asked as she rolled the mat.

"Can you sense my heart now?" Sam asked.

Jillian reached out mentally. "No."

"You won't be able to for a while. On the up side, like all the gifts, the more you use this one, the easier and stronger it becomes. You can only stop one heart now, but in the future, you'll be able to stop two, three, a roomful. But it will take focus. If things are chaotic, you'll still only manage one or two."

"Why can't everyone use the gifts?" she blurted as she lifted one end of the rolled up mat and carried it with Sam over to the wall. "Stopping your heart was easy. So is time shifting and astral projection . . ." Using a gift was simply a matter of clearing one's mind, which she could now quickly do, and thinking about or desiring to leave her body, step outside time, push a concept or command to an animal, stop a heart . . .

They dropped the mat to the floor. Sam straightened. "That's what the first Deiforms thought. They figured it was a matter of recruiting and training. They soon discovered that wasn't the case. Everyone can have a relationship with God, but not everyone is called the way we are. Only other Deiforms can connect with Him in the way we can."

Jillian jumped on the opening Sam had handed her. "Who were the first Deiforms? How old is the Fellowship? How did the cells form?"

"Three siblings. Thousands of years old. Pretty much the same way the gospel spread," Sam replied, ticking off each answer on her fingers. "I think that covers all your questions." A smile played on her lips. "There's a book that covers the Fellowship's early history. I don't know if Roberta told you this, but the Guide is also the Chronicler. Roberta records everything we do. This cell's first Guide also wrote down everything he'd been taught about the Fellowship's origins."

Jillian's mouth dropped open. "You only thought to mention these books now?" She winced at her shrill voice. "How many times have I asked you about the Fellowship?" She'd drawn the three questions she'd just asked from hundreds that begged for answers. Sam had always brushed her questions aside, promising that she'd get her answers later. "Later" had apparently arrived.

Sam held up her hands. "I wanted you to focus on your training."

"I want to read the books."

"You will. In fact, our history is required reading." When Jillian drew breath, Sam quickly continued. "There are two parts to your training. We like to start with learning how to use the gifts, so you can go back into the world and defend yourself. The second part is to learn about the Fellowship itself."

Bring it on! Normally she wouldn't join a group blind, especially one you could never leave. But though Sam would say that those who joined the Fellowship came willingly, Jillian believed it was more a matter of accepting one's fate. The choice wasn't whether to join; it was whether to accept that one *had* to join—a subtle but important difference. The first was a true choice; the second was an acknowledgement that the choice had already been made. Sam would say by God; Jillian would say by fate, or life, or by her biochemistry or genome, or through a means nobody could explain—yet. Her initial encounter with the Fellowship had spun her world out of control, almost landed her in prison for two murders she hadn't committed, and brought her to the attention of the dreaded Beguilers. If not for Sam's gift of healing, Jillian would be six feet under, not standing here discussing the Fellowship's history, the least of her concerns when she'd faced her crossroads. She'd always been damn curious about it, though.

Sam folded her arms. "We're talking ancient books, here. The older records . . . they're in the chapel's undercroft, and that's where they stay."

"So I have to go into the chapel." Something she'd managed to avoid.

"You don't have to go into the nave to get to the undercroft. The chapel is open all the time. You can go whenever you like."

She might not have to go into the nave, but she'd still have to enter the chapel. Why was she being so stubborn about this? Nobody had even subtly pressured her to attend the twice-weekly services, or to spend time in the chapel in quiet contemplation. Was she afraid of being struck by lightning and becoming a believer the moment she passed through the chapel doors? When the Fellowship had brought her to the island without asking, she'd resisted any suggestion of entering the chapel because she'd wanted to make it clear that she was an atheist and not interested in joining their group. That all seemed moot now, so what harm would reading in the undercroft do? The old books—scrolls?—would be fragile. She couldn't insist that Sam bring them to her. "Will you show me where the undercroft is?"

"Sure. Next time we have a free moment. Anyway, I'll meet you in the conference room." Sam strode away.

Jillian stared after her. If Sam ever relaxed and hung out with her for five seconds, Jillian would be forced to admit that miracles did happen.

Chapter Three

ROBERTA GAZED AT Jillian from across the conference table. "Have you heard of the Association of the Sacred Souls?"

The name sounded vaguely familiar. "You mean the soul healers?" Jillian asked, using the term the media had coined for the group.

"Yes."

"I've heard a few things about them, but not recently. Wasn't there some fraud investigation around seven or eight years ago?"

"It didn't go anywhere," Sam said. "Friends in high places."

Jillian twisted toward her. "Did you investigate them?"

"Yes, but not for that reason," Roberta said. "We always take a look at cults that are gathering a large following." She pressed a button on the control panel. The monitor flickered to life. Jillian recognized the photo of the elderly man. Anthony somebody or other, known as the Soul Master to his underlings. She remembered chuckling to herself when she'd read that tidbit in a newspaper article.

"Anthony Lancaster Sr." Roberta jerked her chin toward the screen. "Claimed he could see souls, see the corruption caused by sin, heal it, teach you how to heal it, so you can be closer to God. All hogwash, of course, but he gained a following—and its assets."

"Why didn't you shut him down?"

"Because everyone who joined his group did so of their own free will, and there was no indication that anyone was being mistreated."

But they were all brainwashed. Why else would a grown adult hand over everything they had to a cult?

"We had more pressing concerns, cases in which innocents were being harmed," Roberta said, her eyes on Jillian's face.

Sam clasped her hands on the table. "So what's changed?" she asked.

"Lancaster Sr. died last year. Lancaster Jr. took over his father's . . . work. The cult's focus may have shifted."

Now Jillian recalled hearing about Lancaster Sr.'s death on the news. It had been one of those stories that was all over the media one day and completely absent the next. "You said may. You're not sure?"

Roberta moved to the next photo. "Amanda Gladstone, found dead in a hotel room. Cause of death: drug overdose, but her sister doesn't believe it." Another face appeared on the monitor. "Jane Gladstone. She's one of us, a Supporter. She's asked us to look into her sister's death and expose the cult's culpability."

"I haven't worked with her before," Sam said.

"She lives in the UK. She's here now because of Amanda's death."

Sam laced her fingers behind her head. "Okay, so we have a Supporter accusing a cult of murder, and with no proof, I assume. Otherwise the police would be looking into it."

"Correct."

Jillian noted with interest that not all investigations were divinely inspired. Well, she didn't believe any of them were, but this one was clearly a secular request.

Sam chewed her lip. "Why does Jane think Amanda was murdered?"

"Amanda had recently left the cult," Roberta said. "She went underground for a few days, then called Jane and told her she was out and needed help to get home. Plane ticket, some money, that sort of thing. Jane wired her funds and arranged for her to pick up a plane ticket at the airport. She never did. Hotel staff found her dead when they investigated because she hadn't checked out."

Sam's brow furrowed. "How did she end up at a hotel? Was that where she was for the first few days?"

Roberta shook her head. "She was staying with a friend, but we don't know who. Jane suggested that Amanda stay at the hotel for that last night. She's adamant that Amanda wasn't on drugs and wouldn't use drugs. But the autopsy says otherwise, and the police didn't find anything to suggest foul play."

"How long had it been since Jane had seen her?" Jillian asked. "Do the soul healers allow their members to see family?"

"She hadn't seen Amanda for thirteen years. Amanda wanted nothing to do with her."

"Maybe drugs are a part of daily life for this cult," Sam said.

"We found no evidence of that when we investigated it."

"That was years ago."

"True, but Lancaster Sr. was pretty much a broken record until his death. The cult's dogma remained the same. When the fraud investigation happened, the media would have been all over the drug angle, had one existed."

"But that was seven or eight years ago," Jillian said, echoing Sam. "Maybe things *have* changed under Lancaster Jr."

"Jane doesn't think so." Roberta paused. "But I suppose she could be wrong."

"Leaving a cult can be disorienting," Sam pointed out. "What if an addict helped her escape the cult? Maybe she finally got out because she'd somehow become hooked and couldn't get her fix while part of the group." She quickly discarded her own idea. "No, she'd never be alone long enough to fall prey to a dealer, let alone harbour an addiction."

"Do we have reason to believe that Amanda Gladstone was murdered?" Jillian asked.

"Not at this time," Roberta said. "But Jane has served us well for almost ten years, so we've agreed to investigate. Miriam has already met with Jane and confirmed the details of Amanda's death."

Jillian leaned forward. "Miriam?"

"One of our Jewish Deiforms who happened to be in the city where Amanda died. The soul healers borrow heavily from Christianity, and she's needed elsewhere, so we're going to take the investigation over."

"Does she believe that Amanda was murdered?" Sam asked.

"She doesn't know. She met with Jane and double-checked the details of her story. It's up to us to dig deeper. Jeremy found an article in a local newspaper about the death of another former cult member." Roberta moved to the next photo. "Janet Bailey. Collapsed at a party and later died."

"Let me guess. Drug overdose, and she'd just left the cult." Jillian said.

Roberta nodded. "Someone else at the party mentioned that to the police, but since they found drugs on the premises and Bailey wasn't the only one using them, there was no reason for them to suspect that the cult had anything to do with it. In fact, they thought it could explain the overdose. Someone who'd just left a rigid cult and was cutting loose . . ." She leaned back in her chair. "The deaths of two former cult members under similar circumstances could be a coincidence."

Sam stared at Bailey's photo. "It's not unusual for cults to harass ex-members, but murdering them . . . that would be a whole different ball game."

"There's one other thing you should know." Roberta sipped her coffee. "Jane used to belong to the soul healers."

Sam's eyes widened. "You're kidding."

"No. It's how we first made contact with her. We came across her when we were investigating another cult. She's become something of an expert on mind control."

"How long has she been out?"

"Over fifteen years."

"Were both Jane and her sister in at the same time?" Jillian asked.

"Yes. Jane tried to get Amanda out, but Amanda wasn't interested in leaving."

Jillian cleared her throat. "If I can be cynical for a minute, blaming the cult for Amanda's death could be a knee jerk reaction. Or maybe she's asked you to investigate because she's hoping you'll end up shutting down the cult. She must hate them."

Roberta's eyes bored into Jillian. "You know, the day will come when you'll use 'we,' instead of, 'you,' when referring to the Fellowship."

"I know." She sometimes already did. At first, she'd felt as if she were pretending to be someone she wasn't. Now it felt more natural to use "we" and "us." It still wasn't automatic, but it would be.

"But your point is taken. Jane has not only asked us to investigate her sister's death, she's also taken her accusations to the Internet and anyone who'll listen to her. Since she doesn't have any proof, nobody's taking her seriously—except the soul healers. The Internet is one of their fishing holes. They're not happy about what's popping up in the search engines. She's also confronted one of Lancaster Jr.'s inner circle. He threatened to file for a restraining order, but he hasn't done so." Roberta pursed her lips. "I want you to meet with Jane, assess her story for yourselves, and determine whether we should investigate her sister's death any further."

"If we decide not to, what will she do?" Sam raised her brows. "Since she's a Supporter . . ."

"We'll do what we can to help her accept that the cult wasn't responsible. But we're getting ahead of ourselves. Meet Jane, learn about the cult, draw your own conclusions."

Sam frowned. "You want both of us on this?"

Roberta nodded.

"I could work this alone," Sam said quietly. "You know that."

"You're working this together," Roberta said, her steely look making it clear that she wouldn't entertain any protests from Sam.

"Fine." Sam's tone belied her words. "I just figured that we shouldn't risk sending Jillian back into the world so soon if we don't have to."

Jillian gave her a sidelong glance. She didn't believe for a moment that Sam would prefer to work alone so that her trainee would remain safe on the island. Sam wanted to work alone, period.

Roberta's tone softened. "Given what happened to Jim and her run-in with Lilibeth, I agree with you that we need to be cautious. That's why you'll both work on this."

Surprisingly, Jillian dreaded leaving the island. Her first visit hadn't been a voluntary one; the Fellowship had drugged and brought her here. When Roberta had ordered Sam to take Jillian back to the mainland to clear her name, Jillian had vowed to never return. She would walk away from the Fellowship, no matter what the cost. Working with Sam wouldn't make a difference. Seeing a Deiform in action, witnessing the gifts, wouldn't sway her. A short time later, she'd hugged Mom and Danny for the last time while Sam hid in the back seat of the rental car. Then she'd driven to the rendezvous point and let the Fellowship kill her. She'd choked up as she'd removed her watch, slipped her wallet from her pocket, and slid her topaz ring from her finger. If she could have hung on to one thing, it would have been that ring. But the authorities had needed to find enough of her to believe that she'd burned to death, so she'd relinquished her earthly goods and boarded the plane with only the clothes on her back. No jewelry, no ID, no life.

The second time she'd arrived on the island, she'd come willingly, knowing it would be her home for the rest of her life, and the Fellowship her family. Jillian Campbell no longer existed. She was dead, and Jillian had studiously avoided thinking about what that meant—until Warren had returned. He'd stayed behind to ensure that Mom and Danny didn't have any unwelcome visitors, had watched the police show up on their doorstep, the news reports, the visitation and funeral, the stoicism after everyone had paid their respects and returned to their lives. She'd managed to hold it together as he'd recounted what had taken place the week following her death—until he'd told her where Mom and Danny had laid her charred remains to rest. Not with Dad. In the pretty cemetery a five minute drive from their home, in a new plot Danny had bought for the three of them.

She'd lost it. A family at last—in death. It didn't matter that a deceased Fellowship member would lie with her parents for eternity. Being buried with Mom and Danny was exactly what she would have wanted; that Mom and Danny had known deepened her loss. Why couldn't they have connected more fully with each other? Why was it always too late? And good on Mom for passing on the plot Dad had bought. She belonged with Danny.

It was normal to grieve; all newcomers to the Fellowship did so, Roberta had assured her. After all, everyone and everything they'd known was gone forever. What had it been like for Sam, a nineteen-year-old wondering what the hell was happening to her? She'd said that she hadn't fully grasped the reality that she'd never see her family again. When had it hit her? In the early days, had she dreaded going back into the world because of the temptation she'd face? The moment her feet hit the mainland, Jillian would once again fight the urge to call Mom.

"I don't expect you to leave the island immediately," Roberta said. "Jillian, you have a lot to learn about cults. There are plenty of books in the library. Sam, select a couple of former cases involving cults and review them with Jillian."

"Why don't you spend some time at the target range?" Sam said to Jillian, failing to mask her irritation. "I'll take a look at what we have on the soul healers. We can meet back here after dinner and go through it."

Jillian wanted to protest. She'd like to find out more about the soul healers, too. But if Sam wanted her to spend more time at the range before they left the safety of the island again, so be it. Jillian didn't want to worsen Sam's mood. "Sure. I'm already a lot more comfortable with a pistol," she said, hoping to convey that she could see using one to defend herself, "but more practice never hurts."

"Good." Sam marched from the room.

Jillian gazed at Roberta. Their relationship had warmed somewhat, but Roberta still intimidated her. It didn't help that, whenever they were alone, Jillian wanted to blurt out a question that constantly nagged at her. The likely answer—God—wouldn't satisfy her. How had Roberta known? "Thanks for giving me something substantial to do."

Roberta's brows shot up. "You're a Deiform. You're the heart of the Fellowship. You still have much to learn, but you're ready to do what the Lord has chosen you to do." She raised a finger. "As you work on this case, remember this. Survival is your primary goal. No heroics, no testing the gifts to see how far you can go. The ideal outcome is you alive and mission accomplished, but if you run into problems or find yourself in a dilemma, save yourself."

"I understand."

"I mean it," Roberta said, an edge to her voice. "Deiforms don't come along every day. Losing a single battle will cost us much less than losing you." She rolled back her chair and rose.

"Roberta."

Halfway to the door, Roberta turned.

If Jillian didn't ask, she'd burst. "How did you know I was gay?"

Roberta was silent for a moment. "Ask me that question again when you know the answer." She left the room.

Deflated, Jillian stared after her. That was helpful—not. If she knew the answer, she wouldn't have to ask. God, she hated riddles. Now she couldn't wait to get to the target range. Nothing was clearer and more real than pointing a gun at a target and pulling the trigger.

Chapter Four

J ILLIAN'S HEART POUNDED when the plane descended through the clouds and she spotted land. Almost there. She felt like an engorged sponge. She'd managed to absorb the books she'd read and the discussions with Sam, but she needed a break and had welcomed the news that it was time to go back into the world. But now that they were almost there . . . She crossed her legs and smiled weakly at Sam, who was sitting across from her. "I'm still worried about running into someone I know."

"We'll be hundreds of kilometres away."

"It could still happen."

"They'll start to wave, then remember that it can't possibly be you. If not . . . refuse to acknowledge them. Say you don't know them. But it won't happen." Sam looked out the window.

"Have you ever run into anyone you know?"

"No. I doubt anyone would recognize me now, even if I did."

"Where are you from?" When Sam looked at her with confused eyes, Jillian said, "Where did you live? Before the island?"

Sam folded her arms. "Let's leave our former lives in the past."

"But you know about my former life. You know everything about me."

"And I told you a little about me. Why do you need to know where I lived, or what my favourite toy was?" Sam growled. "All that matters is who we are now."

But that was the problem. After spending at least a few hours a day in Sam's company for months, Jillian hardly knew anything about her. During training sessions, Sam was all business. She threw in the odd word or two at meals, and Jillian knew Sam liked her eggs sunny side up—whoop-de-doo. If Sam wasn't reading in the study or sequestered behind her closed bedroom door, she was in the chapel, or enjoying the island's natural beauty by herself. Jillian had managed to coax her into the odd walk, usually with Puck and Raven, the Fellowship's Labradors, along, but her attempts to draw Sam into conversation had gone the way this conversation was going. Impersonal topics: okay. Anything else: shutdown.

Sam scratched her nose. "If we have time before dinner, we'll stop at a music store."

Jillian's breath quickened. "Why?"

"You said you want to take up the guitar again."

Disappointment tempered Jillian's surprise and excitement. She'd thought she was about to learn something about Sam.

"I found one in storage, but it's pretty beat up." Sam shrugged. "You might as well buy one."

"Thank you for looking," Jillian said, astonished that Sam had searched for one. Jillian had mentioned her desire to relearn the guitar once, in passing, while babbling on one of their walks, so the silence wouldn't grow awkward.

"It's good for you to pursue an interest. You need to balance work and play."

Jillian bit her tongue. Though reading was a recreational activity, she supposed. And for all she knew, Sam spent her time in her bedroom belly dancing. She couldn't stifle the smile that sprang to her lips.

"What?" Sam asked.

"Oh, I'm just thinking about getting a guitar." Jillian cleared her throat and thought about something else. When she'd worked the Taylor case—she inwardly snorted. Worked? She'd warmed a courthouse bench for a few weeks, and when she wasn't doing that, Sam had kept her on a tight leash; Jillian had remained in the safe house and watched TV or read. Indications were that she'd have more freedom this time. "So the credit and debit cards Jeremy gave me . . . do they actually work?"

Sam's eyes widened. "Of course they work. Your Jillian Westwood identity is what we call a deep identity. It would take some digging and brain power to figure out that Jillian Westwood doesn't exist. Occasionally, when we're in a hurry, we'll throw together a shallow identity." Her brow furrowed. "Like we did for Peter, when he rescued you."

The damsel in distress implication made Jillian bristle, even though she'd needed rescuing. "Where is Peter?" She hadn't seen him since her very first night on the island.

"He's helping Brian."

She didn't know Brian very well. He'd brought in Sam, but she wouldn't dare ask him about that. Hopefully her friendship—or was it acquaintanceship—with Sam would grow to the point that Sam would share more details about when she'd joined the Fellowship and what she'd done since then.

Jillian Westwood sounded posh. So did Samantha Westwood, the name Sam would use. Jillian's surname was a deliberate match. If anyone bothered to investigate, they'd discover that she and Sam were half-sisters. They shared a father. Sam would say they shared a Father. When a giggle bubbled up inside her, Jillian knew her nerves were getting the best of her. "At least I'm used to juggling last names. That'll come in handy when I get more identities."

"Unless your Westwood identity becomes compromised or we don't want you to use it for some reason, that won't happen for a while."

"Why not?"

Sam took her time answering. "We won't just be working together on this case. Roberta wants us to work together for a while. After what happened to Jim . . . Anyway, we'll use our Westwood identities for now. Being related could come in handy if one of us gets into trouble." Her tone was even. Too even.

"How do you feel about us working together for longer than usual?"

Sam's face remained smooth. "Roberta talked to me about it before we created your Westwood identity. If I'd had a real problem with it, she would have punted you to Warren."

Punted her? What was she, a freaking football? *Calm down.* Sam was a loner with a capital L. The fact that Roberta had spoken to her about it, rather than telling her to do it, spoke volumes, as did Sam's use of "real problem." Just a problem, then, but she'd agreed to it, or Roberta had talked her around. Okay, so Sam had grudgingly agreed to team up with the new Deiform and probably wanted to punt Jillian out the plane window. "Do you think the Beguilers will come after me this time?" The first time she'd left the island with Sam, she hadn't believed the Beguilers existed or were interested in her. This time, she believed every damn word Sam had ever said about them.

"If they do, you have the gifts now."

"I haven't used them much."

"You can defend yourself, and you have to believe that you can defend yourself. We're working together, but that doesn't mean we'll never have to split up."

Did Sam worry that the gifts would elude her at the worst possible moment? Probably not, because Sam believed they came from without, not from within. If her energy was low or she was distracted, it wouldn't matter. God would come through. Jillian would have to nurture the same faith in herself. And the Beguilers? *Believe in yourself.* Let the sons of bitches come after her. If they thought she'd lose her cool and cower in their presence, they had one hell of a surprise coming. She was no longer a naïve Fledgling. She was a trained Deiform.

JILLIAN WAITED FOR Sam to disarm the safe house's alarm, then followed her into the hallway. Her new guitar would stay in the trunk. Rather than assaulting Sam's and everyone else's ears, she'd postpone getting reacquainted with the instrument until she could find a quiet spot on the island. "Are you going to teach me all this?" Jillian asked as they entered the living room.

"All what?"

"The safe house locations. How to get into them. How to call home, if I'm separated from my cell phone."

"Yeah, I will." Sam put her hands on her hips and glanced around the room. "Doesn't look like she's here. I'll go downstairs and see if anyone's been lurking outside."

"Is security always in the basement?"

"Usually." Sam went back into the hallway.

Feeling peckish, Jillian strolled into the kitchen and pulled open cupboard doors until she found the pantry. Good, it was stocked. A package of chocolate chip cookies beckoned to her. She reached for it—

Something hard pressed against the back of her head. A gun cocked. She froze. *"Sam!"*

"Don't move," a woman said quietly.

Jillian remained still but pushed out another thought to Sam. *"I have a gun pointed at my head."*

"What's your name?" the woman asked.

Huh? She grasped the implication and recovered quickly. *"Jillian. I'm here with Sam."*

The pressure against the back of her head eased. Jillian slowly turned around, in time to see the woman holstering her pistol while behind her, Sam crept into the kitchen, her pistol drawn.

Sam lowered her gun. "What are you doing?"

The woman turned to her. "One can't be too careful, after Jim. I wanted to be sure." She shifted her attention to Jillian. "I apologize. You look like your photo, but I don't take any chances."

"Do you greet all new members like that?" Despite her pounding heart, Jillian managed to sound amused. "Miriam, right? You look like your photo, too. Pleased to meet you." She stuck out a steady hand.

Miriam shook it. "And you."

Sam leaned against the kitchen counter. "If she wasn't one of us, do you honestly think I'd just buzz off into the basement? I wouldn't even bring her into the safe house."

"They caught Jim off guard. As I said, I don't take any chances."

"Where's your car?" Jillian asked. Sam had driven into an empty garage.

"Around the corner. Since you're staying, I figured I'd leave the garage to you."

"See any Beguilers hanging around?" Sam asked.

"No."

"Maybe you scared them off," Sam said to Jillian. "You beat Lilibeth."

"Quite the accomplishment." Miriam quirked a brow. "I hear you're an atheist? I wonder how long that will last."

Jillian's jaw tightened.

"I wonder if she'll get a boon," Miriam said to Sam, which irritated Jillian further. She hated it when people talked about her as if she wasn't there. On top of that, she had no idea what Miriam meant by a boon, something she wouldn't admit. When Miriam's eyes met hers again, Jillian refused to look away.

Miriam's eyes narrowed. "I doubt you'll get one. It's difficult to accept a blessing from someone you don't believe is there."

"Why don't we get down to business?" Sam pushed away from the counter. "We read your report. Anything else you can tell us?"

"There's a crusade this weekend that's worth checking out. The soul healers might show up and fish."

Jillian recalled her reaction when she'd learned that the soul healers attended Christian rallies and tried to recruit those who went to the front. Talk about nerve.

"We're not planning to go inside yet," Sam said, "but thanks for letting us know."

"Also, Jane has heard rumours that Lancaster Jr. is losing it."

Sam's brows knitted together. "Losing it?"

Miriam nodded. "Someone let slip that his behaviour can be erratic. One of his inner circle might be calling the shots."

"Not necessarily. It could mean they're all terrified of him."

"Assuming the rumours are true," Miriam added. "Without being inside, nobody really knows what's going on."

"Anything else you can tell us?" Sam said.

"Just to be careful. If they *are* killing people who leave, they won't appreciate you poking into their affairs. I've warned Jane to back off, but she's not the type to sit around and do nothing." She checked her watch. "I have a flight to catch. If you need anything, I'm only a phone call away."

At the front door, Miriam turned to Jillian. "Next time I run into you, I promise I'll be friendlier. Bye." With a wave, she was gone.

Sam plunked into one of the living room chairs. "She could have told us that on the phone," Jillian said, opting to sit on the sofa.

"She wanted to check out the new recruit."

"Do they all get the gun in the back of the head treatment, or was that a special welcome for me?"

Sam gave her a wilting look. "Miriam's okay. I've worked with her a few times. Everyone was shocked by Jim's death."

Jillian was more angry with herself than with Miriam. She should have reacted, instead of freezing like a scared rabbit and calling for Sam. "I should have shifted."

"Yeah, you should have. It's one of those times you don't care if someone sees you disappear. You're usually not gone for long, anyway. When the person moves, you shift back in and take them out."

"So you wanted me to shift and kill Miriam?" Jillian said, smarting because Sam was right. She silently thanked Sam for not calling her out in front of Miriam.

"Not kill her, because she was an unknown entity. In this case, you would have turned the tables by pointing your gun at her head . . . if you were armed. Other times, you know who you're dealing with. Depending on the circumstances, you incapacitate or kill."

Jillian blew out a sigh and threw up her arms. "You're right. I screwed up."

Sam's forehead creased. "Don't beat yourself up over it. Like anything, it becomes automatic over time. You'll shift without thinking." She paused. "Anyway, you sorted things out before I got there."

"She spoke to me telepathically, I guess to see if I could hear and answer her." Wait a minute. "You used telepathy with me before we'd met," Jillian said, remembering her shock as she'd waited to meet Sam in the library.

"Deiforms can use telepathy with Fledglings, so I figured I'd try. When I actually spoke to you, I could tell by your face that it had worked."

And she'd thought she'd masked her confusion well. "Then why did you need to see whether I could shift with you?" she said, recalling Sam's test in the car.

"Shifting always clinches it for me, maybe because that's what Brian first did with me."

She wanted to press Sam for details, but figured she'd have a better chance with a question that wasn't about Sam. "What did Miriam mean by a 'boon'?"

"It's a unique gift given to each Deiform. Well, unique among living Deiforms. You usually receive it when an act of faith is required."

"What do you mean?"

"When you're in a tight spot and you call out to the Lord. It doesn't always happen that way, but 99 percent of the time, that's how one discovers their unique gift."

"Do you know what yours is?"

Sam looked down at her hands. "I do, but only our Guides need to know who can do what. You don't need to know unless we find ourselves in a situation in which I have to use it." She held up her hand. "I'm not trying to dodge your question. We tend not to talk about our boons because it could sound like we're bragging."

Bullshit. Sam just didn't want to tell her. "But you find out about them—"

"*We* find out about them."

"We find out about them," Jillian said, despite knowing that Miriam was right and she wouldn't have a boon, "when we're out of options and we're about to be killed or something like that?"

Sam nodded.

Jillian wondered what the circumstances were for Sam. "I won't get one."

"You might."

"No." She'd have to rely on herself. For some reason, she felt disheartened. What was she doing? She wasn't like the other Deiforms. What if her gifts failed her at the worst possible moment? Why had she accepted Sam's bullshit about a hungry person accepting a meal not caring about the motivation of the one offering it? That might be true, but the version of Christianity Jillian had learned said that accepting Jesus as Lord and Saviour, and not good works, would get one into heaven. Then again, Sam hadn't claimed that her actions would earn her brownie points, and Jillian wasn't trying to get into heaven. Sam had essentially said that Jillian would feel at home within the Fellowship despite her atheism, because she shared its values. But what about boons? What about acting on behalf of someone who didn't exist? What about following Roberta without question? "How do Guides come in? How do they know they're Guides?" Considering the power they wielded, there must be some way to verify their claim to the role beyond "take it on faith."

"They find us."

"What do you mean?"

"At some point, someone will show up on the island, saying they were told to come to us."

Huh? "How do they know where the island is?"

Sam stared at her. "How do you think?"

"So God tells them, go to such and such an island, you're a Guide?"

"Yeah. Or another cell's home base. If they have to ask someone where we are, they're not a Guide."

"And you just take their word for it? What if someone just happened to, I don't know, get lost, and they paddle to the first land they see?"

Sam frowned. "Someone like that would say, 'I'm lost, can you help me?' not, 'Are you the Deiform Fellowship? The Lord commanded me to come to you.' They'll also know other things that only Guides know."

"So Roberta just showed up one day?"

"I wasn't there, but yeah, that's how it would have happened."

"If a Guide were to show up on the island, would that mean that Roberta's—" Jillian stopped herself. The question would be insensitive.

"No, it wouldn't mean Roberta's about to die," Sam said, finishing the question for her. "You've met Patrick?"

Jillian nodded. She'd learned that the residences on the western side of the island housed older Deiforms and those like Peter—Fellowship members dead to the world. Three—well, four, counting herself—Deiforms worked out of the island, but a couple of retired ones also called it home.

"Patrick is our former Guide. Roberta consults with him all the time. God hasn't stopped speaking to him."

Too busy training and settling into her new home and routine, Jillian hadn't thought about what would happen to her as she aged. "I guess we won't be running around defending Good when we're eighty."

Sam's mouth twitched. "Not as often as we do now. An older Deiform occasionally ventures into the world, though."

Sam seemed more willing to answer questions than usual. Any other time, Jillian would take advantage of her talkative mood, but right now, she needed to focus on something real. "I was checking out the pantry when Miriam pounced. Do you want something to snack on?" As Sam shook her head, Jillian rose. "Thanks for answering all my questions. You must grow tired of it."

"We all have our crosses to bear," Sam said, without cracking a smile.

HER LEGS ACHING, Jillian followed Sam up the apartment building's stairs. Why couldn't Jane be meeting them in an apartment on the second floor, rather than the tenth? Jillian understood the need for all the cloak and dagger; they didn't want anyone in the cult to associate them with Jane. Her legs would have preferred the elevator, though.

They finally reached the tenth floor and emerged into an empty corridor. Sam knocked at Apartment 1013. Jillian suspected they were being scrutinized through the peephole. The door swung open; Jane Gladstone motioned them inside. "I didn't expect two of you," she said as she quietly closed the door.

"You should be more careful about who you let in," Jillian said, surprised that Jane hadn't asked who they were. They could be from the cult.

Jane smiled. "I've worked with the Fellowship for ten years. I know a Deiform when I see one. You exude a certain . . . something. Power? Righteousness? Something."

Jillian resisted the urge to give Sam a sidelong glance.

Jane squinted at Sam. "You look familiar. I might have seen a photo of you, years ago."

Sam shifted her weight. "I'm Sam. I spoke to you on the phone."

Jane nodded and turned to Jillian. "I don't recognize you."

"I'm new. My name's Jillian."

"Jillian and Sam," Jane repeated. "Do you want coffee? Tea?"

"Tea, please," Sam said. Jillian nodded her agreement.

While Jane fussed in the kitchen, Jillian surveyed the living room. Jane must be fifty-something, but the furnishings, decor, and framed posters suggested a twenty-something lived here. "Is this her apartment?" she asked Sam.

Sam shook her head. "She's just meeting us here. It's Wendy's. Another Supporter."

"I see," Jillian said, trying not to be miffed that Sam wasn't keeping her fully in the loop. "Where's Jane staying?"

"Closer to downtown, in one of those fully-furnished, short-term lease apartments."

"Why don't we sit in the kitchen?" Jane said from the hallway. "It's cozier."

A teapot, three teacups, and a stack of paper napkins sat on the kitchen table. They made small talk until the tea was ready. Sam didn't waste any time. "What can you tell us about Amanda's death?"

"Not much. She called me out of the blue, said she was out of the cult and needed help. I was ecstatic. When I left, I tried to get her out. But she wouldn't listen, and eventually refused to have any contact with me. After a while, I couldn't . . . I just couldn't." Jane gazed into her cup. "Frankly, it was too painful, being so close, but cut off. I had to move on, to save my own sanity." She lifted her head. "That's when I moved to the UK, or maybe I should say, ran away."

"You're being too harsh on yourself," Sam said. "You tried."

"Would you still say that if I tell you that I'm the one who brought her into the cult?"

Sam didn't hesitate. "Yes, I would."

"I wish I could forgive myself so easily." Jane looked down at her cup again.

"What else did Amanda say when she phoned?"

"She said she was staying with a friend. She obviously knew I was in the UK, but I'm not sure how. I'd tried writing letters while I was still here. They were always returned, so I didn't bother again. I knew there was no point trying to call."

"Do you think she might have contacted one of the groups for former soul healers?" Jillian asked. "Maybe she stayed with an ex-cult member."

"I've spoken to all of them. Nobody heard from her."

"So you don't know who she stayed with?" Sam said.

"No. I asked, but she didn't want to tell me, and I didn't push. I didn't want to risk alienating her. I can't tell you how thrilled I was to hear from her, to hear that she was out. All I was thinking about was—" Jane's voice choked off. She gulped down some tea. "I just wanted to see her again," she whispered.

"You suggested that she stay at the hotel, right?" Sam prompted.

"Yes. I booked it for her, and arranged the flight." Her voice shook. "I stood in the arrivals area, waiting for her. When she didn't get off the plane, I thought maybe she'd gone back into the cult, that somehow they'd gotten to her. I didn't think . . . I'd only just spoken to her the previous day. She sounded okay, and determined to start a new life. When she called the first time, I should have hopped on the next flight. I should have told her, stay where you are, I'm coming. Why didn't I drop everything and go?" Her eyes welled with tears. "Why didn't I do that? Why did the police have to deliver terrible news to make me get on a plane?"

"Because you didn't know where she was, and you didn't want to push," Sam said gently. "If you'd come on too strong, taken over the situation, you might have frightened her."

"I guess we'll never know now." Jane took a moment to compose herself. "Anyway, I'm sure you know the rest. On the way here, I desperately hoped they'd made a mistake, that it wasn't her. But it was.

It was." She lifted her teacup but didn't take a sip. "Amanda would never do drugs. I know what the autopsy showed, and I know what it means. They forced her to do it. They killed her."

"I'm sorry, but I have to ask this." Sam leaned forward. "How do you know she wasn't doing drugs? You hadn't seen her for thirteen years."

"Precisely because I hadn't seen her for thirteen years," Jane snapped. "The soul healers live clean lives. No drinking, no smoking, no drugs."

"Maybe she was revelling in her newfound freedom," Jillian suggested, thinking about Janet Bailey's death. Not long out of the cult, she'd partied.

"She sounded absolutely sober when I spoke to her." Jane's mouth pinched. "And don't you think she'd start with a cigarette, or a beer? Why shoot up? She was looking forward to seeing me, to starting a new life. Why would she shoot up?"

Jillian shared Jane's bewilderment. "How did you get out?"

"I fell in love," Jane said softly. She sipped her tea; her voice regained its vigour. "That's not unusual, or forbidden. In fact, as long as they both don't falter at the same time, couples tend to stay in the soul healers. When one has doubts, the other one talks them through it. But we were never a couple." Her expression grew wistful. "For some reason, falling in love . . . it put me back in touch with the things I'd wanted before I'd joined the cult. A husband. A family. A life. For the first time in a while, having Lancaster Sr.'s blessing wasn't the most important thing to me. The pre-cult me was able to break through to the surface. Once that happens, you can't go back.

"It turns out I didn't get the husband or family," she said wryly. "It was naive of me to think that I could walk away and live as if that part of my life had never happened, especially when Amanda and others I cared about were still inside. But I got my life back. I've *chosen* to spend my life working to bring people out of cults. But I couldn't save my own sister. And now I never can."

"The soul healers just let you walk away?" Sam asked.

"Oh, they phoned me, sent me letters. When I'd show up at the residence and demand to see Amanda, they'd tell me in graphic detail about how my soul would wither and die, that I didn't stand a chance against Satan." She jabbed a finger against her chest. "I'd done the same. I'd made those calls, written those letters, said those words. But I never killed anybody for leaving, nor did anyone ever suggest that I do."

Sam grunted. "Is it possible that only those in Lancaster Sr.'s inner circle knew about any murders?"

Jane shook her head. "Everyone's still alive. Well, I don't know everyone who's left the cult, and some have died in accidents, or of cancer or natural causes. Nothing suspicious." She jutted her chin toward Jillian. "You asked whether Amanda might have contacted an ex-soul healer group. There wouldn't be any groups if they were killing everyone. And *I'm* sitting here. Trust me, if there's anyone they'd like to see disappear, it's me. I've been a thorn in their side since Amanda died."

So why kill Amanda and Janet Bailey? Maybe the cult hadn't murdered them.

"I was close to Lancaster Sr.," Jane said. "I wasn't one of his confidantes, but I was privy to goings-on that most members didn't know about. I'd remember if I'd heard anything that suggested they were eliminating ex-members."

"How did you leave?" Jillian asked. "The logistics of it. Did you leave the residence and not return? Everything I've read says you never go out alone. You usually travel in pairs, or with a group."

Jane chuckled. "I'm sure what you've read doesn't capture life with the soul healers. You have to live it to believe it. Those with the Soul Master's complete trust sometimes venture out by themselves. Everyone else is rarely permitted to leave a residence or cult centre alone. Private time doesn't exist. The bathroom is the only place you get a few minutes to yourself, and even showers are timed. But that's how I got away. I climbed through the window of a public washroom and ran. A kind man in a convenience store let me use the phone to make a long distance call. Thank God my mother answered. She pretty much did what I did for Amanda. Paid for a hotel and a ticket home." Her eyes closed.

Jillian didn't have to be a mind reader to know what Jane was thinking: she'd made it, but Amanda hadn't. "What does your mother think about Amanda's death?" she asked, knowing from Jane's file that her father had passed away a few years ago.

"She says she doesn't want to hear my conspiracy theories, that I'm obsessed with the soul healers and it's time to let go."

Wondering if Sam shared her thought that Jane's mother could be right, Jillian continued to gaze at Jane.

"Amanda was already dead to her for years," Jane said quietly. "I never gave up. My mother got on with her life."

"Did Amanda contact your mother when she got out?"

"No."

"Did you know Lancaster Jr.?" Sam asked.

"Yes."

"What did you think of him?"

Jane's face tightened. "The man's a self-centred, arrogant ass. When I heard the news that the Soul Master—Lancaster Sr.—had died, the first thing I thought was, 'Good.'" She grimaced. "I know that sounds terrible, but that was my first reaction. But a second later, I thought, 'Oh no, that means Junior will be the Soul Master.' I felt so sorry for the people I know and lived with for years. I don't harbour any grudges against them. I know they're not thinking straight, and now they're under the thumb of a tyrant."

"So Junior is definitely in charge now?" Jillian asked, wanting to confirm the news reports.

Jane nodded. "It's payback time."

"What do you mean?"

"Senior was harder on his son than he was on anyone else. So were the rest of us. Public humiliation, followed by repentance, is one of the primary ways cult members purge the blemishes from their souls. It was always better to confess how one had fallen short of the ideal, but if you didn't want to do that, others were always happy to report the transgressions on your behalf. Junior reported every tiny transgression, so we all reported his. Senior called him forward during just about every cleansing session. Humiliated him. Berated him. Told him that he would be the Soul Master one day, and so he had to hold himself to a higher standard. Junior would quietly take it, with hate burning in his eyes—but not for his father. For us. Now he's in charge. You can imagine what those cleansing sessions must be like." She paused.

"The worst thing is, I think he actually believes the BS the cult teaches. I did too, but once I was out and no longer under the cult's spell, I realized that Senior knew darn well he couldn't heal souls.

Junior, though . . . he actually believes he's some type of anointed one, and that anyone who doesn't believe it is unworthy."

"How do you think he reacts when people leave the cult?" Sam asked.

"Not very well. Who do you think made some of those harassing phone calls? Junior probably holds a grudge when someone breaks free. I bet it eats away at him." Jane's voice hardened. "I hope it does."

Sam chewed her lip. "Getting back to Amanda, are you sure you have no idea who she stayed with before going to the hotel?"

"Positive. Like Jillian, I thought maybe it was an ex-cult member, but it wasn't."

"This is going to sound insensitive, but do you have any videos or photos of the funeral, or know anyone who does?"

Jane shook her head.

"What about a guest book?"

"There aren't many names in it, and I know all of them. The soul healers," her mouth twisted, "her supposed family . . . none of them were there. No, I finally got to be her sister and bury her."

"Who was Amanda close to before she went into the cult?" Sam asked.

"Me. A couple of girlfriends she stayed close to after high school. I called one of them, but couldn't find the other one. Amanda might have had close friends at work . . . I don't know."

"What about boyfriends?" Jillian asked. Maybe Amanda had run to an old flame.

"I don't know." Jane balled the napkin she held. "Once I was in the cult, I didn't care about her social life. All I cared about was saving her."

They lapsed into silence. *"Do you have any more questions for her?"* Sam asked.

"No."

"Even though she's spoken to the ex-cult groups, I'd like to do it again, and find those who don't belong to a group. Not everyone wants to hang out with their former brethren. We can have Supporters do the same in other cities."

"Amanda would have stayed with someone here," Jillian said.

"Yes, and that person might have told someone in another city." Sam shifted in her seat. "If you don't mind, I'd like the names in the guest book," she said aloud.

Jane nodded. "Of course. I want you to get to the bottom of this. When I get home, I'll email them to you."

"Miriam told us there's a crusade this weekend that the soul healers might crash," Jillian said.

Jane rolled her eyes. "They started using that technique a few years ago. It's quite ingenious, if you think about it. If you go to the crusade, make sure you answer the call. They won't approach you inside. They're not *that* brazen. They'll get to you in the parking lot."

Sam wanted them to go to the crusade. Jillian cringed at the thought. She wasn't worried that she'd stick out like a sore thumb. Quite the opposite; she'd fit right in.

Chapter Five

Jillian's jaw clenched as Sam pulled into the church's parking lot and slowly cruised along, searching for a spot. They were fifteen minutes early, but the lot was almost at capacity. Parents and children chatted away as they strolled to the church's entrance, their faces alight with excitement.

Since she'd belonged to a church youth group and participated in several crusades, Jillian knew all about those who rushed to the front when the invitation to accept Jesus as Lord and Saviour was issued. Hell, she'd sometimes handed the pamphlets to the newly awakened, murmuring encouraging words and inviting them to attend the next Sunday service. She'd never seen most of them again. The majority of those who came forward during such events were caught up in the moment, maybe expecting to be struck by lightning, or to experience a grandiose epiphany, as they huddled together, pledging their lives to Christ. Or maybe they were lonely, or looking for answers the pamphlets didn't provide. "Do we both have to go up?" she asked. Hypocrisy turned her stomach.

Sam pulled into a spot and killed the engine, then turned to her. "If only one of us goes up, the soul healers might not approach us."

"If they're even here. And they'll have tons of people to choose from. They might not target us."

Sam studied her. "You'll have to get used to being someone you're not, Ms. Westwood. Sometimes you'll have to be someone you don't like or respect."

She used to do that all the time at work, but pretending to admire greedy people didn't offend her sensibilities as much as pretending to seek the Lord. She almost laughed out loud. Hello? She'd joined the

Fellowship, for god's sake. But she wasn't being dishonest. The Fellowship knew she didn't believe in God, but had wanted her anyway. Playing the role of spiritual seeker hadn't bothered her when she'd investigated Jim, and it shouldn't now. "I'm not praying out loud."

"Everyone draws the line somewhere," Sam said, her eyes bright.

Jillian wanted to slap her. She'd bet Sam was loving this, dragging her to an evangelical rally. Wait—just because she hated the thought of pretending to answer the call didn't mean she couldn't like or respect those who believed . . . like Sam. Is that how Sam thought Jillian viewed her and the others in the Fellowship?

Hoping Sam wouldn't choose seats near the front, Jillian followed her down the aisle of the church, each footstep cushioned by an immaculate cream carpet. Varnished pews gleamed on either side in a space large enough that it could be mistaken for a modern auditorium. No whiff of history here. Gospel music blared from large speakers, two gigantic screens hung above the stage, flanking the podium, and a drum kit, guitars, and piano sitting to the right of the stage told Jillian that live music would accompany any singing during the service.

Sam hadn't asked why Jillian refused to step foot into the island chapel's nave but didn't have a problem with entering this church. Maybe she assumed that Jillian would do whatever it took when it came to an investigation. She'd only be partly right. Here, Jillian was pretending to be someone else. On the island, she was herself.

Sam sidled along a pew in the centre section, about fifteen rows from the front. Jillian would have sat in the aisle seat, so they wouldn't have to climb over everyone when they were invited to come forward. With luck, their entire pew would rush to the front. "Slick presentation," she murmured.

Sam grunted and opened the program a greeter had handed to her. Jillian did the same. Her mind wandered as she flipped through the glossy pages and peered at the professional photos. That afternoon, they'd met with most of the ex-cult members in a downtown living room, and had left no further ahead. Nobody knew who'd sheltered Amanda after she'd escaped the cult. Had Amanda lied to Jane? No, that didn't make sense. Why claim to be staying with someone, when she wasn't? So if an ex-soul healer hadn't taken her in, where had she been from the time she'd left the cult to her arrival at the hotel? She could have lied about the date she'd broken free, but there was no disputing the date on which she'd initially made contact with Jane.

Ex-members in other parts of the country had also been a dead end, but Jeremy had provided them with a few names from Amanda's work life, people she'd abandoned for her new "family." He'd also located the second high school friend. Jillian wasn't optimistic that Amanda's secret helper would be among them, though. Nobody on the list had come forward to offer Jane closure, or shown up at the funeral.

The pews rapidly filled. The chatter in the church almost drowned out the music. After returning the smile of the man who sat next to her, Jillian buried her head in the program and slowly turned the pages without reading them. When a frisson of anticipation ran through those gathered, she looked up. The band members were taking their positions. She glanced at her watch. Only a couple of minutes to go. Sam stared at the podium, her program resting on her lap.

Several men and women filed onto the stage. Each stood in front of one of the chairs lined up to the left and right of the podium. The crowd buzzed with excitement when a man in a clerical collar bounded up to the microphone. Jillian recognized him from the photos in the program: Pastor Michael Morris, this church's leader. He motioned for the crowd to settle down. After the inevitable coughing had subsided, Morris said a few words of welcome, finishing with, "Let us pray."

Jillian bowed her head and listened to Morris ask God to be with the visiting pastor as he spoke, and to bless everyone present. At least he hadn't prayed for everything from world peace to comforting those who suffered in countries thousands of miles away, while beggars sat outside the church's front doors and children up the street went to school with no breakfast. She forced herself to quash the familiar indignation that would make it impossible for her to go up to the front and not bite everyone's head off.

Breathe! Mingling with religious folk and attending church services would be par for the course from now on. Jesus, she lived with a bunch of religious fanatics. But not hypocrites, which made all the difference. She'd have to stop thinking about Dad and everything wrong with organized religion every time someone mentioned God or she stepped into a church; otherwise her hands would be permanently clenched and her teeth constantly gritted.

"And now it gives me great pleasure to introduce Dr. David Fields." Morris swept his arm toward the steps on the left side of the stage. A smattering of applause grew into a crescendo as Fields, in casual business dress, strode onto the stage.

"Thank you so much, Pastor Morris." Fields removed the microphone from the podium and strolled from behind it. "Let's get into the spirit by singing that glorious and mighty hymn, 'Onward Christian Soldiers.'" The words appeared on the large screens.

Everyone rose to their feet. The band played. Jillian mouthed the words, knowing that her singing would clear the church faster than a fire alarm. Plus, someone nearby had the voice of an angel, so clear and pure and perfectly pitched that it gave her goosebumps. *Wait.* She turned to her left and tried not to gape at Sam. Okay, if Sam hadn't been in the church choir, Jillian was Mary freaking Poppins. It had been a while since she'd received a revelation in church. She forced her eyes forward and vowed to never, ever sing a word in Sam's presence. Embarrassment wouldn't begin to describe it.

The service that followed was typical fare: you're asleep—wake up, you're in the dark, come to the light, the usual. Maybe the guy was genuine. Not every religious leader was a money-grubbing hypocrite, but the honest ones usually laboured unseen. They didn't make the headlines or hold splashy crusades. There were exceptions—she'd always believed Billy Graham was the real deal. But most of those in tents and on stages: hypocrites. It was only ever a matter of time before they were caught with an air-conditioned doggy house in their landscaped backyard, or with their pants down in a motel room.

Uh-oh. Here came the call to commit one's life to Christ. What would she do if those waiting to reel in those seeking to be born again wanted to pray with each person individually? As long as they didn't want her to repeat a prayer after them, she'd be okay.

Sam nudged her arm. Right, time to stand up and follow the sheep down to the supposed shepherd. Her worries about praying were instantly banished when she reached the aisle. Half the church must be responding to Fields' invitation; making her way down to the front was worse than driving in rush hour traffic. No way would the greeters be able to pray with each person. They'd pledge their lives to Christ as a group and receive the literature that Jillian assumed was in the boxes at the greeters' feet.

When she finally reached the front, a harried-looking woman directed her to the right. She joined the group gathered in front of a middle-aged greeter and waited with Sam until their section was full. As she'd suspected, group prayer; she mouthed the appropriate words after the greeter, then accepted several tracts held together with an elastic band, and managed to smile when the greeter welcomed her to the church.

"Let's hang around here a bit, give anyone who might be here time to notice us," Sam said, flipping open one of the tracts.

With a sigh, Jillian rifled through her pile. She snorted to herself when she came across a tract about the sin of homosexuality. Were they still handing out this crap? Did they know that the woman standing next to her reading this garbage could heal, and time shift, and communicate with their cats, astral project . . . Jillian could too, but if there was a God, her being a Deiform must be the punch line for some divine joke. Sam was the real deal.

"Let's go."

Jillian fell into step with Sam as they walked up the centre aisle. Nobody accosted them; they'd be run out of the church if they tried to snatch up the newly-converted here. She and Sam were almost at the car when they heard running footsteps behind them. They both turned around.

A clean-cut man and a smiling woman, both twenty-something, strode up to them. "I see you answered God's call to be born again and walk the path less travelled," the man said.

"We know how challenging it can be in the beginning," the woman added, "and how important it is to belong to a supportive group who understands your calling—who gets it."

"That's why we hold a prayer and support meeting every Tuesday night."

As if on cue, the woman held out two flyers. "Do join us. And tell others who also want to walk the spiritual road."

"Thank you," Sam murmured as she and Jillian accepted the flyers. Jillian expected Sam to engage them in conversation, so she was surprised when Sam said, "Good night," and turned back to the car.

"Good night," the man and woman said in unison. They moved on to their next victims.

"They didn't ask for our phone numbers or anything," she said to Sam.

"They don't want to harass anyone. They're on church property. This is a fishing expedition, not a serious recruitment attempt."

Jillian climbed into the car, dropped the tracts into her lap, and peered at the soul healer flyer. She could make out a phone number and several website addresses in the dim light. "Are we going to call them?"

Sam started the car. "No. But if we ultimately decide that we need to get someone inside, we now have an easy and unsuspicious way to make contact."

"I thought maybe you'd talk to those two."

"To what end? They wouldn't have known anything about Amanda, and I didn't want us to stand out in their memory. Most will do what we did—take their flyer and go home."

Yeah, and Jillian supposed it was naive to have hoped that Sam would say the magic words that would open the cultists' eyes right there on the spot. Deprogramming wasn't so simple.

Sam swung out of the parking lot. "I hope the service wasn't too trying for you," she said, her tone light.

Should she tell Sam that she'd attend more services with her just to hear her sing? Sam's voice had been the highlight of the evening. "It's not as if I heard anything I hadn't heard before." Many, many times. "The speaker came across as genuine." That didn't mean he was, though.

"I liked that he didn't make any grandiose claims or put on a show, like healing people." Sam chuckled. "It always cracks me up when I see that. If any of those so-called healers were genuine, they'd collapse after the first two or three."

Remembering how much healing her gunshot wound had drained Sam's energy, Jillian nodded. Her own limited experience with healing made her wonder how she'd feel after healing a serious wound or affliction. Healing a small cut had made her want to nap. Sam had said she'd grow more resilient with each heal. That had better be true; there would be no point to healing herself or someone else in a tricky situation, if she couldn't walk afterward.

JILLIAN STOPPED NEXT to Sam and scanned the busy cafeteria for the two women whose photographs she'd studied that morning—Janet Bailey's close friends, or at least they'd been close before the cult had sunk its claws into her. "Over there," Sam said, tipping her head to her right. They made their way to the table.

"Excuse me," Sam said. The two women looked up. "I'm Sam."

"Hi," the woman Jillian recognized as Sheila said.

Sam gestured toward Jillian. "This is my associate, Jillian."

"Sit down." Rosie, the other woman, slid a stack of books out of the way.

"We couldn't believe it when you called last night," Sheila said. "We don't know anything about the soul healers."

"Janet tried to get us to go to a meeting, but we weren't buying it. I zoned out whenever she talked about it," Rosie added.

Sheila gazed across the table at them. "Rosie said you're working for a family?"

"Yeah. A couple of families hired our firm. They want to get their kids out," Sam said, repeating the cover story she'd told Rosie on the phone last night.

"Good luck," Sheila snapped. "You don't stand a chance, though. Everyone's brainwashed in that cult."

"You won't get near them. Fucking cult is probably paying off the police and making large political donations." Rosie grimaced. "Pardon my French."

"Tell me about how Janet became involved with them," Sam said, as Jillian listened quietly. They'd agreed that Sam would take the lead.

Sheila and Rosie both started talking at once, then stopped and looked at each other. "You go," Sheila murmured.

Rosie heaved her shoulders. "It was Janet's first time away from home, and she was struggling. Her grades weren't good, and—"

"Her parents were brutal," Sheila said. "They wanted perfection. She wanted to transfer to a university closer to home, but they said no, this university has the best program."

Sam clasped her hands on the table. "So she was homesick."

They both nodded. "She signed up for some course on the Internet, to do with finding your inner strength and persevering through hard times," Rosie said. "For a few weeks she actually seemed happier, and said she was getting everything under control."

"Then she started hanging out with them." Sheila's lips pressed into a thin line.

"First it was Friday nights, then weekends, then she was never available. Her grades started to slip even more, but she didn't care. When her parents called, she didn't pick up. Next thing we knew, she was dropping out and moving in with her new," Rosie formed air quotes with her fingers, "friends. We couldn't talk her out of it. The more we protested, the more she dug in her heels."

"We tried to keep in touch, but we weren't good enough for her anymore." Sheila's mouth twisted. "When we did occasionally run into her, she was always with someone else, and all they did was talk about how wonderful life was. But Janet wasn't herself. She was . . . subdued. She kept regurgitating the same old propaganda."

"It was like talking to a brick wall." Rosie shook her head. "I'd try to bring up stuff she was interested in, and sometimes I'd see a spark in her eyes, but then the wall would come down again."

"We gave up on her," Sheila said, her voice heavy with guilt.

"How did she get out?" Sam asked, verbalizing the question in Jillian's mind. "Something must have happened."

Rosie's eyes teared up. "She called me one night. She was babbling . . . said she didn't have much time. I didn't catch a lot of it. I kept telling her to slow down, but it was clear she wanted out. She said her life was in danger."

"Are you sure?"

"Yes. I thought she was exaggerating, because she could be a bit of a drama queen at times. But a week later, she called again and said she'd gotten away. We met, and she looked terrible. I swear to god, someone had beaten her, but when we asked, she denied it."

Sheila shifted in her seat. "We wanted her to come back to the residence with us, but she wouldn't. She wanted to go home. She called her parents and flew out the next day."

"Yeah, after their precious baby had dropped out of school and moved in with a bunch of crazies, her parents were suddenly more receptive to her going home," Rosie said bitterly.

"We were happy for her. She was talking about re-enrolling in the fall. I was going to visit her during March break." Sheila's face fell. "Then we got the call . . ."

"I couldn't believe it when I heard it was a drug overdose," Rosie mumbled. "But in a way, I wasn't surprised."

"Why not?" Sam asked.

"After living with those nut cases, anyone would be confused. I figure she couldn't deal with being out. I don't think she was getting therapy, and she wanted to make new friends, to fit in . . . someone offers her pills at a party, says it'll be fun . . . I don't know . . ."

Sheila's face crumpled. "She should have stayed here. We were her friends. We would have supported her."

Rosie slipped an arm around Sheila's shoulders. "We tried. We tried."

"Not hard enough." Sheila picked up a napkin and wiped her eyes.

"You have nothing to feel guilty about," Sam said. "You tried to keep her out of the cult. You tried to keep in touch. When she needed your help, you didn't turn your backs on her. You were there for her."

Both women nodded, but Jillian could see that their guilt wouldn't be assuaged that easily. She could relate. When she was younger, she'd often wondered if she could have somehow prevented Dad's suicide. It hadn't mattered that she'd only been eleven at the time, and ignorant of her father's crimes and of how low he'd sunk. As she'd grown older, she'd accepted that the choice was his, that she couldn't have swooped in and saved him from himself. What about Mom, though? Did she still torture herself? Jillian would never know.

"I hate to say this, but . . ." Sheila turned to Rosie. "I haven't even mentioned this to you, but if they're going to get anyone out, they need to know."

"What?" Rosie said, her eyes wary.

"I wasn't surprised that she overdosed. She sometimes acted spaced out when we saw her," Sheila said tentatively.

"Because she was brainwashed, not because she was stoned," Rosie snapped. "She didn't touch drugs until that party."

Sheila backed off, but her eyes remained uncertain.

Sam chewed her lip. "Anything else you can think of that will help us deal with the cult?"

"No," Rosie said, as Sheila shook her head.

"Do they recruit on campus?"

"No," Rosie said again. "If I ever see them here, I'll report them to security. They stick to the Net and suck people in." Her eyes widened. "Can you believe students here still sign up to get their e-books, even after what happened to Janet?"

"Because the police say it wasn't the cult," Sheila said scornfully. "And now everyone's curious about them."

Rosie's eyes brightened. "Maybe you can do more than get people out. Maybe you can close the cult down."

"One step at a time." Sam pulled two business cards from her pocket and handed one each to Rosie and Sheila. "If you think of anything else, give us a call."

"Sure." Sheila smiled weakly.

When Sam rose and murmured a good-bye, Jillian did the same. The two women eyed her curiously, probably wondering why she hadn't said a peep. She strolled from the cafeteria with Sam.

"Are we going to shut the cult down?" she asked when she was sure they were out of earshot of anyone.

"We don't have enough information yet."

"What if it is employing mind control techniques?"

"As long as its adherents are healthy and not being abused, we probably won't do anything."

Jillian turned to her. "Even though people are trapped?"

"I don't like it either, but we have to keep our eye on the bigger picture. As long as the cult isn't a danger to its members or society," she held up her hand when Jillian drew breath, "we usually leave it alone. I know, mind control could be considered a danger to its members, but if they're healthy, eating well, and not abused, we have worse things to worry about."

Jillian didn't like it, but there was no point in arguing. "What's on the business card you gave them?"

Sam pulled another one from her pocket and handed it to her. *Sam Westwood, Private Investigator*, with a number that routed through Jeremy to her. Jillian snorted and handed it back.

"So what did we learn?" Sam asked.

"Nothing." Jillian shoved her hands into her pockets. "All right, she sounded afraid when she called them, but since she'd had it drilled into her that leaving the cult would be the same as embracing evil, she was probably paranoid about what might happen when she took that step. As for the drug overdose, if they'd both been completely shocked, maybe a red flag would have gone up, but they weren't. They said she sometimes seemed spaced out."

"Cult members can come across that way when they're regurgitating the same words for the thousandth time. But I agree. They didn't say anything that indicates the cult played an active role in Janet and

Amanda's deaths."

"Nothing beyond recruiting them and stealing their lives, anyway," Jillian said wryly.

Sam's mouth twitched.

"What now?" Last night, they'd also called Amanda's former co-workers. Nothing.

Sam pulled out her phone. "Let's pay Amanda's high school friends a visit."

"Jane already spoke to one of them."

"I want to talk to both of them myself, in person."

While Sam called them, Jillian walked next to her and turned the case over in her mind. Yes, it was strange that Amanda had called Jane and then overdosed in a hotel room, but as Rosie had said, those who'd just fled a cult might not be thinking straight. Part of them might still be tied to the cult, still wanting to believe and return, while the other part battled for freedom. Jane was grieving and felt guilty because she'd brought Amanda into the cult. Could she not accept that Amanda had been responsible for her own death? Did she want to hurt the cult that had taken years of her life and claimed her sister? If they proved that the cult had killed Amanda, how would that help Jane? She'd still beat herself up for introducing her sister to the soul healers, but if the Fellowship shut the cult down . . .

"We can meet one of them tonight," Sam said, bringing Jillian back to her surroundings. "I left a message for the other one."

They reached the car. "I wish we didn't have to lie to people about why we want to talk to them," Jillian said as she pulled on her seatbelt.

Sam turned to her. "Well, if you'd like to tell people we're Deiforms, you can try that, but they probably won't be interested in talking to us. They'll slowly back away and direct us to the nearest mental health hospital."

True, but she still didn't like it. "We're not seeing anyone this afternoon. Do you want to do something?"

"Like what?"

"See a movie. Go for a walk downtown. Visit a museum." Anything but sit around the safe house. She was tired of reading, watching TV, and surfing the damn Internet.

"You're vulnerable outside the safe house," Sam said.

For god's sake! "You can't keep me locked in a cage forever. You said yourself there will be times when we have to split up. At some point, I'll have to leave the safe house by myself. I know the gifts. I'm not some helpless . . ." Her voice trailed off when she looked at Sam . . . Sam's tight face, her grip on the steering wheel . . .

"Has anyone told you about Kristin?" Sam asked.

"No."

Sam was silent for a moment. "She came in a few years after I did."

"What happened?"

"You know what happened."

Yes, but . . . "How did they get her?"

"Kristin disobeyed Brian," Sam said. "If she'd done what he told her to do, she'd probably be alive. She should have shifted, but instead she got into a shoot-out, and lost."

"They shot her."

"Yeah, they shot her." Sam's voice was harsh. "They would have preferred to take her alive and draw it out, but the ultimate objective is to kill the Fledgling or green Deiform, and that's what they did. Brian had shifted. As soon as he realized she hadn't followed him, he shifted back in, but he had to shift right back out or he would have been killed." Her voice dwindled. "It must have been horrible for him."

"Maybe she tried to shift and failed."

"It's possible, I suppose, but apparently she was headstrong during training, too. Believed she was untouchable. You're not like her. You know you're vulnerable."

And she'd never disobey Sam. She trusted Sam implicitly. If Sam said shift, she'd shift. "What about the boon?"

"If she thought she was invincible, she wouldn't have asked for help. Or . . . she asked, and the Lord declined the request."

"Declined the request?" Jillian gaped at Sam's dry language. "Why would He look the other way when she's about to die?"

"To teach her a lesson."

"That's one hell of a harsh lesson."

"Only because you don't believe that life continues after death."

She drew breath to retort, then conceded the point, supposing that if one did believe in life after death, then death wouldn't be the ultimate smack down. Still . . . tough love didn't begin to cover it.

"We didn't recover all of her remains."

Jillian swallowed. "What do you mean?"

"By the time it was safe for Brian to shift back in, the Beguilers had gone. I'm sure they would have liked to take her whole body, but then Brian wouldn't have known for sure that she was dead." Sam grimaced. "They left her head."

Jesus. Jillian didn't want to think about what they'd done with the rest of Kristin.

"We buried it in the graveyard."

"I'm sorry."

"I didn't know her. When she came in, I was away. I came back to the island a few times, but she was always busy training with Brian. I saw her at breakfast, and that was all."

Jillian knew from experience that communal breakfast with Sam meant little or no interaction.

"I couldn't believe it when I called in and Roberta told me the Beguilers had killed her." Sam glanced at Jillian. "I never spoke to Brian about it, because I didn't want to upset him. But I read his report. I always want some idea of how it happened, so I don't get caught off guard."

"Why haven't you told me about this before?"

"I didn't want to spook you." Sam shrugged apologetically. "Your room used to be Kristin's room."

Jillian snorted. "I'm not that fragile. I'm not fatalistic, either. Did whoever had the room before Kristin meet an early death?"

Sam waited until she'd changed lanes to reply. "No."

"Neither will I." And she liked her room, thank you very much; it had a great view. She and Sam were the only ones who slept on the second floor. She'd noticed that Warren didn't live in the main house, and neither had Jim. Jillian didn't know if she'd ever have the option of moving out on her own, and finding out wasn't a priority. She was the new kid on the block and happy where she was. Maybe one had to earn the privilege of living alone, but if that were the case, surely Sam, Roberta, and Brian were in a position to move. Jillian could understand why Roberta chose to live in command central, but why wasn't Sam living by herself? She would have thought Sam would jump at the chance to have personal space larger than a bedroom. As for Brian . . . Jillian had her suspicions about him and Roberta.

"Brian's never forgiven himself, even though it wasn't his fault." Sam said. "Kristin ignored his warnings and didn't pay much attention to anyone else, either. The Lord gives us the gifts and expects us to use them. If Kristin had practiced more, understood that the gifts are the Lord's way of bailing us out . . ."

Until this moment, Jillian hadn't fully appreciated the burden on Sam's shoulders when they were out in the world, clearing her name. Well, the Fellowship had cleared her name. Jillian had merely been along for the ride, with Sam as her protector. "If He exists . . . you believe He exists . . . why let a Deiform die so early? Why call her, train her, and then let her die? If He's omnipotent, He could have protected her. He could have saved her."

"Are you suggesting that God should protect His Deiforms from all harm?"

"I'm not suggesting He do anything, because I don't believe He exists. But you do. When Kristin died, didn't you ask yourself why He'd let that happen?"

Sam's voice rose. "Of course I did. I'm sure we all did. But imagine what life would be like if there were no challenges, no difficulties, no risks, because everything was handed to you, and if you ran into trouble, someone swept in and took care of it for you. We'd all be a bunch of spoiled, entitled children with no compassion for others."

Jillian could agree, but . . . "Some people have to endure so much, though. Others seem to lead charmed lives."

"I won't pretend to know why," Sam said flatly.

Jillian liked that Sam didn't claim to have all the answers and was unapologetic about it. No "God works in mysterious ways," or "Our minds our too puny to understand God's plan for us" bullshit. Okay, so Sam was petrified that the Beguilers would kill her trainee, and she'd blame herself for the rest of her life if that came to pass. Jillian would drop her plea to leave her cage—for now. Especially since she didn't have a rock-solid faith in the gifts, unlike other Deiforms. "Do you ever worry that the gifts will fail you?"

"No."

See?

"Do you?" Sam asked.

How honest should she be? "Yeah, I do. I don't believe in Him," she said, grateful that they weren't having this conversation face to face.

"You're not making sense. Since you don't believe in Him, you can't believe that He's responsible for the gifts. Therefore, for you—*for you*—believing in Him shouldn't be a prerequisite for the gifts to work. You don't believe in Him, and they *are* working for you."

Intellectually, she grasped that, and wasn't surprised that Sam had responded to her logically, rather than seizing the opportunity to proselytize. They had an unspoken agreement to not pick at each other's viewpoints when it came to the God question; frankly, Sam was better at biting her tongue. Her response made sense, and Jillian had told herself the same thing, so why did she still worry? "What do you think about that?"

"What?"

"The gifts working for an atheist? I'm not trying to score a point, here. I'm genuinely curious about what you think."

Sam didn't hesitate. "Just because you don't believe in Him doesn't mean He doesn't believe in you. He chose you, and I respect that."

"What about the others? Miriam didn't seem as accepting."

"It'll depend on who you talk to. But no matter what anyone thinks, you're a Deiform. They can't deny that He's chosen you. They'll respect it, too."

Now Jillian wasn't sure whether Sam was okay with her atheism, or forcing it down with a spoonful of sugar and gagging the entire time. She didn't want to know. "I guess I can watch TV this afternoon."

"Will grocery shopping do?" Sam said, surprising Jillian. "Because we need a few things." She paused. "You can push the cart."

Jillian smiled into the side view mirror.

Chapter Six

JILLIAN TRAILED AFTER Sam as they walked around the corner to where the car was parked. Amanda's former high school friend hadn't sheltered her; she hadn't seen or spoken to Amanda in years.

"No luck," Sam said, her phone still pressed to her ear.

Former friend number two still hadn't gotten in touch. "You only left a message this afternoon," Jillian said, picking up her pace and falling into step with her.

"I just left another one. Hopefully she'll get back to us soon. You up for visiting the hotel where they found Amanda?"

"Sure! But we have the police report." Unfortunately, the investigators hadn't viewed any security camera footage. Since the coroner had determined that the cause of death was an overdose, there was no need. By the time Jeremy had gone looking for the footage, the hotel had recorded over the dates of interest.

"Not everyone will talk to the police. I asked Jeremy for a list of staff who might not want to get involved. Users, illegal workers, parolees. A few are working tonight."

Jillian clenched her hands. "Is there anything else I should know?" she said levelly.

"Sorry, I should have mentioned it to you." Sam glanced at her. "I'm used to working alone." She fired up the engine and pulled away from the curb.

Still miffed, Jillian quashed her childish impulse to snap, "If you don't want to work with me, just say so." She didn't want to risk Sam taking her up on it.

At the hotel, her mood didn't improve when she found out that she'd cool her heels in the lobby while Sam sought out the people she hoped to question.

"Two of us will intimidate them," Sam said, holding up her hand.

Jillian gusted an exasperated sigh. "All right, all right." At least the hotel was connected to a shopping promenade. "How long do you think you'll be?"

"Hopefully no longer than an hour or so. Stay in the lobby."

"Sam, if I'm supposed to wait around for you, I'm going to do what I want. It's only eight o'clock. There are lots of people around. I'll be careful. The most I'll do is wander around the promenade, okay?"

Sam's jaw tightened. "Don't hesitate to call me."

"I won't. See you soon." She turned away and strolled toward the promenade, then looked back to see if Sam was still there. Jesus, she was. Jillian wanted to scream. Honestly, the Beguilers weren't going to kill her in the middle of a crowded promenade. But marching among the crowd a minute later, she was acutely aware that anyone could approach her from behind or dart out from a store. Her heart raced at every little noise. She glanced over her shoulder, searched the faces around her, almost bolted when someone jostled her from behind. The pistol she wore didn't make her feel any safer. Shit, would she ever relax when she was alone in public again? She hadn't felt this way when she'd walked from the car to the courthouse, and she hadn't been armed, either. But she'd known that Sam was just around the corner. Annoyed with herself, she bought a newspaper, returned to the lobby, and sat where nobody could surprise her from behind.

She'd finished the newspaper and twiddled her thumbs for ten minutes before Sam came back and tipped her head toward the revolving doors. Jillian left the newspaper for someone else.

They didn't speak until they were inside the car. "Did you find out anything?" she asked Sam.

"Amanda had a male visitor the night before she was found dead."

"That wasn't in the police report."

"Like I told you, when it comes to the police, some people don't want to get involved."

Jillian frowned at her. "Who told you?"

"One of the room service people. Apparently he rode the elevator up with the guy and saw him go into Amanda's room."

Jillian lifted an eyebrow. "He remembered after all this time?"

"People who know something but don't divulge it to the police . . . it can weigh on their minds. They don't forget it. Not everyone feels guilty, but fortunately this guy did. It doesn't get us much further ahead, though. I have a description of the visitor, but he could be a friend, maybe even the one who took her in."

"The friend we're trying to reach is a woman," Jillian pointed out, then she wanted to kick herself. So what? Anyone could have helped Amanda. The mysterious visitor was as likely a candidate as former friends.

"Thirty-something, around five feet eleven, slim build, short brown hair, clean-shaven . . . We should run the description by Jane, see if it jogs anything. Do you want to call her?"

"Sure."

Her call went through to voicemail. "Hi Jane, it's Jillian. I visited you with Sam," she added, feeling that she lacked authority within the Fellowship. "We'd like to run something by you. Can you give me or Sam a call, as soon as you can?" She recited her and Sam's phone numbers, said good-bye, and disconnected. "Maybe we should give the description to Jeremy and Emma. It's so general that it'll probably match hundreds of cult members, but you never know, we might get lucky."

"Call them."

She felt like snapping a salute, then inwardly smiled when Sam added, "You're getting the hang of this."

JILLIAN SWALLOWED A mouthful of cereal and raised her brows when Sam lowered her phone and shook her head. "I'm not leaving another message," she said. "According to Jeremy, she works from home. Let's head over there. I would have preferred to arrange a time to meet, but since she's ignoring us . . ."

"Everyone's ignoring us." The lack of response from Amanda's former friend Sherry didn't surprise Jillian, especially since Jane had already spoken to her, but . . . "I expected Jane to get back to us right away."

"She might have been out last night, and it's only—" Sam glanced at her watch "—8:15."

True, but Jane was desperate for clues about her sister's death. Unless she'd returned home after midnight, Jillian suspected she would have called them. It would certainly be the first thing on her agenda for this morning.

Half an hour later, they parked in front of Sherry's house. "No Bibles this time?" Jillian said when Sam started up the path without detouring to the trunk.

"When you want people to open the door, you don't use Bibles," Sam said, making Jillian chuckle. Sam rang the doorbell. When nobody answered, she rang it again. A car sat in the driveway and Jillian could hear a TV, so Sherry was home.

They'd been waiting for at least a minute when the door cracked open. A woman studied them suspiciously. "Yes?"

"My name's Sam Westwood. I left you a couple of phone messages."

"What do you want?" the woman said flatly.

"Are you Sherry Singleton?"

"What do you want?" she repeated.

"We're looking into Amanda Gladstone's death." Sam reached into her back pocket, pulled out a business card, and held it where the woman could see it. "My card. If you like, you can call my office and confirm who I am."

The woman squinted at it. "What do you want with me?"

Sam lowered the card. "We're trying to find who Amanda stayed with before she went to the hotel where she was found dead. We're checking in with all her friends from before she entered the cult."

"The cult?" The woman swung the door open. "You'd better come in."

Apparently "the cult" was a synonym for "open sesame." Jillian exchanged a glance with Sam, then followed her into the home.

"I didn't return your calls because I wondered if you were from the cult. But if you were, you wouldn't call it a cult, would you?" Sherry led them into the living room and turned off the TV. "Are you looking into this for Jane?"

"Yes."

Her face darkened. "Well, since you're here . . ." She gestured toward two armchairs. "Sit down."

As Jillian sank into a chair, Sam said, "This is my associate, Jillian Westwood." She smiled. "It's a family business."

She was such a smooth liar—but then, she wasn't lying. They *were* a family business, of a sort. They *were* investigating Amanda's death for Jane.

"She stayed with me," Sherry blurted.

Jillian struggled to mask her surprise. No teeth pulling or clever questioning required.

"I should have told her not to go to the hotel. If I'd told her to stay that night, she might be alive. But no, when Jane arranged the hotel, I encouraged her to go. It's closer to the airport, I said, as if I cared about it being more convenient for her." Sherry shook her head. "The truth is, I was relieved that she was leaving. It was a weird few days." She rubbed her forehead and groaned. "This is one of those times I wish I hadn't quit smoking."

Sam leaned forward. "Let's start at the beginning. Amanda contacted you . . ."

Sherry nodded. "I don't even know how she got the number. I hadn't spoken to her for years. When she went into the cult, she tried to reel me in. Needless to say, I stopped returning her calls. She must have called information, or maybe my mother."

"How did she sound on the phone?"

"Agitated. Desperate. Afraid. She was all over the place. It took a few minutes to calm her down and find out what she wanted. When she said she'd left the cult and needed somewhere to stay, I told her that she could stay here, that I'd pick her up. She was terrified that the cult would find her first and drag her back, so she hid in an alleyway we used to play in when we were kids. Took me back." Her voice dropped. "Now she's dead."

"Did she say why she left the cult?" Jillian asked.

"That's the weird part. I'm not sure she did." Sherry tapped her temple. "Not up here. She was still brainwashed, that's why she called me instead of Jane. *I* persuaded her to call Jane, and believe me, it wasn't easy. Amanda thought Jane was the devil incarnate. But she made me uncomfortable. She couldn't stay here. I . . . I keep telling myself she would have left sometime, but . . ." Sherry's eyes grew distant.

Sam appeared as perplexed as Jillian felt. "If she still believed in the cult's teachings, why did she leave?"

"She wouldn't say. Something must have made her run away, but she was still loyal to the cult, and it was tearing her up inside. She felt lost outside the cult but couldn't go back to it. Every time I pressed her about why she'd left, she either shut down or became hysterical. I stopped asking. I figured she'd talk about it in her own time—with Jane."

"Did anyone from the cult contact her while she was here?"

Sherry's eyes widened. "They tried to. That's why I wouldn't return your calls and wasn't sure whether I should answer the door. We had to resort to taking the phone off the hook at night, and when we went out to pick up some groceries, a couple of soul healers followed us around the store. They just stared at Amanda. It creeped me out. That's when I knew she had to find somewhere else to stay."

"How did Amanda react? Did she try to talk to them?" Jillian asked.

"She cried. If they were trying to guilt trip her, they were succeeding. Something really bad must have gone down for her to leave, because she still wanted to be with them."

Jillian met Sam's eyes. If cult members followed Amanda to the grocery store, they could have followed her to the hotel. Sam cleared her throat. "Did Amanda do drugs while she was here?"

Sherry drew back. "No! Any sign of that and I would have thrown her out, former friend or not."

"Are you sure? She might have hidden—"

"I'm sure. When I heard the news, I knew the cult had killed her because she didn't use here, and she wasn't suffering from withdrawal."

"Why didn't you come forward?"

"And have the cult come after me?" Sherry snorted. "No, thanks. Amanda's dead. There's nothing we can do for her now."

Sam's face remained smooth. "What about Jane?"

Sherry's mouth tightened. "What about her? She brought Amanda into that farce. She took her own sister's life away from her. Amanda was vivacious, funny, had plans, until her darling sister ruined it for her. So if Jane has to live with not knowing for the rest of her life, so be it. Karma can be a bitch. When she called and I told her I hadn't seen Amanda, I didn't feel guilty at all. She's lucky I didn't give her a piece of my mind."

Jillian shifted in her chair. "You're okay with the cult potentially getting away with murder?"

"Frankly, I don't give a shit what the cult does, as long as it leaves everyone else alone." Sherry's voice rose. "You didn't see Amanda. She was tortured. I don't know if any amount of therapy would have helped her. Am I upset that she died? Yes. Do I feel guilty that I practically kicked her out? Yes. Have I had enough of the soul healers? You're damn right, I have. Let them kill each other off. I don't care. Amanda's at peace now. I'd let it lie, if I were you. Tell Jane to go home." She glanced at her watch. "I really should get to work."

Sam stood and pulled out a business card again. "If you think of anything else we should know, please call us."

"Sure." Sherry took it, but Jillian suspected the card would go into the garbage the moment they left.

She silently walked down the path with Sam, then looked down at her phone with surprise when it rang. She stopped walking. "Hello."

Dead air, then the line disconnected.

"Who was it?" Sam asked.

"I don't know. They hung up without saying anything." Jillian peered at the phone's display.

"Call Jeremy and give him the number."

"I don't have to." She lowered her phone. "It's Jane's number."

Sam frowned. "Call her back."

Jillian did so. "It's going through to voicemail."

"Hang up." Sam pulled out her own phone and made a call. "I need the address of Jane's apartment, and the key." Silence, then: "I want to check on her." She paused. "Tell her we'll be there in around fifteen minutes. Thanks." She hung up. "Jeremy's going to call Wendy and get her to meet us there with the key. Come on." She strode off.

Jillian hurried after her.

THEY SAT IN the car across from Jane's apartment building until they saw a woman with fiery red hair stroll down the sidewalk and enter the lobby. Wendy, Jillian knew. As soon as she'd seen the photo Jeremy sent, she'd known that Wendy's hair would make her easy to spot.

They left the car, jaywalked across the street, and took the stairs to the third floor. Sam knocked on the door for Apartment 312.

"Who is it?" a muffled voice said.

"Sam and Jillian."

The door swung open. "She's not here," Wendy said as they walked in and glanced around.

"When did you last hear from her?" Jillian asked.

"Yesterday afternoon. She calls me just about every day, lets me know if she's found out anything new." Wendy's forehead creased. "I hope nothing's happened to her."

"Were you expecting something to happen to her?"

"No. But if her suspicions about her sister are right . . . she followed cult members around, showed up at their residences . . . she wasn't letting up." Wendy swallowed. "I tried calling her after I got off the phone with Jeremy. I got her voicemail."

"Let's look around." Sam moved farther into the living room. "You've been here before, right?" she said to Wendy. "If you see anything out of place, let us know."

Jillian walked down the hallway and into the bedroom. The lack of personal items reminded her of the bedrooms in the safe houses. Jane had lived here for a couple of months now. She'd dropped everything, packed a bag, flown over, and stayed. Under other circumstances, maybe she would have tried to put her personal stamp on the place, even though it was a furnished temporary residence. But she was consumed with proving that the cult had murdered her sister. And now she was gone.

Ten minutes later, they all met back in the living room. "Everything looks normal," Wendy said.

Jillian agreed. No signs of a struggle or a hasty exit. No half-eaten plates of food; no music playing; Jane's purse and phone weren't here. If not for the strange hang up call and Jane ignoring the news that they had information to run by her, Jillian wouldn't be concerned.

"Thanks, Wendy," Sam said. "If you hear from her or find out where she is, call us right away."

"I will." Wendy bit her lip. "I hope she's okay."

"Me too." Despite her own worry, Jillian gave Wendy a reassuring smile.

They left the apartment, parting ways with Wendy in the hallway. Sam didn't speak until they were back in the car. "My gut says something's wrong."

"Mine too."

"I'm calling Roberta." Sam pulled out her phone. "Hi, Jane's missing." Silence. "No, we're not absolutely sure the cult's involved. We're not sure what's going on." She told Roberta about not being able to reach Jane, the hang up call, and their visit to her apartment. "We haven't found out anything that indicates Amanda was using," Sam said, after a long silence. Jillian could hear a tinny voice responding, but couldn't make out what Roberta was saying. Sam's eyes flicked to Jillian. "I'm not sure that's a good idea." Jillian had the impression they were talking about her. She resisted the urge to lean closer. "Let's talk about it when we're back. Yeah, okay. Bye."

Sam ended the call and looked at Jillian. "We're going back to the island to regroup. We've run out of avenues to explore, anyway."

Jillian bit her tongue as she pulled on her seatbelt. Nope, she wouldn't ask Sam to tell her what Roberta had proposed that was a bad idea. She had the feeling she'd soon find out.

Chapter Seven

WHEN JILLIAN AND Sam entered the conference room and sat down, Roberta was leaning across Jeremy to gaze at his laptop. She lifted her head and straightened. "Welcome back. No activity on her debit or credit cards."

"Her last outgoing call was to you," Jeremy added. "She's had a few incoming calls, but nothing suspicious. Her phone is off. I can't locate it."

Jillian raised a finger. "Can I be cynical for a minute?"

Roberta's eyes narrowed. "Yes."

"There were no signs of a struggle at her apartment, nothing to indicate she left it against her will. Maybe she's dropped out of sight so we'll kick the investigation up a notch. Maybe she worried that we'd decide Amanda's death wasn't suspicious. Maybe we weren't working fast enough for her. I don't know." Jillian paused. "But with her disappearing, we're now taking everything more seriously."

"Or she could be legitimately missing, and they snatched her from somewhere outside her apartment. I understand what you're saying, but I'd rather look for her and discover that she's deceived us, than not look for her and find out that she's captive somewhere, or worse." Roberta leaned back in her chair. "The first logical place to look is the cult, but we need a quick way to get to the top dogs. We'll have to entice them with something they won't be able to resist. Money. We don't want to be too obvious, though, so we're going to start by letting them try to recruit one of us." She focused on Jillian. "You."

Apprehension mingled with excitement. Getting cozy with a cult didn't thrill Jillian, but at least she'd play a key role, rather than follow Sam around and play second fiddle.

"I thought we were going to discuss that," Sam said.

"We are discussing it."

Sam stared at Roberta.

"What will I have to do?" Jillian asked to fill the awkward silence.

"You'll dangle the bait."

"How?"

"You're at a crossroads in your life. You've been bumped up to management at the accounting firm where you work. You hate your new job. It's forcing you to re-examine your professional life, and by extension, your life. You're searching now. You attended a crusade with a friend," Roberta glanced at Sam, "and received a flyer in the parking lot. You went to one of the websites . . ." She turned to Jeremy.

"I took a look," he said. "What a great fishing hole the Internet is. Lost souls, souls in transition, souls searching for the meaning of life—look no further than social networking sites, forums, and chat rooms. They also hang out in places where people with, uh, life problems gather."

"The recently separated, those who have lost their jobs, who are experiencing money problems, grieving over a recent death . . . they're all ripe for the picking," Roberta said.

"No people with chronic medical problems, though." Jeremy shook his head. "They want them healthy."

"So I make contact, attend a few meetings," Jillian said, "and then what?"

"You've discussed your new friends with your mother, who happens to be well-off financially and a bit of a philanthropist. She likes what she's hearing. She's considering a donation. She wants to meet the people who count. And, of course, should her daughter decide to work with the soul healers, she'll expect her to work closely with the leadership."

"They'll definitely have to meet my mother." A dull ache flared in Jillian's chest.

Roberta nodded. "Yes, they will. Ruth has agreed to work with you on this."

"Ruth?" Sam said, her voice tinged with surprise.

Ruth was an older, retired Deiform who lived on the western side of the island. Jillian had waved to her a few times, but didn't know her.

"She infiltrated a few cults in her time." Roberta pointed at Sam. "I expect you to support them. Your first step is to visit one of the soul healers' websites. Get your hands on their material, read it, figure out how to best initiate contact. When you're ready, go back into the world. When you need Ruth, she'll join you."

"Anything else?" Sam asked.

"Jillian will have to be an only child."

Jeremy nodded. "I've created another identity for you to use," he said to Jillian. "It will jibe with Ruth's."

"You'll use the new identity from this point forward, but only for this investigation. That's it for now. I'll leave you to it." Roberta rose and left the room. Jeremy trailed after her.

Sam rolled back her chair. "I'll go get the flyer."

Jillian wondered if Sam was chasing after Roberta to suggest a plan that wouldn't involve her sitting on the sidelines while she watched over her trainee and Ruth. Yes, Sam would be the protector again, and Jillian would be the damsel who might need rescuing. Half the time, she still felt as if she was stumbling around in the dark, so she should be grateful that Sam would be around to pull her ass out of the fire if the situation turned ugly. She'd tell herself that, anyway.

She lifted one of the conference room's laptop lids and waited for the screen to come alive. Fifteen minutes later, Sam returned, sat next to her, and slapped the flyer onto the table.

"You know so much about cults that you should probably be the bait," she said to Sam, curious to see how Sam would respond. "I'm not sure why Roberta wants it to be me." Had she received a vision, seen Jillian in the cult?

This Fellowship cell believed that Roberta, its Guide, received instruction from God. When deciding whether to join the Fellowship, Jillian had worried that following Roberta's orders without question could be a sticking point, especially when those orders involved killing people. She'd have to accept that, over time, she'd come to implicitly trust Roberta, regardless of the source of the guidance and visions Roberta received. Sam trusted her, and Jillian trusted that Sam would always act in accordance with her Christian values—values that happened to match Jillian's, but she'd dropped the Christian label.

"Between the two of us, it makes sense for me to remain outside the cult," Sam said. "First, the Beguilers will have less of a chance of getting to you when you're with cult members than they would if you were alone, supporting me. Second, you're not familiar with all the resources available to you."

So Sam had decided to play nice—or Roberta had ordered her to. "I'm a capable woman, you know."

"I know. But you're not ready to work on your own yet." Sam glanced at her. "If you want, I'll work on this alone."

"No, don't do that." She hadn't left Mom and Danny behind to sit around and sulk. "I guess I'm not used to being the junior member of the team. Did you feel like a child when you first joined?"

"No." Sam rubbed her finger along her lower lip. "Then again, I almost *was* a child. For someone like you, a confident adult who's used to calling the shots in her life, I can understand why you feel the way you do."

Rather than bolstering Jillian, Sam's words made her feel petty. "I'll get over it."

Sam's forehead creased. "Listen, Roberta isn't fobbing you off with trivial work on this one. Your role will be critical." She tapped the paper in front of her. "Jeremy said the third address down leads to the most secular site. I guess they put it there for people who were dragged to the crusade and only went up to the front to please whoever they were with."

Getting the message, Jillian typed in the web address and waited for the website to load. The resulting page promised to reveal how to overcome any problem in return for the visitor's name and email address. She submitted her first name and an email address she'd created at one of the free email sites.

"Now we wait for the free e-book they promised," Sam said.

Jillian checked her email. "I have to confirm my email address first." She did so, then refreshed the Inbox. "Here it is." Sam leaned over to skim the e-book with her. It was filled with the usual clichés about how to harness your inner power and visualize your way out of any predicament. "Do you believe any of this bullshit?"

Sam shrugged. "I believe that people can create their own prisons and hold themselves back. But change takes work. It's not easy."

"Well, I'm on their list now. I wonder what they'll want me to do next."

"They'll want to find out about you, so they can weed out the undesirables. You'll probably get another email today or tomorrow, and at some point they'll ask you to do a survey."

Jillian didn't mind playing a waiting game. Given the choice between staying on the island and making contact with the soul healers, she'd be happy to remain right where she was. "You know, I initially thought the Fellowship was a cult. It does have some of the characteristics of one, don't you think?"

Sam folded her arms. "Like what?"

"Cutting off family and friends, withholding information until the recruit is firmly in the fold . . ."

"We don't demand that you leave your life behind because your family and friends are evil or against our cause. As for withholding information, yes, we do that. But not because we're trying to hide our true purpose and beliefs until someone's joined. You got those up front."

She certainly had, and she was only teasing, anyway. "Some people would say all religious people are brainwashed."

Sam snorted. "You honestly believe that?"

"No." Though when she'd looked back at her time in the church, she'd thought of herself that way. It wasn't true, but a way of absolving herself of responsibility. After Dad's death, Mom hadn't forced her to go to church. As a teenager, she'd chosen to go. Once she'd walked away, she'd allowed her suppressed anger over Dad's suicide to burst to the surface and had blamed the church for everything. But he'd committed the sins. He'd pulled the trigger. Resenting the church, and those who remained within it but didn't shove their beliefs down everyone's throats, was a waste of time and energy. As for all religious people being brainwashed, hell, many of them were hypocrites. Brainwashed people didn't nod and smile, then go out and do the opposite of what they'd pledged to do.

"As for us, everyone must come willingly, and we're very particular about who we invite into the fold." Sam's eyes narrowed. "Sometimes His guidance on that matter is mystifying."

Actually, Roberta had guided them to her—which amounted to the same thing to everyone in the Fellowship but her. She ignored Sam's subtle jab, and it was time to stop yanking Sam's chain. Their nascent friendship—well, Jillian saw it that way; Sam might see it as nothing more than a working relationship—was important to her. "Since there's nothing more to do for now, do you think I can have a peek at those history tomes you mentioned?"

Sam gave her a long look. Jillian wanted to kick herself. She'd just pressed Sam's buttons, and now she expected Sam to trust that her interest was sincere. Stupid! She drew breath to say, "Never mind, we can go another time."

But Sam said, "Okay."

Really? She leaped to her feet before Sam had a chance to change her mind.

HER EYES ADJUSTING to the dimmer light, Jillian followed Sam down the stone steps, bursting with curiosity. Puzzled, she surveyed the gloomy undercroft, with its dingy stone floor and walls, and not a stitch of furniture.

"Everything's in here." Sam led her to a wooden door on the far wall, swung it open, and flicked a switch.

Jillian blinked. She hadn't expected the bright modern room, one that wouldn't be out of place in an office tower. She stared at its contents in awe. Bookcases and display cases stuffed with books and parchments lined the walls, a metal table and chairs stood in the centre of the room, and floor and desk lamps provided illumination. Afraid to touch anything, Jillian carefully moved farther into the underground library. The air felt dryer.

Sam shut the door and gestured to her left. "Here you'll find the investigations we conducted pre-1970 or so." She pointed to her right. "Our history, as recorded by our Guides. Some entries read coherently, others are as clear as the Book of Revelation. Any personal journals left behind by Deiforms and Supporters are also here."

"Am I supposed to be keeping a journal?" Jillian had tried to keep a diary once, and had managed to scribble down the mundane details of her days for about a week before she'd given up.

"No. But if you do, you can say whether you want it to be preserved or destroyed upon your death."

"Do you keep a journal?"

"No."

Sam's answer didn't surprise her. "I take it that the later investigations are stored digitally."

Sam nodded. "Since about 1980. We have hard copies too, but we don't store them here. They're in the main house's basement." She suddenly smiled. "The same applies to personal documents. You don't have to write everything longhand. Most of the later ones are digital. You can write longhand if you want, but . . ." She moved to a metal filing cabinet against the back wall. "Around thirty years ago, we started to create a catalogue of what's in here and where to find it." She slid a drawer open and beckoned Jillian closer.

Jillian read the folder labels: Exorcisms, Murder, False Messiahs, Cults, Hate, False Healings, False Miracles—the list went on, and that was only the top of three drawers.

Sam pushed the drawer shut. "Parchments have to be read on this table." She patted the metal tabletop. "The same goes for the older books. Don't remove a parchment before I teach you how to handle them. Just ask me when you want to read one."

"I don't know where to start."

"You're interested in reading that book about our early history, right?"

Jillian nodded.

Sam wandered over to one of the bookcases. After a moment, she crouched, carefully slid out a book, and laid it on the table. "This one. At some point, someone copied and rebound the book that someone else had transcribed from documents in there." She gestured toward a display case. "The book is still old, though, so be careful with it."

"I will. But right now, I should get back to one of the books you've given me on cults." She wanted to get her required reading out of the way, especially since she'd be rubbing elbows with cult members. "Can you leave the book on the table, or is that against the rules?"

"No, I'll leave it out. You can come down here anytime. The chapel is always open."

"I'll be back soon," Jillian said, meaning it. She wanted to learn everything she could about the Fellowship. It was her life now. She was one of them.

JILLIAN SIPPED HER tea as she watched what she hoped was the tail end of a motivational webinar. After almost an hour of rah-rah advice about visualization, goal setting, and other topics that would enable her to resolve any problem, no matter how large or small, she was ready to nod off, despite the presenter's energetic, perky voice. As expected, after a few vague emails about problem solving and a survey about her goals and challenges, Jillian had received an invitation to an exclusive webinar that would reveal how to tap her inner resources and think her problems away!

Next to her, Sam shifted in her seat. "I think they're moving into the pitch stage now," she murmured.

The presenter changed the slide. "Now, maybe you're saying to yourself, I know what I have to do, but I need someone on my side. I need someone to hold me accountable. I need someone I can trust, someone who will walk with me and guide me to the life I was put on this earth to live. We have you covered. If you're really serious . . . if you want to change your life . . . join others who are on the same path as you."

Sam straightened and nudged Jillian's arm. "This is it."

"With our expert coach guiding you every step of the way, you'll achieve the life you've visualized. All you have to do to take advantage of this opportunity to live the life you've always wanted is to go to . . ."

Jillian's stomach fluttered. She reached for her notebook and jotted down the web address for the coaching program, then surfed to it after the presenter had chirped good-bye. She could see how the slick presentation at the coaching site would attract the desperate and downcast. A video of a handsome man repeating the offer in sultry tones invited visitors to enter their name, email address, and phone number in the form below. But if one wasn't ready for that, perhaps a book or video series would suit?

Sam thrust her hand toward the screen. "They have a good setup going on. Most people won't end up in the cult, but they might buy something. It sure beats standing on street corners selling candles and flowers."

Or worse. One of the books Jillian had read described a cult that forced its female members into prostitution to fund itself. She assumed Roberta wouldn't expect anyone to infiltrate such a cult—at least she hoped not. "It keeps the line of communication open, too. I bet they pitch the coaching in all their products."

Five minutes later, she skimmed the email welcoming her to the program. "Someone named Andy is going to call me," she said, now understanding why the form had required her phone number. "When would be a good time?"

Sam shrugged. "I don't know, tomorrow at seven? You work full-time, remember"

Jillian typed a reply and sent it, then sighed. "I hope I don't blow it on the first call."

"You know what to say."

Yes, but when working for the agency, she'd always played a confident accountant. Then again, to gain her co-workers' trust, she'd sympathized with their problems, sometimes claiming that she'd gone through similar experiences. This would be no different, except this time the point of the conversations would be her supposed crisis.

"Remember, if he thinks you're a promising prospect, he'll invite you to a meeting. Tell him you'll think about it. You don't want to seem too eager." Sam rolled back her chair. "Anyway, I'm going to read for a bit. I'll see you at dinner."

Jillian watched her leave, then drank the rest of her tea. After returning her cup to the kitchen, she went to her room, grabbed her jacket, and whistled for the dogs. Ten minutes later, she sat cross-legged on the same rock on which she'd tried to pry more information from Sam about the gifts; it felt like a lifetime ago. "You two have fun," she said to Puck and Raven. "Don't mind me." She pulled out her phone and practiced her conversation with Andy to dead air.

Chapter Eight

JILLIAN LISTENED TO Andy's closing remarks, not sure how she'd done. Sam hadn't barked any orders into her mind, but she'd whispered a few suggestions based on Jillian's side of the conversation. "Yes, I'll be sure to read the material."

"Good," Andy said in his silky baritone. "I know this is a frightening time for you, Jillian. Now that you're no longer sleepwalking through life, you know that you need to make a change. You feel that you're on the verge of transforming your life, and that's because you are. Jillian, I want to assure you that you're not alone. I want to remind you that contacting me was a brave thing to do. Not everyone would have taken that step, Jillian. Not everyone has the courage to change her life. You do, Jillian. You do."

"Thank you," she murmured, rolling her eyes. She didn't dare look at Sam.

"There are others just like you who want to find their purpose and stop wasting their lives away. Working with a group, belonging to a community in which members support and help each other, makes a huge difference. I lead a group made up of people just like you, Jillian. We meet once a week. Why don't you come to our next meeting?"

"I'd like to read the material you'll send first," she said, trying to sound obedient but not too eager.

"That shouldn't take you long."

"What do you do at these meetings?" she asked, stalling.

"We discuss the challenges we're facing. We support each other. You have a lot to offer the group."

Really? An accountant who hated her management job and who'd expressed vague concerns about the news and the state of society?

"You don't have to decide right now," Andy said smoothly. "Why don't I call you tomorrow?"

"Sure." She paused. "I'll think about going to a meeting."

"I'll be there, so you'll know at least one person, Jillian."

"That will definitely help."

"I'll call you at the same time tomorrow."

"Sounds good."

"I'll look forward to it, Jillian."

"Me too." They said good-bye. Jillian's shoulders sagged. "How did I do?"

"What, do you want me to give you a score out of ten?" Sam wrote a large *9* on a paper and held it up.

"You know, you can be seriously annoying," Jillian said, her smile ruining any hope she'd had of sounding stern.

Sam lowered her score. "You said the right things, he's sending you material, and he invited you to a meeting. He obviously believed you."

"And he knows I'm not too old, or sick, or argumentative."

"You're catching on. Let's listen to the conversation, see what we can pick up." Sam pressed a button on the conference table's control panel.

Jillian settled back to listen and tried not to cringe at the sound of her own voice. Jesus, she did sound sincere. And how many times had Andy said her name? Rather than making her feel special or whatever it was supposed to do, it had irritated the crap out of her.

"He's feeling out your views regarding the establishment and government," Sam said when Andy questioned Jillian about the issues of the day that he could somehow relate back to anything she'd said about her life and bogus job. "You responded exactly right."

Critical and concerned about society and its values, but helpless to do anything about it. Andy would hopefully view her as a potential kindred spirit.

Sam chewed her lip. "Let's see what his reading material is about."

Jillian checked her email and skimmed the attached document from Andy. "It's basically a rehash of what we just discussed, with a questionnaire."

Sam read Andy's questions. "Clever. Another way of sizing you up."

How many tests would she have to pass? "What else are we doing to find Jane? This way could take a while."

"Jeremy and Emma are looking, but she's vanished into thin air."

"Do you think the cult has her?"

Sam shrugged. "I don't know. They're the only ones that would want to make her disappear."

"What if she went willingly?" Assuming she wasn't dead. "I don't mean because she's trying to do the same thing we'll try to do. What if she's one of them again?"

Sam's voice hardened. "She's been out for years."

"Yeah, and has been hanging around them, hoping they'll slip up. She could have succumbed again. If anyone's in crisis, she is."

"Once someone has broken free of mind control, it would be difficult to lure them in again. If she's intentionally joined them, it'll be because she wants to infiltrate and find evidence that they killed Amanda." Sam shook her head. "But I don't see it. They're not stupid. They wouldn't accept that she'd turned from accusing them of murder one day, to wanting to return to the fold the next. If they have her, they took her."

"In that case, they could be trying to bring her over to their side. Even if she's resisting, she won't be at her best." Lack of sleep, poor nourishment, constantly bombarded with cult doctrine and whatever other crap they were throwing at her . . . "Aren't you worried that she'll tell them about the Fellowship?"

"No, because they wouldn't believe her."

"How can you be—"

"You didn't. Jim told you about the Fellowship, and you laughed at him. You didn't say, 'Oh, okay, Jim. I guess I'm a Fledgling. Come right on over and I'll join up.'" Sam's voice was even, but . . .

"Do you blame me for Jim's death?"

Sam's brow furrowed. "What?"

"If I'd believed him and met him that night, he'd still be alive, right?" She grabbed a handful of her jeans in balled hands. "You see, the thing is, I never would have believed him. It wouldn't have mattered what he told me. There's nothing he could have said to me that night that would have made me believe him. Nothing. I wasn't like you. I had no inkling. And, I'm sorry, but someone calling me out of the blue and telling me I've been chosen by God wasn't the best way to make me listen."

They lapsed into heavy silence. Jillian stared at the laptop's screen, but nothing registered. She'd accused Sam of blaming her, when really, she blamed herself. Rationally, she understood that just about everyone would have hung up on Jim and dismissed him as a loon, but it didn't help. At the same time, she couldn't change what had happened and needed to forgive herself. She'd left Mom and Danny; she'd spend the rest of her life making up for Jim's death. She could point out that Sam, a Christian, should forgive her, but she wouldn't stoop to that.

"I don't blame you," Sam said quietly.

"No? That's not what you said when we first met."

"I was upset. Someone I'd known for years had just died, and you weren't the typical Fledgling, on several fronts. But you're not responsible for his death. We don't know what would have happened if you'd met him that night. Maybe you both would have been killed."

Jillian swallowed. After Sam's initial outburst, Sam had protected her, cleared her name, and had never again suggested that she'd gotten Jim killed. And, yes, expecting Sam to have greeted her with a warm smile and open arms was unreasonable. Jillian would have been freaking furious, too—and grieving. This was about her, not Sam. "I'll forgive myself eventually," she said crisply. "If I agree to go to the meeting when Andy calls tomorrow, that means we'll be leaving soon." With no idea of when they'd set foot on the island again.

Sam remained silent. Was she angry? Jillian searched her face, but couldn't glean anything.

"Yeah, we'll be leaving soon," Sam finally said. "Take advantage of the time to relax a bit."

Jillian bit back the same advice. "I will." Maybe she'd visit the undercroft's library, but not right now. "I think I'll go for a walk," she said with a weak smile. Usually she'd ask whether Sam wanted to join her, but she wanted to be alone.

JILLIAN PLAYED THE basic chords once more, then rested the guitar on her lap and gazed out at the water. She didn't know why she always returned to the rock she'd sat on with Sam. No matter where she wandered and how many places she considered resting, she always ended up here. As she sat motionless, listening to the birds sing and the insects buzz around her, she appreciated for the first time what Sam meant by only letting her guard down on the island. Jillian had experienced a palpable sense of security when she'd stepped off the plane. She could close her eyes here, relax; she didn't have to constantly scan her surroundings for threats. She could focus on her guitar playing, if she could refer to it as that. She hadn't played an actual song yet, but her brain was dredging up her previous experience with the instrument. Tomorrow she'd try something short and easy, and probably mangle the hell out of it.

The light breeze tried to lift the pages of the "learn the guitar" book that lay open in front of her, but she'd anchored them with a couple of stones.

"Hello, Jillian."

Jillian looked over her shoulder.

Ruth smiled at her. "I hope you don't mind me interrupting, but since I'm going to be your mother, I thought we should become more acquainted than simply saying hello to each other."

"No, that's all right," Jillian said, moving the guitar to the rock and scrambling to her feet.

Ruth looked up at the blue sky. "Do you want to go for a walk? I think you can leave your guitar here."

"Sure." She fell in next to Ruth as she strolled away, and waited for her to speak.

"I went into a few cults in my time," Ruth finally said. "Don't fall into the trap of thinking that because you're aware of the mind control techniques the cult may use, you're immune to them. I'm sure Sam's told you to, uh, centre yourself regularly when you're dealing with cult members."

Sam *had* advised Jillian to reach for her centre on a daily basis. "I'll keep that in mind." Jillian paused. "Do you know Sam well?"

Ruth's mouth turned up at the corners. "Very well. I trained her. She visits me often. You'll find that you'll always feel a bond with the one who trained you."

Maybe that was why she kept returning to that damn rock. "I thought Brian trained her."

"Brian brought her in, but I trained her. Just as she brought Warren in, but didn't train him." Ruth chuckled. "I don't think she wanted to train anyone. I'm sure it took some persuading on Roberta's part."

Probably because Sam didn't want anyone to feel bonded to her. "Has Sam said as much to you?"

"No. But as I said, I know her very well, and I know that, regardless of how she feels about it, she's taking her role as your trainer very seriously." Ruth's shrewd eyes met Jillian's. "Now, who do you think brought you in?"

Jillian considered the question. "I don't know."

"Jim found you, but you're the only Fledgling I know of who arrived in the company of Supporters, rather than another Deiform. You'll have to scour the records in the undercroft to find out if you're the only one to ever arrive without a fellow Deiform."

Was she the only atheist, too? Maybe atheists didn't qualify for a Deiform escort, though when she'd willingly returned to the island, Sam had been with her. A lightbulb went on. "Sam brought me in."

Ruth's face softened; she almost smiled. "That, she did."

Jillian screwed up her courage to ask Ruth a question that had nagged at her since coming to mind. Ruth struck Jillian as a sharp cookie; she wouldn't appreciate feeble attempts at manipulation, or any white lies. Bluntness, rather than subtlety, would have a greater chance of getting an answer. "Why does Sam live in the main house? I've gathered that she's a loner, so why is she living in a group environment? I would have thought she'd want to live by herself."

Ruth was silent for a moment. "Why do you want to know?"

"Because I'm curious about it," Jillian said, again opting for honesty. "It doesn't jibe with what I know about her. I could ask her, but she won't tell me, and I don't want to annoy her." She glanced at Ruth, and saw the amusement she'd expected to see.

"Well, I suppose there's no harm in telling you, since the answer won't reveal anything you don't already know."

Okay, if anyone else told her she'd get an answer she already knew, she'd scream.

"She asked Roberta if she could move out, and Roberta said no."

A frisson of shock ran through Jillian. She certainly *hadn't* known that tidbit. "Why? I'm sure Sam's earned her own space."

"A thousand times over," Ruth said. "That's not the issue."

"What is, then?" She wouldn't let Ruth dodge the question now.

"As you said, Sam prefers to keep to herself. Roberta worried that if Sam were to live alone, she'd become a hermit. Roberta would occasionally see her, and Sam would continue to visit me, but the others would only ever see her in the chapel."

"I doubt it would be that bad."

"She wouldn't seek company, Jillian."

True. "Has she always been a loner?"

Ruth cocked her head. "More or less. She's always been quiet and preferred her own company, but she wasn't always as eager to return to her room and shut herself away."

"She sometimes reads in the study."

"If the study suddenly becomes popular, she'll move," Ruth said, making Jillian smile. "Sam came to us many years ago. She's seen and heard terrible things, witnessed unimaginable horrors. Her faith in the Lord has never wavered. It's stronger than ever. But it wouldn't surprise me if she's lost faith in everyone else. Have you wondered why she reads so much?"

Jillian shook her head.

"Her books are order in the chaos. She can choose to lose herself in stories in which Good wins, Evil loses, and everything is tied up in a neat little bow. She needs that, so she can return to the world and face Evil again."

"She reads a lot of non-fiction. She was reading about the Tudors once. They weren't exactly model citizens. They chopped people's heads off at the drop of a hat." Given the context, Jillian snickered at the idiom.

"Not every book she reads has to wrap her in a blanket and offer her milk and cookies. But her time alone, and stories that remind her of the good in this world, have a rejuvenating effect. Socializing doesn't. It drains her, and that's the last thing she needs when she comes home after having her soul pummelled yet again." Ruth's voice cracked. "The purer the Deiform, the more it hurts."

Jillian shoved her hands into her jacket pockets. She had to stop being so sensitive when talking to Sam. Who'd want to work with an adult who regularly throws temper tantrums? She needed to keep her pride in check. "She must hate working with me." When Ruth didn't answer, Jillian's eyes flicked to her, then back to the path. Maybe Ruth was deciding how honest she should be.

"I've no doubt it's sometimes . . . challenging for her," Ruth said, "but not because it's you specifically. I'm glad Roberta has the two of you working together. You have an excellent teacher, and I'm hoping that Sam will share her feelings about an investigation with you, rather than internalizing it all."

Jillian wanted to laugh. She was lucky if Sam shared what type of cereal she liked.

"That will take time, though."

Yeah, a million years—minimum.

As they walked on in silence, Jillian reflected that Ruth was right. She hadn't learned anything new about Sam; Ruth's answers had merely deepened her understanding of what she already knew. Could she apply that to Roberta's cryptic answer when she'd asked how Roberta had known she was gay? Roberta had known before they'd met . . . or had she? Sam had said that she'd read about Jillian's sexual orientation after Roberta had called her in. Roberta could have added the information to Jillian's file while Jillian was sleeping off the drug Peter had given her. Still, what could Roberta have gleaned from seeing her unconscious? Had she seen a vision? Sensed something? The jury was still out regarding how Jillian felt about Roberta's abilities, but assuming she did have extrasensory perception, what would she have sensed or seen?

Ask me again when you know the answer.

Maybe that meant it wasn't something Jillian knew at this point, but would learn later. Considering she didn't have a clue how Roberta could have known she was gay, she'd go with that for now.

Ruth stopped outside a brick bungalow. "Here we are. Would you like to come in for tea?"

"I'd love to. We're supposed to be getting to know each other better, but all we've talked about is Sam."

Ruth quirked a brow. "I don't know about you, but I've learned quite a lot."

Chapter Nine

Jillian experienced a sense of déjà vu as she hopped off the plane and walked with Sam to the sedan. How long would it be until she didn't flashback to the first time she'd arrived on the mainland with Sam, not sure if she was with a friend or a liar, and determined to never return to the island? She chuckled to herself. The last thing she'd expected to do was return from the island months later with a cult meeting on her agenda for later that evening. Crazy.

As she settled into the car's passenger seat, another familiar urge taunted her. Would she ever not want to call Mom and Danny? Would she forget they were alive? Would she look up one day and realize that she hadn't thought about them for months? The latter possibility frightened her. She didn't want to forget her history, her former life . . . but in ten, twenty, thirty years, would any of it feel real? Would she wonder if it had actually happened? Would Jillian Campbell truly be dead?

They drove the ten minutes into town in comfortable silence, listening to the radio. Unless someone else had stayed at the safe house since their last visit, the pantry and fridge should still be stocked. "When should I start staying at the apartment?" she asked, referring to the address she'd give to cult members, if they asked.

"I doubt they'll follow you around, so you'll only have to be there if you invite anyone over."

"But what if they do follow me?"

"They won't. They'll have no reason to." They stopped at a traffic light. "Every time we drive through this intersection, I marvel at how magnificent that church is," Sam murmured. "Looks like a morning service is starting soon."

Jillian gazed at the people climbing the stone steps up to the entrance of an old, majestic church. "You want to go in there, don't you?"

Sam took her time answering. "I wouldn't mind a look inside sometime."

"Why not now? It's only," she glanced at the dashboard clock, "9:50. From the looks of it, there's a cemetery. I can stroll around it while you're inside."

"No way."

"I'm going to the meeting tonight by myself."

"That's different. You'll be outside on your own for a minute or two. Here, you'll be completely exposed, and there's too many people around. A Beguiler could easily blend in."

"On the other hand, there's too many people around," Jillian said, throwing Sam's observation back at her.

"No."

A retort to the effect that Sam should trust God to protect her died on Jillian's tongue. She wouldn't manipulate her in that way, and He hadn't protected Kristin. The light changed. "Pull into the parking lot," she barked. To her surprise, Sam complied. She waited until they'd parked, then twisted toward her. "You can't be with me twenty-four hours a day. You know that."

Sam remained silent, her face reflecting her inner struggle.

"It's time to kick the baby bird from the nest, okay?" Jillian pressed. "You're not responsible for me anymore. I want this to be a partnership of equals, not a babysitter and her charge. I still have a lot to learn and you're more experienced than I am with the types of situations the Fellowship investigates, but I'm responsible for myself."

"And I'm responsible for keeping you safe."

Jillian's frustration mounted. "It's time for me to face my fear that I'll run into a Beguiler, and for you to face your fear that one of them will kill me," she blurted. *Damn it!* She held her breath and waited for Sam's denial, but Sam didn't react. "You've already saved me once. You've done your bit." Nothing. "You've taught me the gifts I can use to defend myself. That's all you can be expected to do. If something happens to me, it won't be your fault."

Sam stared out the window at the church. The silence stretched.

"I know you haven't been going to church when we're here because you don't want to leave me alone in the safe house." She'd gathered that based on something Sam had said the very first Sunday they'd spent back in the world. "I'm trained now, and by a damn good teacher. How am I supposed to believe in my gifts, if you don't? You have to trust that I can take care of myself."

Jesus, Sam still wasn't saying anything, and Jillian didn't want to beg. If Sam ever wanted to work alone again, she'd have to overcome her exaggerated sense of responsibility toward her charge.

"I'll just stay for the service," Sam finally said. "I'll come back another day to look around."

Jillian released a relieved sigh. "No, take your time."

Sam's eyes met Jillian's. "You could come with me."

"You know I won't do that." Jillian softened her voice. "Even if I was into it, I'd say no. I want to spend some time outside. At least half an hour."

"Take this." Sam removed her hoodie, unstrapped her holster, and handed it to Jillian.

She hesitated, then took it and strapped it on. No need to mention that she'd only shoot someone if there was no other way out.

"If you get yourself killed, I'll be really pissed off," Sam said.

And Sam would struggle with guilt for the rest of her life. Jillian had two reasons to stay alive.

Sam pulled out her phone. "I'm setting it to vibrate. If you run into trouble, call me."

"I will." She adjusted the holster to a more comfortable position and zipped up her jacket.

They got out of the car. "Call me when you're done, and I'll meet you back here," Jillian said. "Give me at least half an hour, okay? See you in a bit." She willed herself to walk away and not look back.

Wandering down the first path she saw, she jumped when two birds suddenly took flight in front of her. Maybe she shouldn't have sent Sam away so quickly, but she didn't want Sam to resent her. *Deep breath.* Hoping to occupy her mind with something other than being ambushed, she left the path and walked along the nearest row of headstones, reading as she went.

FORTY-FIVE MINUTES AND umpteen epitaphs later, Jillian paused and reflected on what she'd read, not at all bothered that Sam hadn't called. Sunlight dappled the ground beneath the trees, but it wasn't too warm. Cemetery workers weeded, pruned, and mowed. People were everywhere, visiting their departed loved ones. Jillian felt so fortunate to be alive. Every time she'd read yet another old tombstone for a child, she couldn't help but think about how she'd cheated death. Hell, in a graveyard not too far away from Mom's house sat a tombstone with her name and birthdate on it, but that wasn't what she'd thought about when she'd stood in front of yet another old family plot and realized that most of the children hadn't seen age five. No, she'd flashed back to when she'd clutched her bleeding stomach and known her time was up. If Sam hadn't been there . . .

She shook herself and refocused on the tombstone in front of her. Another child. 1886–1887. Jesus. "Nobody should have to bury a child" was a modern sentiment. As recently as one hundred years ago, holding a dying child in one's arms wasn't unusual, and the average life expectancy was around fifty years. At thirty-six, she would have been one of the lucky ones. Her eyes welled with tears. She wasn't usually this sentimental, but she couldn't help but think about Mom, who'd buried a child, or at least believed she had. Jillian was suddenly acutely aware of the phone in her front pocket. *Don't even think about it.* She moved on to the next headstone, mercifully for someone who'd seen old age.

Footsteps, behind her! She whirled. "Good morning," said the man approaching her. Jillian's heart raced. She wanted to run away. Out of all the people in the cemetery who could have struck up a conversation with her, why did she have to get the guy in the clerical collar? She couldn't help but think of Dad—and how some of the most ungodly and morally bankrupt people wore a damn collar. Politeness took over. "Morning," she said, wondering if he was associated with the church that had enthralled Sam.

"Are you here to visit someone in particular?" he asked.

"No, I'm just looking around."

"Interested in history?"

She nodded, her heart still pounding. When he clasped his hands behind his back and strolled toward the next tombstone, she felt obligated to go with him.

"This is one of the cemetery's oldest sections," he said. "We have graves here from the 1700s."

"I noticed that." She read the next tombstone as she passed it. A teenager who'd died in 1905. "Too many children are buried here."

He nodded. "Makes you appreciate modern medicine and our improved life expectancy, doesn't it?"

"Yes," she murmured, blood pounding in her ears. Why was she so stressed out? Okay, she'd rather be talking to anyone else but a man of the cloth, but her heart was practically leaping from her—her blood ran cold. Shit. Shit, shit, shit! She gave him a sidelong glance and forced herself to focus on what he was saying.

". . . stone in the adjacent section. Would you like to see?"

"Sure." If he was a Beguiler, why wasn't he making a move? Probably for the same reason she wasn't reaching for her gun. They were in a public place, surrounded by people. Mass panic would ensue. If he intended to capture her, drawing attention would only make removing her from the cemetery more difficult. Yes, capture her, because he wouldn't kill her here; if he'd wanted to, she'd be dead by now—a quick knife to the belly, a gun to the head. He'd taken her by surprise. No, Beguilers were like cats. They played with their prey, both before and after death. They only killed when toying with their target wasn't possible.

"This one's not as old, but as you can see, the detailed engraving is exquisite."

She gazed at the stone he'd led her to, but her mind was too busy to appreciate the engraver's handiwork. Maybe she was wrong. Maybe it was just the collar. Should she reach into her pocket and try to quietly call Sam? No, he'd hear her voice when she answered.

". . . short walk away."

She turned to him. "Pardon me? I'm sorry, the family over there caught my eye." *Yep, we're not alone, buddy.*

"I asked whether you'd like to see the old chapel that's not too far away."

So that was where he hoped to pounce—inside a chapel. "I'd like to, but not today. I should be going. I'm meeting someone."

"I don't think so."

"Excuse me?"

He tipped his head to the right. "That family you referred to . . . have another look."

Puzzled, she glanced at the man, woman, and two girls in their Sunday best, huddled around a grave.

"Now look over there, at the monument," the Beguiler calmly said, pointing.

She did so, and didn't see anything suspicious. "What about it?"

He pulled out a phone, punched in a number, and pressed the phone to his ear. "Wave to Jillian."

She looked back at the monument. A man who'd appeared to be reading the inscription waved. In a fit of bravado that defied her growing panic, she waved back.

The Beguiler snorted. "Walk away, and he'll shoot the girls."

"You wouldn't dare," she said, using every ounce of control she possessed to keep her voice level.

"Do you want to find out?" When she didn't move, he said, "I didn't think so. Now, let's go visit the chapel."

She had no choice but to stroll at his side. Why the chapel? Why not lead her to a car and drive off with her?

"Oh, if you were thinking of doing that disappearing trick your type are so fond of, don't. If I don't call my associate every five minutes, the girls die. If you take me out or disappear, I won't be making any calls."

There went time shifting. Would they really shoot children in the middle of a crowded cemetery? Probably not, but the bastard was right. She couldn't take the chance.

When a young couple strolled by and smiled at the Beguiler, Jillian's blood boiled, especially when the woman murmured, "Father." This son of a bitch wasn't taking her down. She needed to estimate how long it took to reach the chapel. They'd already walked for a couple of minutes. When she spotted the stone building, about four minutes had passed. If she ran, she could make it to the monument in three, perhaps?

Ignoring the large sign that said the chapel was closed to the public, the Beguiler pushed the wooden door open and motioned for her to go ahead. Jillian stepped into the dim sanctuary. The door thumped shut behind her. A gun pressed against the side of her head. "Raise your hands," another man growled.

She did so. A deadbolt clicked into place behind her. While the fake pastor unzipped her jacket and relieved her of her gun and phone, Jillian's eyes adjusted to the reduced lighting. Layers of dust covered the pews, the floor, the table holding candles that hadn't burned for years and a couple of old Bibles.

"Let's pay our respects at the altar," the Beguiler said with a sneer.

The other man—his lackey—pushed Jillian forward. She lowered her hands and followed the Beguiler to the front. Her breath caught in her throat. She struggled to keep the horror from her face. Metal objects lay in a row on the altar—a hook, knives, chains, a saw . . . Jesus. The chapel had become a medieval torture chamber. She wanted to wince and turn away but kept gazing forward, focusing on a point behind the altar. Without thinking, she'd stopped walking. "How original, gutting me on the altar." She forced a snicker. "I think I've seen that in almost every B horror movie I've watched."

Pain exploded in her right cheek. Her vision went white. She staggered back a step, but managed to remain standing, then gingerly felt around with her tongue. All her teeth were still there. Lackey moved into her field of vision, his gun levelled at her.

Rubbing his fist, the Beguiler stared coldly at Jillian. "Your death can be quick, or excruciatingly slow. Renounce your god, and I'll be merciful."

Jillian snorted. "You don't know the meaning of the word." Knowing what was coming, she tried not to cringe. His fist smashed into her left cheek. She gasped and dropped to her knees. The bitter taste of blood filled her mouth. She spit on the floor and swallowed, then quickly stood and defiantly met his eyes. "Go to hell." A punch to her stomach doubled her over. Sucking in air, she clutched her abdomen. *Look the bastard in the eye.* Gritting her teeth, she straightened and braced herself.

The Beguiler placed her gun and phone on the altar. He lifted a chain. "Let's get started."

Lackey grabbed his crotch with his free hand and leered. "Why don't we have some fun first?"

"Later. When she's more . . . receptive." A smile played on the Beguiler's lips. "I like it better that way."

Jillian fought her revulsion. *Don't give the bastard the satisfaction.* She cursed herself when he lashed the chain at her, making her flinch.

He grinned. "Oh, my. You're in for a rough time, Jillian."

A phone rang. Everyone froze. Jillian recognized the ring tone. "It's . . . Samantha. If I don't answer, she'll know something's wrong."

The Beguiler hesitated, then lifted Jillian's phone from the altar and handed it to her. "One word, and I'll tell my associate to shoot the girls, do you understand?"

She nodded. "Hello."

"I'm done," Sam said.

"I wish I'd gone with you."

Sam snorted. "Sure you do."

"Seriously, I do. You were right. I shouldn't skimp on my prayers. Next time I'll listen to you, Samantha."

Silence, then, "Are you in trouble?"

"Yes, I am. I'm still in the cemetery. I spent most of my time walking around one of the older sections."

"Do the Beguilers have you?"

"Uh-huh."

The Beguiler drew his finger across his throat.

"I have to go. I'll see you back at the car."

"I'll find you."

"Bye." Knowing the chances that Sam would stumble across the chapel in time to help her were lower than her chances of being struck by lightning, Jillian hung up. When the Beguiler held out his hand, she gave him the phone.

He turned it off and set it on the altar next to a tarnished brass candlestick, then turned back to Jillian. "Now, where were we?"

"I believe you were about to torture me, but you know what? I think I'll just disappear. You should have called your friend by now, and that family could be gone. You're bluffing."

His face darkened. He pulled out his phone. Jillian flicked her eyes to the lackey, then back to the Beguiler. There was no margin for error. When he hung up, she had five minutes to incapacitate them and get back to the monument. If she failed . . . two girls could die, or she'd be missing a few of her vital organs by the time Sam found her laid out on the altar as some type of sick offering. But she wouldn't fail. She'd do it. *Deep breath. Ignore the throbbing pain. Focus.*

"Checking in," the Beguiler said. "Still got the girls in your sights. Good. If they leave, just shoot anyone. The younger, the better." He disconnected, slipped the phone into his pocket, and lifted a padlock from the altar. "Time to leash the dog," he said, approaching Jillian with the padlock and chain.

She glanced at the lackey. He might inadvertently shoot her, but she didn't have a choice. *Focus.*

The Beguiler circled behind her. "Hands behind your back."

Now! At the same time the lackey with the gun pitched forward, she whirled and smashed the base of her hand into the Beguiler's nose. He staggered backward. She whipped the chain from his hand, darted behind him, threw it around his neck, tightened it. The padlock fell to the floor. Gurgling, he clawed at the chain. Her muscles straining, she inched her way toward the altar, dragging him with her. *Come on, come on, I don't want to kill him. Pass out, already.* The lackey's heart would soon start to pump again. Almost there. She loosened the chain and kicked the Beguiler forward. As he fell to his knees and retched, she reached for the candlestick and bashed it over his head. He tumbled onto his side and remained still. Jillian retrieved her gun from the altar, then patted him down. She tucked his firearm into the back of her pants and slid his phone into her back pocket.

One down.

Problem number two was still prostrate. Shit. Training her pistol on him, she snatched her phone from the altar and dialed Sam. "I'm okay," she said as soon as Sam answered. "But there's a guy near a monument who's going to shoot two children if he doesn't hear from his boss in the next few minutes, and his boss is out cold."

"Where is it?"

"Near one of the older sections. It's some guy on a horse. I'll head there myself in a second."

"I don't think I'm that far away." Sam hung up.

Jillian went to the lackey, rolled him onto his side, and felt for a pulse. Relief flooded through her. He must have landed badly and hit his head. She picked up the gun that had skidded into the base of a pew and shoved it into her jacket pocket, then holstered her gun and raced from the chapel. How much time did she have? Hopefully she hadn't taken more than a couple of minutes to neutralize her captors. The guy wouldn't shoot as soon as time ran out. He'd hesitate, give it another minute or two—she hoped.

Adrenaline powered her. Her lungs threatened to burst. "Hey," a man yelled when she almost barrelled into him. *Keep running.* As she rounded a bend in the path, a gaggle of honking Canada geese near a tree caught her attention. Wait. *Follow! Help! Danger!* They ran and took flight. If only she could tell them to go to the monument and stop the evil man, but that was too complex to convey. How long had she been running? It felt like an hour. *"Sam!"* No reply.

She could see the monument! The geese honked overhead. The family still stood at the grave. The man waiting for a call looked at his watch. Jillian focused on him and summoned a final burst of energy. *Danger! Danger!* The geese swooped around him. He lifted his arms to protect his head. *Calm!* she commanded and ran straight at him. He looked up; his mouth opened. She threw an arm around his neck, gripped the gun in her jacket pocket, and jabbed it into his stomach. Anyone watching would mistake them for a couple. "That phone call you're expecting? It's not coming," she said.

He stared at her, fear in his eyes.

"You're not shooting anyone, either. There's no point now, is there?"

Perhaps figuring she wouldn't shoot him in cold blood in the middle of a public place, he backed away, then whirled—and froze at the sight of the geese that had landed behind him. He turned back to Jillian and showed her his palms in a gesture of surrender.

Thank you, Jillian sent, not sure the geese would understand. *"Sam! Sam!"*

"I see the monument," Sam said.

Good. "We need to chat," she said to the man as she disarmed him. She already had three guns on her, for god's sake. She shoved the fourth gun into her other jacket pocket and scanned for Sam. There she was, jogging up a path to join them. The geese waddled away.

"There are two more, in an old chapel a few minutes from here," Jillian said to Sam as she discreetly handed her one of the pistols. "When I left, they were both unconscious."

Sam shoved the pistol into her hoodie pocket. "Let's go see if they're all right," she said, her voice even. She nudged the man. "You'll come with us too, of course."

"Come on." Jillian thrust the gun in her right pocket forward to remind him it was there, although, faced with two Deiforms, his fear had turned to sheer terror. His face ashen, he obediently fell into step with Sam. What did he think they'd do to him? They weren't like him and his ilk.

Nobody spoke on the way to the chapel. As soon as they stepped inside, Jillian and Sam pulled out their pistols. Someone groaned. Motioning for lackey number two to walk ahead of them, they cautiously approached the altar. Lackey number one had regained consciousness and was bent over the Beguiler, who hadn't moved. Lackey's back was to them, but their footsteps alerted him to their presence. He stiffened.

Sam surveyed the scene and raised appraising brows at Jillian. "Over there, against the wall," she said. The one they'd cornered at the monument immediately followed Sam's order. Lackey number one pushed himself up from the floor and shuffled over to his side, rubbing his forehead. Jillian levelled her gun at them while Sam bent over the Beguiler.

Sam grunted. "I think he'll be okay."

Jillian breathed a silent sigh. She hadn't killed him or turned him into a vegetable, but she'd express her relief later. She wanted the two men glaring at her to see a badass Deiform.

Sam moved to the altar, saying, "I bet they have smelling salts."

Jillian's jaw clenched. Why, so they could torture her until she passed out, then bring her around and do it all again? Bastards. They were damn lucky she was on the side of Good.

"Yeah, here they are," Sam said. Silence, then coughing and groaning.

"Samantha," the Beguiler croaked. Then Jillian heard him spit.

Sam barked a laugh. "I'll give you a point for bravado. I'd work on your aim, though. You. Come help your friend over to the wall."

Jillian stepped back to give herself a wider field of vision. Sam had stepped away from the Beguiler, her pistol aimed at him. Lackey number two pulled the Beguiler to his feet, slung one of the Beguiler's arms around his shoulder, and helped him over to lackey number one. The Beguiler pressed his back against the wall and slid down to a sitting position.

Sam stepped to Jillian's side. "I haven't seen you before," she said to the Beguiler. "Do you have a name?" When he spat at her, she pulled out her phone and snapped a photo of him and his two accomplices, then turned to Jillian. "We should take all their toys with us. There must be a bag somewhere. Why don't you gather everything up while I have a talk with these gentlemen?"

Jillian lowered her gun and went to the altar. She found a duffel bag behind it and listened to Sam while she scooped the disgusting items off the altar.

"I'll make this quick," Sam said. "This is the second time you've gone after Jillian, and the second time it hasn't ended well for you. She resisted Lilibeth, and she didn't have any trouble dealing with you, even though she was outnumbered. I'd give it up. Next time she might not show you any mercy."

No response, but Jillian doubted Sam had expected one. She tossed the firearms she'd confiscated from her opponents into the bag, then zipped it closed and carried it over to Sam.

"You two, lie on your stomachs and put your hands behind your head," Sam said. *"The Beguiler isn't in any shape to pursue us, and I doubt the others will come after us, but when I say let's go, sprint out of here."*

"One second." Jillian dropped the bag to the floor and strode over to the Beguiler. "You make me sick," she said as she reached behind him to unfasten the clerical collar. She yanked it free and marched back to Sam. *"I'm ready to leave now,"* she said, picking up the bag.

"Let's go."

Jillian jogged to the door and out into the cemetery, feeling as if she'd emerged from darkness.

"We're clear," Sam said. They slowed to a walk. "You all right?"

She wasn't sure. Right now, all she wanted to do was return to the car and get the hell out of here. But she said, "Yeah, fine." When they reached the parking lot, she tossed the clerical collar into a garbage can. Sam took the duffel bag from her and put it into the trunk. Jillian sank into the passenger seat, pulled the door shut, and closed her eyes. Safety. She hugged herself . . . and trembled.

JILLIAN MANAGED A small smile when Sam handed her a cup of tea. "Thanks," she said, setting the cup on the kitchen table and curling her fingers around its warmth. "Tea has always been a comfort drink for me."

Sam pulled out the chair across from Jillian and sat. "My mother always said a cup of tea makes everything feel better. House burned down? Have a cup of tea. Someone died? Have a cup of tea."

Jillian chuckled, surprised that Sam had divulged that personal tidbit. She must be worried about her, or suffering from the "what if?" malaise.

"The Deiform Jillian is getting quite the reputation," Sam said.

"Good," Jillian said, sounding braver than she felt. "You think they'll keep coming after me?"

"They've failed twice now. Let's hope today was it."

"They must have followed us from the airstrip."

Sam rubbed her lower lip with her finger. "Yeah. I should have spotted them."

"You weren't alone in the car, you know. They might have had lookouts along our usual route."

"We shouldn't have driven the same route to the safe house."

Jillian didn't want to live like that, but did she have a choice? "No harm done." Sam would still beat herself up; Jillian wished she knew how to stop her. "I can't believe he had a freaking clerical collar on. They didn't have a lot of time to plan."

"Who knows what they drive around with?"

Yeah, not many people drove around with a duffel bag filled with torture instruments.

"At least we've added him to our collection," Sam said. "Everyone will recognize him now, no matter what he's trying to pass himself off as."

"If he hadn't been wearing a collar, I would have realized earlier that he was a Beguiler—not because I believe everyone in a collar is a saint, but because I thought him being a clergyman was making my heart race." Had he chosen to wear a collar for that reason? Did the Beguilers understand that much about her, or had he figured the collar would make her lower her guard? Maybe the location had influenced him?

Sam leaned forward and rested her elbows on the table. "So what exactly happened?"

Jillian recounted what had taken place, from the time the Beguiler had approached her in the cemetery to when she'd arrived back at the monument. "If I'd failed to stop his heart, I would have been screwed."

"But you didn't. And that was gutsy. Aren't you glad you didn't chicken out, now?"

She nodded. "How would you have handled the situation?"

"If my gifts were at the same strength as yours, the same as you did."

Pleased, Jillian said, "We reviewed a lot of scenarios. You taught me well." She stifled a smile when Sam's face flushed, not wanting her to know that she'd noticed. "What about the threat they made to shoot the girls? Do you think it was real?"

Sam grimaced. "Probably not. If you'd run or incapacitated them, shooting someone would only have drawn attention. Well, you would have felt bad, I know—"

She would have tormented herself for the rest of her life.

"—but the cost would have been too high for them. Having said that, I would have done exactly what you did. I would never risk playing with an innocent's life." Sam paused. "I might have asked the one at the monument to show his gun."

She'd remember that, if there was a next time. "What else do Beguilers do, apart from going after Fledglings and green Deiforms? Do they have a home base? Who leads them?"

"From what we know, they entice vulnerable people, those hard on their luck, to join their ranks. They're organized similarly to us, with small groups scattered around the world. Most of the time, they sow mischief—plant seeds of mistrust between spouses and business partners, egg on the conspiracy theorists. But their favourite sport is picking us off—when they can. Fortunately, their windows of opportunity are small."

"So they're not out there sacrificing humans over a pentagram?"

Sam's mouth twitched. "No."

"Why don't they go after our families?"

"What good would that do?"

"It would demoralize us."

"Or make us angry." Sam paused to sip her tea. "When we get back to the island, remind me to show you another book in the undercroft. Early on, they tried going after the families. We normally don't dole out retribution, but we did that time. We just about wiped them out. The details are all in the book, and they're not pretty. But we had to send a message, and they've kept their hands off our families and Supporters since then. If Joanna hadn't been helping Jim to bring in a Fledgling, she'd still be alive." Sam raised her hand. "You're not to blame. I'm simply stating a fact."

That didn't make her feel any better. "Who leads them? And I don't mean Satan. I mean here. In the flesh."

"I'm sure they have their group leaders, as we do."

Jillian's encounter with Lilibeth came rushing back. She wouldn't ask who gave the Beguilers their "gifts." If Deiforms could draw on the good within themselves, she figured Beguilers could draw on the evil. "Has a Deiform ever switched sides?"

Sam frowned. "What do you mean?"

"Gone over to the Beguilers."

"No. Once a Deiform has made the choice, by resisting being turned or beginning to train, Beguilers can only try to kill them. But Fledglings are vulnerable. Not many can resist an enchanting. That's why the Beguilers go after them with such zeal."

"So if Lilibeth had managed to turn me, I'd be one of them?"

Sam nodded. "You'd be a Beguiler, not a sidekick."

The thought curdled her stomach. Back then, she hadn't understood what was at stake, because she hadn't taken Sam seriously until that night.

"I don't waste a lot of time worrying about Beguilers," Sam said, her eyes on Jillian's face. "To me, they're like flies. I swat them away and focus on what I have to do. You should do the same."

"I'll try."

"Are you sure you still want to go to the meeting tonight? I'll understand if you want to put it off until next week."

"No, I'm okay." She lifted her hand and gingerly touched her left cheek.

"There's a small bruise. We'll cover it."

"We could use it. Maybe I have a boyfriend knocking me around."

Sam shook her head. "If you did, I doubt you'd pursue life coaching."

True. Since she was taking concrete steps to improve her life, her self-esteem wasn't in the toilet. The first thing she'd do was dump the boyfriend, not take group coaching with a bunch of strangers.

"Plus, it would make you less attractive to the cult. They wouldn't want some jealous, violent boyfriend showing up."

"You're right." Jillian sighed. "At least I did something right today."

"Listen, not only did you best them, but we added three photos to our collection. Everyone will know his face now, and the faces of his two lackeys." Sam slowly nodded. "You truly do belong to the Fellowship. You truly are a Deiform."

The Deiform Jillian. She could live with that. In her own way, she'd embrace it.

Chapter Ten

As Jillian slowed down to make a right turn, she glanced at the passenger seat. Man, it felt weird to be driving, especially alone. She slowed as she approached the address Andy had given her, then pulled into the parking lot next to the modern building and found a spot. A mixture of excitement and anxiety made her heart skip a beat. She took a deep breath and reminded herself that she was Jillian Harwick, a disgruntled accountant wondering what to do with her life and concerned about the state of society. She'd gone undercover many times, but this operation meant something to her, and she had a new "employer" she wanted to please.

As for the Beguilers . . . they wouldn't strike again so soon—the only reason Sam had decided to remain at the safe house, rather than risk a cult member spotting her in the car with Jillian, or hanging around the building. At least Jillian didn't have to worry about a sniper taking a shot at her the moment she stepped out of the car. Funnily enough, the Beguilers' desire to capture and torture her was a positive; she'd always have time to fight for her life. Plus, her run-in with the Beguiler had done wonders for her confidence. She could beat them. She wouldn't let her guard down, but she could walk alone without jumping at every sound.

Her mind wandered back to the conversation with Sam about Kristin. *Imagine what life would be like if there were no challenges, no difficulties, no risks, because everything was handed to you, and if you ran into trouble, someone swept in and took care of it for you. We'd all be a bunch of spoiled, entitled children with no compassion for others. And there'd be no growth, no rising confidence, no sense of accomplishment. Don't get cocky.*

Enough stalling. She lifted her satchel from the passenger seat, climbed out of the sedan, and strolled to the building's entrance. The large sign hanging above it read *Discovery and Development Centre*. Her skin crawled when she swung open one of the glass doors and strode inside. She wasn't wired. No microphone, no camera—and no gun. Her objectives were to observe and keep herself in play. "Go with your instincts. Play it by ear," Sam had said. "Remember, the worst that will happen is that they'll decide not to recruit you." Yep, she wouldn't worry that Andy would bundle her into a van and drive her to some cult compound—at least, not yet.

It was almost 7:00, but the sun still shone outside. Jillian lifted her sunglasses onto her head and waited for her eyes to adjust to the new lighting. A woman sat behind a gleaming silver counter. New age music softly played. "Good evening," the woman called out as Jillian strode to the elevators. Jillian smiled at her and pressed the Up button. In the elevator, she adjusted her business suit's jacket and squared her shoulders. Thanks to the painkiller she'd taken, her cheek felt fine. Healing it had been out of the question; it would have been a frivolous use of the gift.

A minute later, she stepped onto the seventh floor, walked to Suite 722, and opened the solid mahogany door. The receptionist's dazzling smile made Jillian want to lower her sunglasses back over her eyes. "Welcome, welcome! You must be Jillian."

"Yes."

"Andy's so looking forward to meeting you. Do you want something to drink? Coffee, tea, water, juice?"

Sam had once said, "I'm careful about what I eat and drink. The only place I let my guard down is on the island." Jillian lived in that world now. "No, thank you. I just had dinner," she said to the receptionist.

"Maybe later, then." She punched a button on her phone and lifted the receiver. "Jillian is here, Andy." The receiver went down. "He'll be right out."

The receptionist wasn't kidding. Andy bounded into the waiting area. "Jillian, it's so good to finally meet you in person," he said, pumping her hand. "Come on, let's get started."

She followed him down a carpeted corridor, pleased that she'd accurately sized him up on the phone. In his thirties, clean-cut, blue shirt and cotton pants, loafers, no wedding ring. Something about him nagged at her; she couldn't put her finger on it. She counted six doorways and glimpsed a woman talking on a headset through one of them. Another "coach"?

Jillian tensed when she heard the chatter coming from a room at the end of the corridor. She hated walking into a room full of strangers; it didn't matter that she'd done so many times.

Andy stopped outside the doorway and swept out his arm. She forced a smile and stepped into the room. Heads turned. Unfamiliar faces swam before her. "This is Jillian," Andy said from behind her.

"Welcome, Jillian," voices said in unison.

"Please, sit," he said, swinging the door shut.

Self-conscious, she sat in one of the two vacant chairs in the circle and glanced around. A water cooler sat on a table in the corner with a stack of paper cups next to it, and several framed prints of grinning couples and groups hung on the cream walls.

Andy dropped into the remaining empty chair. "Now that everyone is here, let's get started."

Jillian lifted her sunglasses from her head and slipped them into the side pocket of her satchel, which she'd leaned against the side of her chair. She wanted to fold her arms, but didn't want to come across as defensive. She quickly counted heads. Fourteen, including Andy and herself. Since the receptionist had known who she was, was she the only non-cult member here?

"Since we have two new people joining us, why don't we begin by introducing ourselves?" Andy said, answering Jillian's question. He turned to the woman on his left. "Why don't you start, Carol, and we'll go clockwise around the circle."

Good, that meant she'd be third to last. As each person introduced himself or herself, Jillian memorized the names and their associated faces, a skill she'd improved during her agency days. She cringed when Christine, a university student, breathily announced that she was here for the first time and thrilled that she'd found a group of kindred spirits. As much as she wanted to, Jillian couldn't warn her that she'd landed in the middle of a cult recruitment meeting—and that set her teeth on edge. She forced herself to relax. Was it terrible of her to hope that the soul healers *had* murdered its ex-members, so the Fellowship would shut down the cult and free everyone?

When the man sitting next to her introduced himself, Jillian moistened her lips. Everyone shifted their attention to her. "My name is Jillian," she said, pleased at how strong her voice sounded. "I'm glad to be here." She wouldn't gush.

"Welcome, Jillian," everyone murmured.

"You all know me," Andy said when his turn came. "Now that we've introduced ourselves, I want to again welcome our two new members to our enlightened group. You don't realize it yet, but you've just taken a step toward the life you're meant to live."

A round of applause greeted his words. Jillian smiled and glanced at Christine, who appeared pleased by the attention. Great; she was ripe for the picking.

"Why don't we start by talking about the challenges we've experienced this week. Christine and Jillian, when we get to you, perhaps you can tell us what brought you here tonight. And for the benefit of our two newcomers, I'll remind everyone to just listen. We'll have a discussion after everyone's had their turn." He glanced at the woman sitting to Christine's left. "Liz, let's start with you."

Shit. Jillian had hoped the other newbie would go first. She forced herself to listen as Liz recounted how she knew she was put on the earth to do something special, but was having trouble identifying what she should be doing with her life. Jillian wondered whether any of it was true. Next, Doug, who was struggling with being resentful when those around him didn't appreciate what he did for them, especially at work. He felt undervalued and underutilized.

As her turn approached, Jillian mentally reviewed her story. When Andy's eyes met hers, she clasped her hands together, so she wouldn't fidget. "What brought you here tonight, Jillian?" he asked quietly.

"I guess you don't mean what car I drove," she said, to polite chuckles. Her lame opening had been deliberate; she didn't want to come across too poised. She drew a deep breath. "Well, I've been wondering about my life lately . . . wondering if I'm on the right track. I don't know, I've always known that I'm missing something, but my job kept me busy and I had a great boyfriend. Until recently. It seems like everything's fallen apart at once. We broke up . . . it came out of the blue." She heaved a sigh and lowered her voice. "I thought we'd get engaged."

Those in the circle made sympathetic noises.

"At work, I was promoted. You might think that's a good thing, but now I'm doing a job I hate, and there's too much overtime."

"It looks like you came straight here from work," Andy said.

"Yes, I did." The business suit had done its job. "My mother is also becoming a problem. My father left her well off, and she's suddenly giving her money away to charities. Don't get the wrong idea. I'm not after her money. But word's getting around, and now all sorts of groups are holding out their hands for cheques, including some dubious ones. I'm in an awkward situation. Every time I try to talk to her about it, she says I'm being greedy, that I don't want her to squander my inheritance. Anyway, enough about my problems."

Hopefully she'd dangled enough carrots that they'd pursue her. Broken heart, dissatisfied at work, a rich mom giving away money like water . . . they'd be nuts not to pounce on her. "I came here because something needs to change. I feel like a zombie, getting up every day, going to work, coming home, sitting in front of the TV, rinse and repeat. I've been reading a lot of self-help books, but, I don't know . . . my friends say I'm wasting my time. I could relate to something Sandy said, so I'm glad to be here." She cleared her throat. "That's it."

Andy nodded at her. "Thank you. Donna?"

Relieved to be out of the spotlight, Jillian listened to the others. She winced at Christine's shaky voice and her obvious need to fit in somewhere. Her best friend had rejected her for a cooler university crowd. "I'm not the clubbing type." Christine picked at her jeans. "She said I suck all the fun out of a room."

Ouch.

Curiously, Andy didn't bare his soul. After everyone else had taken a turn, he spoke about needing to find one's purpose and, most importantly, a community that supported it. "How many people don't live their purpose because their parents wouldn't approve, or those around them," he gazed at Jillian, "mock them, or their friends, the ones we expect to be loyal," he shifted his attention to Christine, "make us feel as if there's something wrong with us. A supportive circle is everything."

Nothing about religion or souls, but Jillian had contacted the cult through its secular website, and had only mentioned the crusade to Andy in passing. This group was obviously geared toward the self-help crowd. It wouldn't reveal its true nature until someone was succumbing to its overtures.

"At this point, we usually ask for one or two volunteers and help them come up with an action plan for the week, but why don't we welcome our two newcomers instead, get to know each other a little better."

Derek raised his hand. "We should invite them to our retreat."

Bob nodded. "We should."

As if on cue, people moved their chairs. Half the room surrounded Jillian, and the other half besieged Christine. Jillian smiled self-consciously at Andy, Derek, Bob, Carol, Sandy, and Donna. "What do you think of the meeting so far?" Andy asked.

"It's nice to be with people who've been where I am and understand how I feel," she replied. "I'm used to being dismissed."

Sandy nodded knowingly. "By your friends?"

"Yeah."

"That's such a difficult situation with your mother," Bob murmured. "It's so hard to watch those we love being taken advantage of. We faced something similar with Carol's father."

Carol nodded. Jillian glanced at her and Bob's left hands. Yep, married.

"He wasn't throwing his money at bogus causes," Carol said. "He kept ordering everything advertised in those TV infomercials. Almost remortgaged his house. I had to take over his finances." She looked genuinely pained. Was this a truth mixed with fiction? Had Carol overseen her father's finances before she joined the soul healers, or because the group wanted his money? Or was it an outright lie? Jillian reminded herself that cult members looked for weaknesses, manipulated the potential recruit, said whatever it would take to bring someone into the fold.

Derek leaned forward and looked at his hands. "I can identify with the job situation. Sometimes being promoted can be the worst thing to happen."

"What do you do?" Bob asked Jillian.

"I'm an accountant. Or at least, I was. They've bumped me into management." Jillian frowned. "I hate it. But I'm stuck there."

"No, you're not," three voices stated in unison. The group laughed.

Bob met her eyes. "You believe—"

Christine's group clapped. "Christine's coming to the retreat," someone shouted. Those with Jillian also applauded. Christine grinned from ear to ear.

Jillian hid her dismay and seized the opening. "What retreat?" she asked, pretending she'd forgotten Derek's mention of it.

"Every few months we hold a brainstorming retreat," Andy said. "We work together, come up with plans to tackle our challenges."

"We've all felt that we're trapped. It's a lie." Bob's eyes bored into Jillian. "But we often need others to show us the door."

"You're in luck. Our next retreat is happening next weekend. Why don't you come? You'll see that you're not stuck." Andy touched her arm. "By the time you leave, you'll be bursting with possibilities."

"Oh, I don't know," Jillian said. "I can't ask for a demotion. You want to hear the worst part?" They all nodded. "I'm good at management. I'm good. And I'm much better off than many people. I'm paid well. I have a good work environment—my own office! I shouldn't complain."

Bob shook his head. "Don't do that to yourself. You deserve better. Isn't that why you came tonight? Because you know you're not living your life purpose? You think to yourself, this can't be all there is, and you're right. But you're surrounded by people who want to keep you exactly where you are." He raised a finger. "Still, you read the books. You look for answers. But you can't soar, with so many holding you down. Imagine what you could do if you surrounded yourself with those who want to lift you up."

"You can change your life."

"We'll help you."

"Don't stay in your rut."

"You know you were put on this earth to do more."

Jesus. Once again, she understood how someone at a low point in their life, or searching for meaning, or fed up with the tedium of day to day living, could be swept away by the notion that they had a special purpose and could change the freaking world.

Andy steepled his fingers and studied her. "From our conversations, I've gathered that you're a spiritual person."

"Yes."

Andy was silent for a moment. "We discussed on the phone how society seems to be deteriorating."

"It is. I almost can't bear to watch the news these days. But what can we do about it? That's why my job is bothering me. I should be doing more. I want my life to have meaning."

Bob nodded. "Come to the retreat and find out what you have to offer. If you don't, you've already given up. Every time you crack open one of those self-help books, you'll feel condemned, because you'll know you could have done more."

"If you really want what those books promise, you'll grab the opportunity to work with people who want the same things you do," Carol pressed.

"It's just a weekend," Andy added. "One weekend out of your life."

Jillian surveyed the eager faces around her, then said, "All right. I suppose it would be silly not to go. But I might not have anything to contribute."

"Don't worry about that," Andy said amidst happy applause. "Jillian's coming to the retreat," he shouted.

She beamed when the other side of the room cheered. Its mission accomplished, the group around her relaxed. Andy, Bob, and Carol had apparently been assigned to her; she spent the next hour gamely answering their subtle questions about her life. She stuck to the script regarding Mom. "My friends say it's Mom's money and I should stay out of it," she said, in response to a query from Andy. "I agree. It *is* her money. I'm just concerned about where some of it is going."

"Your friends sound like they're comfortable with the status quo," Carol said.

"That's them to a tee." Jillian glanced at her watch. "Wow, I can't believe the time."

Andy raised his brows. "Time flies when you're having fun, eh?"

She chuckled. "I should go. Work tomorrow."

"Yeah," everyone grumbled. Jillian wondered if it were true. Did any of them work, and if they did, was it for the cult? She glanced over Christine's way and inwardly sighed. Surrounded by a group hanging on her every word, Christine showed no signs of leaving. Her eyes shone; her face was radiant. She'd either join the cult or face another betrayal. Life sucked.

Andy insisted on walking Jillian to her car. "I'm so pleased that you're coming to the retreat," he said as they strolled through the parking lot.

"I need to know where it is," Jillian said.

"I can give you a call and fill you in."

"There won't be a meeting next week?"

"There will be, but I'd like to keep in touch with you, see how your week is going."

"Oh, that sounds good," she said, doing her best to sound enthusiastic. When they reached her car, she said, "Thanks for walking me here. I'll talk to you soon." Without waiting for a reply, she unlocked the door, slipped into the driver's seat, and waved as she pulled away. He wasn't the only one who'd consider the evening successful. So far, so good.

JILLIAN STRODE INTO the living room, plunked onto the sofa, and folded her arms. Watching the news, Sam didn't glance at her, but Jillian would bet that Sam had watched her drive into the garage. When the anchor finished reading a story about a municipal politician, Sam reached for the remote and turned off the TV.

Jillian didn't wait for her to ask. "It went well. I'm off to a retreat next weekend."

"They're moving quickly. Any meetings until then?"

"Just the one next week." But who cared? She wanted to talk about what had bothered her all the way back to the safe house. "I didn't consider other people. I should have realized . . ."

Sam's brow furrowed. "What do you mean?"

Jillian unfolded her arms. "There was another new woman there. Christine. A student. She was lapping it up. She's going through a hard time, and the bastards are taking advantage of it." She blew out a sigh. "She's going to the retreat, too. I don't know if I can stand by and watch."

Sam straightened in the chair. "You'll have to."

"Why? Why can't I pull her aside and warn her?"

"Because you don't know whether she'll turn around and report you to them. Do you think she wants to hear right now that her new best friends are cultists? And she won't be the only one. Once you're inside, there will be more new members coming through the door. Heck, you might have to recruit some of them."

Jillian leaped to her feet. "I don't know if I can do this."

"We went through all this."

"I know, but it was different when it was only hypothetical. If it turns out that the soul healers don't have Jane and we decide to let the cult continue on its merry way, how will I live with that?"

Sam looked up at her. "Nobody said this would be easy."

"I don't understand why we don't shut the cult down."

"Because we can't do everything. You don't think it bothers me when we have to look the other way, or go after the greater of two evils? I wish there were thousands of Deiforms. Then maybe we could go after the smaller fish."

Jillian gaped. "Smaller fish? The soul healers don't heal souls, they steal them and stuff them into airless boxes. Metaphorically speaking."

"They don't force people to join them. We investigated them, remember? We have to choose our battles wisely."

Jillian's hands clenched. "They might be killing people! They might have kidnapped Jane, and god knows what they've done with her."

"That's why we're investigating them again."

"And if it turns out they're not murderers, we'll let them go on ensnaring people—again."

Sam chewed her lip. "There's still time for you to pull out. I can do it."

"No. You were right. I don't know enough to provide support yet."

"I meant I'd work this alone."

Jillian glared at her. "That's what you really want, isn't it? I'm sorry Roberta insisted that we work together. I know you'd rather I not be around, okay?"

Sam's expression didn't change. "I've never felt completely comfortable with you being the bait."

"Why not? You don't think I can do it? I've been going undercover my entire freaking life."

"I'm concerned because you're exactly the type of person cults try to recruit, and I'm not speaking hypothetically."

Jillian stared at her.

"Think about it. You're in transition. You've just lost your family. Your life has changed—it's still changing. Everything is still new. You're still getting your bearings."

"So you think I'm susceptible, that I'll actually believe their crap?" Jillian wanted to smack her. Sam was the one who believed in fairy tales, not her! "I'm not some naive student."

"It's not a matter of intelligence or sophistication. Nobody knowingly joins a cult. If someone said, 'Hey, come join our cult,' everyone would run the other way, screaming. No, they dribble out just enough information to make you think you're taking up a noble cause, or joining a religious community, or working with like-minded people to effect positive change in your life or the world. By the time you find out what the group's really about, you're utterly committed and not thinking clearly enough to see through the bullshit." Sam pressed her hand to her chest. "I used to think that only gullible people would fall for a cult. I haven't believed that for a long time."

"You're forgetting one tiny detail," Jillian said through clenched teeth. "I already know what the soul healers are. So there's no need to worry. I won't fall for their nonsense. I—" What had nagged at her about Andy suddenly hit her full force. "He matches the description of the guy who visited Amanda," she breathed.

"Who?"

"Andy!"

"It's a vague description. It matches tons of men."

"Not tons of men in the soul healers." She sank back onto the sofa. "What if he killed her?"

Sam raised her index finger. "Don't jump the gun, and keep your priorities straight. We want to find Jane. I suspect finding out what happened to her will answer the question of whether Amanda and Janet Bailey were murdered."

"And until then, I'll stand by while Christine throws her life away. Not only that, I might end up recruiting others. Just helping the soul healers with a meeting will make me an accessory to the fact." She'd soon want to bury herself in books, too.

"Once we know what's happened to Jane, if we're not going to shut down the cult, we'll get Christine and anyone else you helped to recruit out."

Jillian stared at her. "But you just said—"

"It would bother me, too. In fact, it has bothered me," Sam mumbled. "Which is why I sometimes stay around an extra day or two after an investigation to . . . clean up. But I'm usually working alone. If Roberta gets angry about it, I'm the only one on the hook."

"Why wouldn't Roberta want us to undo any damage we might have done?" Jillian asked, digesting the information that Sam sometimes acted of her own accord to set things right.

"It takes time. It delays anything else she wants us to look into."

"Has she ever found out?"

Sam's voice grew quiet. "She knows, Jillian. She knows."

But . . .

"She pretends she doesn't because I'm cleaning up my mess, not going rogue in the sense that I'm doing things she wouldn't condone."

"What would she do if you did something she didn't condone? She needs you." Roberta had said herself that Deiforms were the heart of the Fellowship.

"She wouldn't have to lift a finger. He'd strike me down, and anyone else who abuses the gifts."

"Kill you, you mean?"

"It would depend on the severity of the transgression. Sometimes death isn't the worst punishment." Sam's voice lifted. "But we don't have to worry about that, because we won't abuse the gifts. We might not be able to save everyone in the soul healers, but we'll try to save Christine and anyone else you feel you've helped to recruit. There might not be anyone else. I doubt the upper levels are directly involved in recruitment."

"So what are we going to do for the next week?"

"Stay here. I bet Andy said he'd call you."

"He did."

Sam nodded. "He'll want to meet for coffee or something. Go along with it."

"I hope you're not expecting me to date the guy."

"He'll just want to keep the dialogue open, find out if anyone close to you is trying to talk you out of going to the group, or the retreat."

"He'll also want to find out more about my rich mother." Her tension draining away, Jillian chuckled to herself. Sometimes her life felt surreal. If someone had told her this time last year that she'd be trying to infiltrate a cult because she belonged to a religious fellowship that investigated such matters, she'd have asked them if they were also seeing psychedelic bunny rabbits and rainbow unicorns.

"Did you date people when you worked for the agency?" Sam asked.

"No," Jillian said, knowing that Sam was asking about her former job, not her personal life. "I thought you knew everything about me."

"I don't know the details of all your cases."

"I flirted a lot. You'd be surprised at how batting your eyelashes can get a man talking." Or maybe Sam wouldn't be surprised. "How about you?"

"No!"

Dare she ask whether Sam meant that she never flirted to further an investigation, or never flirted, period? Why rock the boat when, as Roberta would say, Jillian already knew the answer? Sam, flirting? Did not compute. Which reminded her . . . "I have access to all the Fellowship's digital files now, right?"

Sam hesitated. "Yes."

That meant she could read Sam's file, and would bet all her earthly possessions—which currently amounted to clothes, a couple of books, and her guitar—that Sam had hesitated for that reason. "I've already read everything you gave me on the soul healers. Can you show me how the files are organized, so I can read other cases involving cults?" She wasn't lying. When she'd first met Sam, she would have jumped at the opportunity to read her file. Her curiosity about Sam hadn't waned, but Sam would hate it—*hate it*—if Jillian invaded her former life. Right now, Jillian's friendship with Sam was more important to her than snooping through Sam's background.

"Sure," Sam said tersely.

Bringing up the files had soured the conversation. "I'm not going to read your file. I'd rather learn about you from you."

Sam blinked at her. "There isn't much to learn."

Bullshit.

Chapter Eleven

Fighting the urge to chew a fingernail, Jillian paced in the apartment's living room. "They stocked the cupboards. The place actually looks lived in." She checked her watch. "I never imagined I'd be doing something like this."

Lounging in a chair, Sam looked up at her. "When I wrote essays at school about what I wanted to be when I grew up, I didn't write about Deiforms." She gestured toward the sofa. "Sit down and relax."

"I can't." Jillian glanced at her watch again. "He should call any minute. I wish I was driving myself."

"They want to control when you leave."

She knew that. She would have been surprised if a cult member hadn't insisted on being the chauffeur, but she didn't have to like it.

"You'll do fine. All you have to do is hang out with them for a weekend and appear interested. Remember to invite Andy over for a coffee."

"I already met him for coffee." Albeit with Derek, but Andy had done most of the talking. "I don't want him to think I'm interested in him."

Sam's mouth turned up at the corners. "That's why you'll invite a few others, too."

She'd rather not invite anyone, but she had to be friendly. "I need to familiarize myself with the place a little more. It'll be kind of odd if I don't know where the coffee maker is." Another swing by the window—not that she could see any cars from the apartment, because it didn't face the street. "Any last words of advice?"

Sam stood and folded her arms. "No matter what happens, don't panic. Think things through. And if you feel confused, always, always, reach for your centre. Depending on how much they throw at you, that could be the most important thing you do. Okay?"

"Yeah."

"And remember, there will be times when you'll have to profess to hold viewpoints that you personally don't hold."

"Right." Jillian predicted much clenching of teeth over the weekend.

"Keep your eyes and ears open."

Yep, gathering information was her number one priority. Don't push, but seize opportunities to ask subtle questions, and for god's sake, don't blow her cover. She wanted to be an asset to the Fellowship, not a liability.

Her phone rang. She tensed. "Hello."

"Hi, I just wanted to let you know we're a few minutes away," Andy said.

"Thanks. I'll be waiting in the lobby."

"See you soon," he said cheerfully.

She hung up. "Do you think they'll let me keep my phone?"

Sam shrugged. "I don't know. They won't take it away until you're there, so don't worry. Jeremy will track it until it's turned off, and I'll be following you, anyway. If it's a large enough facility, I'll check in there. Otherwise, I'll find a nearby motel. But you won't need me to do anything. They're not going to kill you this weekend." Sam motioned for Jillian to follow her. "Let's go."

Jillian lifted her bag from the floor near the front door. "What will you do all weekend?" she asked as they stepped into the empty elevator. "Aside from read," she added with a forced chuckle.

Sam sighed. "I don't know. I'm going to ask Jeremy if there's anything I can help him with from a distance."

Jillian bit back an apology. "Why don't you kick back and watch TV, or a movie, or—"

"I'm sitting around too much already, and it's only going to get worse." The elevator door dinged open. They entered the lobby. "See you in a couple of days." Sam pushed open the lobby door.

Jillian moved closer to the windows and watched her stride down the sidewalk. She dropped the bag to the floor and flexed her fingers. This retreat was a test. If she couldn't endure two days with the soul healers, how would she pass as one of them for weeks, potentially months? This weekend, she'd have to ingratiate herself with Andy and everyone else, and in the end, it could all be for nothing. The deaths could be coincidental. The soul healers might not have anything to do with Jane's disappearance.

Well, in her agency days, she'd been stuck in some pretty toxic workplaces with people she couldn't stand. Because she'd needed to be around when alcohol or pettiness loosened lips, she'd had to be one of the gals and socialize, too, but at least she'd had her own place to return to at the end of the day. This time, she'd see her "friends" as victims, until she gained access to the cult's higher echelons and insinuated herself with those who were either delusional, or knew it was all bullshit. She'd have to keep her goal in mind when she wanted to scream.

A blue sedan pulled up in front of the apartment building. When Sandy rounded the car and started up the path, Jillian picked up her bag and hurried outside.

Sandy beamed. "Hi. You can put that in the trunk."

Jillian added her bag to several others already there, then slid into the backseat next to Andy. "I thought you'd be driving," she said to him as she snapped on her seatbelt.

"Hello to you, too," he drawled. "It's Derek's car."

"Hi," Derek said, waving absently, his eyes on the side view mirror. He merged into traffic.

Jillian wondered if Sam was behind them and whether Christine was in another car. Maybe she'd decided not to go after all—Jillian could hope. But given that Christine had still been enthusiastic about the retreat at the last group meeting, it was more likely that the cult separated newbies and surrounded them with cult members. She cleared her throat. "How long will it take us to get there?"

"About an hour and a half," Andy said. "You'll love the resort."

"We'll be sharing a room," Sandy said brightly.

Great.

Her companions stuck to neutral topics on the way, perhaps so she wouldn't demand that they turn around and take her home. It was almost dark by the time they drove down a dirt road and pulled into a makeshift parking area that was almost full. At least they weren't in the middle of nowhere; they'd passed a gas station and store less than five minutes ago, and Jillian could see lights through the trees.

After everyone had pulled their bags from the trunk, she crunched along a gravel path with the others. "That's where we're staying," Andy said, pointing to a five-story rustic building.

"Are you sure I don't have to pay anything?" Jillian asked innocently. "You said not to worry about it, but I'm sure staying here isn't free."

"That's the thing, Jillian. We believe in our program so much that we all chip in and cover the costs for people attending their first retreat. We wish everyone would come. At our next retreat, you'll pay it forward."

Suddenly Jillian was a white-collar crime investigator again. Maybe she was wrong, but she doubted the soul healers owned this resort, and staying here would cost a pretty penny. How was the cult funded? She knew about the books and the "educational" programs, first on tape, then on DVD, but there had to be more. Did everyone really hand over their assets to the soul healers? In addition to investigating Jane's disappearance, maybe the Fellowship would want her to play her usual role. She'd cozy up to Lancaster Jr. and his inner circle, and follow the money trail. She hoped not. Despite naturally considering the same angle she would have investigated in her agency days, she hadn't joined the Fellowship to do exactly what she was doing before, though preventing the average Joe from losing money to a cult con man would be a slight improvement over chasing down chump change for corporations.

"There's a picnic area down that way," Andy murmured. "After we've all checked in, let's meet there. We'll have marshmallows."

Sandy slipped her arm through Jillian's. "Sounds great."

Jillian smiled weakly. "Yes, it does."

It only took five minutes to check in, drop her bag in the third-floor room, and claim the bed on the right. Sandy was ready to rush back out, but Jillian used the bathroom first, mainly out of necessity, but also to steel herself for the socializing to come. She couldn't call Sam and tell her the resort's name. Sandy had just asked for her phone, explaining that they wanted everyone to focus on the sessions. Jillian hadn't panicked. If Sam hadn't been able to follow them without being detected, Jeremy or Emma would have tracked Jillian's phone as she travelled here. It was too late for Sandy to hide the phone's location by turning it off. They could have asked Jillian for it in the car, but she might have freaked out and insisted that they take her back to her apartment.

As Jillian strolled down the path that led to the picnic area, she only half-listened to Sandy. The trees standing at attention, silhouetted in the dusk sky, made her encounter with Lilibeth rush back. Would she ever get over having her private fantasies exposed and used against her?

Voices brought her back to her surroundings. The group emerged into a clearing. "Hey, everyone," Sandy shouted, waving.

Jillian waved too. In the light cast by the fire roaring in the central fire pit, she spotted Christine sitting with her group at a picnic table.

"You made it!" Christine said, giving her a thumbs-up.

Jillian inwardly cringed. Centering herself would protect her against mind control, but it wouldn't do anything for her guilt.

JILLIAN LAY IN the dark and listened to Sandy's rhythmic breathing. She didn't have to wait until Sandy was asleep. The worst that could happen was that Sandy would try to shake her awake, and Jillian would take a while to respond. But what she intended to do wouldn't take long. Given the late hour, she doubted anyone would be awake, but why not check?

She flipped onto her back and slowed her breathing, relaxed her jaw, her arms, her legs . . . willed herself to float . . . A wave of nausea washed over her and receded as quickly as it had come. She moved toward the wall, passed through it, floated by the still lump she could make out on the bed. Through another wall, past another dreamer . . . and into brightness. Andy, on the phone. She hovered and listened.

". . . going well. We have five potentials here, all good prospects. I'm confident they'll want to take the next step." He paused. "I wish there were more, too. But we can't save them all."

Save them all? He sounded as if he actually believed the cult's teachings. She wasn't surprised. He wasn't a top dog; he'd be living in a group residence and working his butt off to save souls. Would he kill for the soul healers? Did his dedication run that deep? As for the other three newbies, she'd met them around the fire. Andy's coaching group wasn't the only one reeling in prospects in the city.

"Yes, I'm meeting with the other group leaders before breakfast." Another pause. "I will. And I agree that we may be able to help with her mother."

If she could feel them, her ears would be burning. They'd help her mother empty her bank accounts, but Mommy would want her daughter taken care of in return.

"Yes, I'll call you again tomorrow. Good night." He hung up.

Oh well, she hadn't expected to hear him say, "I just checked on Jane Gladstone at such-and-such location."

Andy started to unbutton his shirt. Time to leave. She vainly checked several more rooms, then used the corridor to head back to her own room, too worried that she could catch a couple in an uncompromising position. The sensation of astral projecting hadn't felt as she'd expected; it was a bit like swimming underwater. Was Sam here? If she was, she'd probably be on another floor and at the other end of the long building. She might have to play the role of friend at some point and so would want to stay out of sight.

Jillian tried not to look at herself when she re-entered her room, but a morbid curiosity always made her take a quick peek—and immediately regret doing so. Bracing herself for the brief wooziness she'd experience, she allowed herself to float into her body. Her eyes fluttered open. The room spun. She sucked in air and flexed her fingers and toes. Maybe this would feel routine someday, but she was still in the "Oh my god, am I connected to my body again?" phase.

Heart pounding, she laced her fingers behind her head and calmed her breathing. *I agree that we may be able to help with her mother.* A sincere sentiment, or did "help" mean bilk her out of her money? Even if Andy truly believed the soul healers to be a worthy cause, the person on the other end of the phone might not. Her astral journey had warned her to prepare for another conversation about her rich and generous mom, but she'd learned nothing about Jane. She'd known it would be a long shot, and the weekend was only beginning. With that lovely thought, Jillian rolled over and closed her eyes again.

FEELING HERSELF DOZING off, Jillian snapped back to the lecture and focused on Ross, the speaker who'd now droned on for—she sneaked a look at her watch—over two hours. It would help if he made sense. She stifled a yawn. Her mind wandered again. She'd spotted Sam's car in the resort's parking lot on the crack of dawn walk Andy had dragged everyone on that morning, so that was one question answered. Sam had probably still been asleep, and blissfully alone. Jillian would love five minutes to herself. Sandy had stuck to her like glue all day. She was surprised that Sandy hadn't squeezed into the bathroom with her.

Throughout the day, Jillian had tried to telepathically reach Sam, with no luck. What was she doing right now? Reading in her room, maybe? Helping Jeremy? Whatever she was doing, it had to be more interesting than the gobbledygook Jillian had listened to and the workshops she'd participated in. So far, the group hadn't revealed itself as the soul healers, but they'd said grace at all the meals. Jillian had done what she did at the Fellowship's breakfast table: acknowledged that she was fortunate to start off her day with a plate of food, something many in the world were unable to do. She inwardly smiled. Sam abandoned her usual reticence when it was her turn to say grace. Jillian sometimes forgot how devout Sam was, and wondered how often she bit her tongue when they were together. Probably a lot. Sam must say grace in her head when they ate alone together, too.

So far, Roberta hadn't asked Jillian to say grace. She was pondering whether to propose that she take her proper turn and say a secular thank you. If Roberta turned her down, she wouldn't take it personally. Did everyone on the island ask God why the hell Jillian was there?

Damn, she was doing it again. *Stay awake and focus.* She wasn't addled, just tired and bored. Were the other new people actually taken in by this tripe? Considering they'd all been kept up until past midnight and woken up at 5:30 this morning, she supposed that a combination of fatigue, a yearning to belong, and the repetitive nature of the material could dull someone's senses.

". . . goes deeper than that. It goes to the essence of who we are, to our very souls."

Jillian straightened. *Here we go.*

"It's not enough to treat the symptoms, to change the superficial. No, you need to go deeper, get to the core of the problem, heal the underlying disease. And that takes dedication, and courage, and a supportive community. You're here because your soul, the essence of who you are, is in pain. To live your life's purpose, you must first heal your soul." Ross turned to look at Christine. "You've taken the first step. You're already on your way. Don't turn back now." He shifted his attention to Jillian. "Don't take the path most travelled. Thank you."

Jillian enthusiastically clapped along with everyone else, and smiled and nodded when Sandy hissed, "Isn't he brilliant?"

Andy twisted toward her. "Why don't we go for a stroll before dinner?"

"Yes, let's," Sandy said. Suddenly Derek, Bob, and Carol were there, too. Feeling surrounded, Jillian listened to them babble about Ross's lecture as they walked to the lobby. Had they listened to a different speaker? Because all she'd heard was circular rhetoric that hadn't made sense half the time. According to her companions, she'd just listened to an inspired and visionary speech by one of the world's great orators. But she played along. She even managed to repeat Ross's more coherent points when they asked her which parts of the lecture had resonated with her the most.

Outside, the tone of the conversation changed. "You've mentioned your mother before," Bob said. "Are you close?"

Jillian nodded.

"How long ago did your father pass away?" Andy asked.

She softened her voice. "A few years ago." Those with her murmured their condolences. "Mom still doesn't know what to do with herself. Dad left her financially independent. She can travel and take up any hobby she desires." She paused to let the information sink in. "But she's still living in the same house, hasn't gone anywhere, and keeps talking about how she'd like to use the money to make a difference."

"Your father must have left you some money," Bob said. Jillian gave him a point for keeping his voice level.

"Yes, he did. I splurged on a vacation and invested the rest."

"Typical accountant," Andy said. Jillian chuckled along with the others. "Have you told your mother where you are this weekend?"

"Yes. I usually call her every day, so I had to let her know that I might not call her over the weekend. She's not infirm or anything. In fact, she's in great health for her age. I just like to talk to her, keep in touch, you know?"

Her companions nodded.

"It's helped, too, knowing that if I can't find a job and I burn through my investments, Mom will help me out. She wouldn't leave me destitute." She noticed Andy catching Bob's eye. "Anyway, I'm glad I came to the retreat. I'm impressed with what I've heard so far."

The conversation returned to Ross's lecture. Jillian threw in the occasional "yes" and nod as her escorts repeated the same old, same old. They continued to drive home their points during dinner and during a workshop that night, which consisted of everyone sharing their determination to transform their lives, or explaining how belonging to the coaching group had helped them to do so. When Jillian's turn came, she told them what she suspected they wanted to hear, then agreed that spending time with like-minded people had made her wonder what she could achieve by joining some of the more intensive programs touched upon over the weekend. As for society, people who believed in traditional values were under siege. They needed to band together, support each other. The applause was deafening. She hoped her grin didn't look fixed.

"I can't believe a day has already gone by," Jillian said when she and Sandy returned to their room after spending another couple of hours in the picnic area. "It's peaceful here. Too bad we're leaving before dinner tomorrow. I wouldn't have minded another evening around the fire."

"Actually, we have a surprise planned for you that's not on the agenda. Something special." Sandy smiled. "Don't worry, you'll still be home before dark."

Jillian hoped her answering smile appeared genuine. *Don't freak out.* She'd still be getting out of here tomorrow, hopefully in one piece.

Chapter Twelve

Jillian tried not to fidget as she watched most of the others file from the meeting room. Another speaker, the same message—and now everyone was heading home, except her and her ever-present entourage. Andy turned to her. "Tom would like to meet you. In fact, he came here for that very purpose."

"Tom is our spiritual mentor," Carol said. "He keeps in touch with all the groups. Through him, we know what everyone is doing."

"Why does he want to see me?" Jillian asked.

"We'll let Tom explain that to you," Andy said, motioning for Jillian to follow him.

As they all walked to the elevator, she didn't have to fake her interest. "When did Tom arrive?"

"Late last night."

"And he really came here just to meet me?"

"You'll like him, Jillian," Sandy said. Andy nodded. "He's so supportive. He wants to see everyone live the life they were meant to live."

Her companions led her to Room 225. Andy knocked at the door, then swung it open. "Go ahead."

Expecting the others to follow, Jillian stepped over the threshold and took in her surroundings. The room was actually an apartment suite; she stood in the short entry hallway. When she heard the door close behind her, a glance over her shoulder told her that she'd meet Tom alone.

Rustling, then a smiling middle-aged man, graying at the temples, approached Jillian with his hand outstretched. "Jillian!"

She shook his hand, then tensed when he didn't let go of her fingers, but clasped her hand between both of his. *Relax.*

"I'm so glad you've come to see me. The others have been raving about you. I always want to hear about special people, and the moment I heard about you, I knew I'd meet a kindred spirit."

His velvety baritone and empathic green eyes would probably have a straight woman swooning. The man certainly had charisma, a magnetism that would draw lost and searching souls to him—to be crushed. *Don't jump the gun.* Apart from the Fellowship's suspicions that ex-members were being helped into their graves, there wasn't anything to suggest that the people she'd met were involved in a nefarious scheme. She couldn't allow her preconceived notions to blind her, or she'd miss what was actually there in favour of what she expected to find. She wanted to prove herself to the Fellowship, not screw up her first operation.

Tom finally let go of her hand. "Come in and sit down."

She entered a bright sitting area, sank onto the leather sofa, and cursed herself when Tom sat next to her; she should have sat in one of the chairs. Acutely aware that she and Tom were alone, she weighed her chances of getting to the hallway before him. *Stop being paranoid.* Threatening or assaulting a potential recruit wouldn't be prudent and could land the cult in a boatload of trouble. She crossed her legs and waited for Tom to speak.

"What did you think of your stay here?" he asked. "Did you enjoy meeting the others, and the workshops and lectures?"

"Very much so. I'm glad I came. I was surprised when Andy said that you'd come to the resort to meet me, though. I don't know why. Others contributed to the workshops much more than I did." But they didn't have rich mothers, or were already within the fold.

Tom flashed her another dazzling smile. "As I said, Andy and the others speak highly of you. We'd love for you to become more involved. I wanted to speak with you personally because I know that when you're balanced on the precipice, the doubts begin to surface. This is when the weak turn back, and those who could make a difference silence themselves. I don't want that to happen to you."

"I want to change my life."

"I know you do." He met her eyes. "Andy believes you're a spiritual person. Do you believe in God, Jillian?"

She and Sam had suspected that this question would come up at some point. "Yes."

Tom nodded, giving Jillian the impression that she'd passed a test. "Have you considered that everything that's happened to you recently has been God's way of trying to tell you something?"

She almost laughed. As it was, she had to duck her head and stifle the smile threatening to spring to her lips. Thank god Sam wasn't here.

"That question hits home, doesn't it?" Tom said in his velvety voice.

She raised her head.

"You see, you're special. God has led you to this point. He's chosen you. You're at a crossroads, a critical point in your life. Will you take the familiar path that you've already walked and discovered leads nowhere, or will you realize your full potential and seize your destiny?"

"I *do* want to live the life I'm meant to live."

"Good." Tom rubbed his finger along his lower lip. "What do you know about the Association of the Sacred Souls?"

Careful. "You mean the soul healers?"

His face darkened. "That's what the media calls us. As usual, they mangle what they don't understand. The first step to reclaiming your life is to free yourself from regret, remorse, the limiting beliefs holding you back. Those aren't physical illnesses, they're sicknesses of the soul. Through our program, and with the help of God, you'll heal your inner self."

"I didn't realize your group was primarily a religious one. I was given a flyer at a crusade, but I was mainly there for a friend. I joined your self-help group, not your religious one. I thought . . ." She trailed off.

Tom's brows drew together. "You're disillusioned with religion. You see it as obsolete, ineffective, indifferent."

"Yes, I do."

"But you're a spiritual woman. You want to do God's work."

"Yes."

"Spirituality is still acceptable in our society. Believing in God is still somewhat acceptable, depending on what definition is used. Adherence to the major world religions is not. At this point, it's merely tolerated. I asked you about God so I could see how strongly society's war on religion has claimed you."

War on religion? Please. "I'm not a church-goer. I don't see the point. Churches are filled with hypocrites who pick and choose what they follow." Her honesty wouldn't knock her halo askew; she'd deduced that the soul healers saw the church in the same light that Jesus had seen the Pharisees.

"I understand your scorn toward the church, Jillian. It's doing nothing while the world crumbles around it."

"It should be taking action."

"Exactly." Tom leaned toward her. "We don't stand on ceremony, don't wear robes and collect fine art. We've gone back to the basics. Unfortunately, the prejudices against religion, the lies God's opponents perpetrate against the faithful, can deafen and blind those who are meant to join God's army. They turn away without listening. They reject their destiny based on misinformation."

Deciding to go for broke, Jillian blinked at Tom. "What can I do? So far, I've sat through lectures, workshops, and round-table discussions. Talk isn't action."

"Precisely," Tom roared. "We need special people like you, those filled with the fire of the Holy Spirit. You *can* do more. The world needs you. Take the next step and cleanse your soul. Then help us to spread the word. Isn't that what Jesus commanded us to do? With each cleansed soul, we draw nearer to a cleansed society. God has chosen you for this work. The future of our world depends on you." His voice grew urgent. "Meet with Andy. Tell him your time has come. He'll guide you through the next steps."

"I've invited him and a few others over for coffee."

"That's wonderful. There's a time for socializing . . . and a time for spirituality."

"I'll talk to Andy about where to go from here."

"Excellent. Well, I won't keep you from your friends. I know they're waiting for you in the lobby." When Tom stood, Jillian did too. "I hope to see much more of you, Jillian."

What should she say in response to that? She chose to merely smile and murmured a good-bye.

The moment she stepped off the elevator and into the lobby, her new best friends swarmed her.

"Isn't Tom wonderful!"

"He doesn't ask to see everyone, Jillian."

"Tom knows you're special."

Curiously, none of them asked her what they'd discussed.

JILLIAN CLOSED THE apartment door and took a moment to savour the silence. She'd survived the weekend without grinding her teeth down to her gums. The rich mother plan had better get her close to the leadership quickly, because the prospect of living in a cult residence for months made her want to cry. In the living room, she lowered her bag to the floor, flicked on a lamp—and almost hit the ceiling. "Jesus! You scared me."

Sam looked up at her from the sofa.

"What are you doing, sitting in the dark?"

"I didn't know if anyone would come up with you. You're supposed to be living alone, remember."

Jillian dropped into a chair and slowly exhaled. "I didn't expect you to beat me back."

"I left when I saw you loading up the car." Sam straightened. "How did it go?"

"Good, I think. I've been invited to take the next step." She filled Sam in on her weekend, including her astral exploration and her meeting with Tom. "I can't tell who honestly believes it," she said, when she'd finished. "I'm sure everyone who isn't a group leader does. But Andy and the rest . . . I don't know."

"Sounds like they'll want to meet your mother."

"Yeah. I'm surprised Tom didn't bring it up, but I guess they don't want to be too obvious." She stared down at her hands. "Those who believe what the soul healers teach, who honestly do believe that the program will heal their souls . . . they think they're following God, just like you do. How do you know you're right? Maybe they're right. I'm not saying the Fellowship is a cult . . ."

Sam blinked at her. "What are you saying, then? Do I have to worry that you actually believe their nonsense?"

"No. I'm saying that you don't have any more proof than they do that what you believe is right."

"Oh, it's proof you want," Sam drawled. "Sorry, can't give it to you."

"If there's a God, where is He? If He wants us to know Him, why doesn't He show Himself?" Jillian shrilled. "Where is He during famines, and wars, and natural disasters? Why doesn't He stop His precious children from torturing and killing each other? How do you explain it all away? What mental gymnastics do you have to perform?"

"My faith isn't rational, Jillian," Sam said, sounding bored, not annoyed. "I don't care about your intellectual pooh-poohing of my faith or anyone else's. Don't bother nitpicking at the inconsistencies and historical inaccuracies in the Bible, either. Not only would it show that you have absolutely no understanding of what the Bible is, but if every word in the Bible was proven to be crap tomorrow, it wouldn't change anything for me. It wouldn't take away my experience of God. I'm sorry you've never experienced Him. I'm sorry you've never known Him. And that's all I'm going to say on the subject, because we have to work together. So let's get back to the matter at hand. What's the next step?"

Realizing that her fingernails were digging into her legs, Jillian consciously relaxed her fingers and tried not to glower at Sam. Why did she leap at every opportunity to pick at Sam's beliefs? Sam didn't do it to her. Was it insecurity? Jealousy? Did she wish she could still fool herself into believing that there would eventually be order in all this madness, that justice would prevail and everything would make sense? Why? "I believed once," she heard herself say.

Sam silently studied her. Was that sympathy in her eyes? Pity? Sadness? *Am I looking into a mirror?*

"I know you did," Sam said softly. "What's the next step?"

Jillian swallowed. "I've invited Andy, Carol, and Bob for coffee tomorrow night. We'll discuss me undergoing a more intensive program, which will probably involve cleansing my soul."

"And quitting your job. And moving into a cult residence."

"I hope my rich mom gets me to the top quickly. I don't know how long I'll be able to stand it."

"Fortunately you'll only have to stay in until you've determined one way or the other whether they have anything to do with Jane's disappearance." Sam raised her brows. "You could be out fairly quickly. It might not take Mom long to get you access to the upper echelons."

Jillian nodded. "If they don't bring her up tomorrow, I will. I can be worried about her, right?"

"You're supposed to be worried about her. Anyway, let's go back to the safe house."

She showed her agreement by rising and picking up her bag. She wanted to apologize, but it would only make things worse. Somehow she had to keep her mouth zipped. Sam wasn't going to change. Jillian didn't want her to.

JILLIAN PERCHED ON the edge of the sofa, waiting for the apartment buzzer to sound. She expected her coffee group to be prompt, which meant they'd be here in five minutes. As the time crawled, she mentally reviewed the conversation she'd had with Sam over dinner, and reminded herself that her accommodating, smiling friends belonged to a cult that might be murdering its own. And here she was, trying to ingratiate herself with them. *Get in, find out, and get out. Survival is your primary goal.*

She jumped when the buzzer announced the arrival of her guests, then went to the intercom. "Yes?"

"We're here," Andy said.

Why wasn't she surprised that they'd arrived en masse? "Come on up." She buzzed them through, opened the door, and waved to them when they spilled into the hallway from the elevator. "Welcome," she said, ushering them into her apartment. They smiled; Carol patted Jillian's arm. She liked that they weren't a touchy-feely group. Neither was the Fellowship. Roberta hugged everyone, but she was the exception. Maybe they were more demonstrative in the chapel. Not that manhandling everyone was required to be a close-knit group or devout. When Jillian had attended church, she'd always felt that the hugs and arm squeezes were pretense. She would have preferred to slap some of those she'd embraced.

Her guests milled about in the living room. "Please sit down. What can I get you? Coffee? Tea?" After listening to who wanted what, Jillian went into the kitchen and put the kettle on; she'd brewed the coffee in advance. She carried a plate of cookies into the living room and set it on the coffee table. "Help yourself."

Andy reached for a sugar cookie. "How long have you lived here?"

Five minutes. "A couple of years." She forced a self-mocking laugh. "I finally moved here to be closer to my job, and now I'm thinking of quitting." The others clucked their tongues in sympathy. "Where do you all live? Andy, you said you live near the coaching centre?"

He nodded. "You can't beat a two-minute walk to work. I moved in with some other group members. It's better than living alone."

"We live just up the road from him," Carol said.

Jillian wondered if, as a married couple, they were entitled to their own place, or just their own room. They made small talk until the kettle whistled. After providing everyone with a coffee or tea, Jillian sat on the sofa next to Andy, sipped her tea, and waited for someone to take the lead.

"My head's still buzzing from everything we learned over the weekend," Bob said, to murmurs of agreement. "Have you discussed the retreat with anyone, Jillian?"

She hadn't expected the perfect opening to land on her lap so soon. "I told my mother about it. She seemed quite interested." She sighed. "But when I told Lisa, a close friend . . ."

Everyone grew still. "What about Lisa?" Andy said.

Jillian stared down at her tea. "She's asking a lot of questions. I told her that I'm at a crossroads, that I want my life to *mean* something. I don't want to push paper while my soul despairs."

"But she didn't understand," Carol said.

"No." Jillian caught Andy and Bob glancing at each other.

"Lisa's reaction isn't unusual," Andy said. "When someone wants to make a change, a real change, in his or her life, those closest to the person are often the most critical. You're on the verge of answering the call, of doing what you're meant to do, of fulfilling the purpose God has for you. You're at your most vulnerable. This is when those who oppose God, who oppose bringing God's vision into the world, will push back. They'll say or do anything to make sure you turn your back on your destiny. They might not even realize they're doing it."

"Satan will use your family and friends against you," Carol said.

Jillian smiled wanly. "My mother isn't reacting badly. I'm not sure she understands the steps I'm considering, but she sounded supportive. As for Lisa . . ." She sighed. "Her sensible friend is suddenly talking about how she might like to do something more meaningful with her life, rather than work a nine to five corporate job. I've told her I want my life to count, but she thinks I should slow down, spend my time looking for another job, and volunteer with your group when I can. You all work, right?" she said innocently. She knew Andy's coaching was a recruitment vehicle.

"We work for God," Andy said. "We dedicate ourselves to bringing His healing light into the world. You can't partly commit to doing God's work, to answering His call. You're either committed, or you're not. We all use our skills differently now." He pointed at himself. "I used to be a high school counsellor."

"I used to work in the IT department of an insurance company," Bob said. "Before that, I worked for several small software start-ups."

Carol gazed at Jillian. "I do administrative work. Phone calls, letters, that sort of thing."

"Doing the books for a socially responsible group does sound appealing," Jillian said.

"Of course it does. It's what you're meant to do," Andy said. "You need to recognize when those around you are trying to steer you down the wrong path, and resist them. God has chosen you to do His work."

"Your mother knows better than your friend," Carol said.

"Can we meet your mother?" Andy asked. "I hope you don't mind, but I mentioned your concerns about her to Tom. I know you're worried about her." He touched her arm. "You're not alone now, Jillian. You have us. We can help. We'll add our voices to yours, help guide her to make better choices regarding her investments and charities."

"Bring her to our downtown learning centre," Carol suggested.

"I might be better off bringing Lisa," Jillian said. "If anyone needs to see the good work you're doing, she does."

Andy shook his head. "Lisa will look for reasons to pick apart everything she sees and hears. You need supportive people around you right now, not those who want to thwart your true purpose in life." Everyone's head bobbed.

Carol lifted a chocolate chip cookie from the tray. "Bring your mother. She'll become an even stronger ally. She'll give you the strength to do what you know in your heart you should do." She nibbled on the cookie.

"I'll ask her." Jillian dipped a sugar cookie into her tea. "I had a question about something I read in the literature Ross gave out at his workshop."

Everyone straightened. "What would you like to know?" Andy asked.

Nothing, really, but she'd prepared a list of questions, to demonstrate that she'd read the material. They also needed something to talk about for the next hour or two. She'd rather pass the time listening to them expound on the same points she'd now heard a million times, than field more questions about her life.

Chapter Thirteen

JILLIAN SLOWED TO stop at a traffic light and glanced at her passenger. Gazing out the windshield, Ruth said, "How are you adjusting? I know it's difficult in the beginning, especially when you're back in the world. Do you think about contacting your family?"

"Sometimes."

Ruth grunted.

"But I won't." Mom and Danny had already been through the hell of burying her, and what would be the point?

"Do you have brothers and sisters?"

"No." Ruth either hadn't read her file, or wanted to hear it from her. "Just my parents. Well, Danny is my stepfather. My father . . . passed away when I was eleven."

"I'm sorry."

"It's old news," Jillian mumbled. "What about you? Do you have family out there?"

"I don't know anymore," Ruth said. "My parents, aunts and uncles, and siblings are all gone. I don't know about cousins. When I came in, I didn't have any nieces or nephews, and I've never asked."

"But you know who's died."

"You'll be told when someone you were close to passes away. There's no need to know about those you'll never meet."

Jillian accelerated through the intersection. "What about children? Has anyone ever had to leave children?"

"No. Usually Fledglings come in youngish, and I gather our Lord doesn't choose those with children. Supporters sometimes have them, but we try to avoid that. Children make one vulnerable, and we need our Supporters to be responsive. We can't always wait until the next day."

"That's why we have to leave everyone behind, I suppose." In her peripheral vision, Jillian saw Ruth nod.

"Imagine if we didn't. Holidays, birthdays, family crises, deaths, illness . . . we'd constantly feel pulled between our familial duties and our true purpose."

True purpose. Jillian couldn't help but think of Andy and company. "It would also be difficult to explain what we do for a living and why we're always going away." Keeping her role at the agency a secret from Mom and Danny had been a strain. She didn't like lying.

"That, too."

"Sam seems to have a lot of regret around leaving her family."

"Did she tell you that?"

"Yes."

Ruth didn't speak until they'd almost arrived at the soul healer's learning centre. "I wish she could sit down with her family and clear the air. She's either being much too hard on herself, or there's something we don't know. Either way, she can't seem to forgive herself. I doubt she ever will."

What could have happened that prevented Sam from letting go? Maybe she'd argued with her parents before she left them? From what Sam had told her, tension had existed between her and her family. She'd thought she was going crazy; they'd dragged her to a psychiatrist, received a diagnosis of schizophrenia, and started her on medication—which she'd refused to take. Or was it simply what Sam had said: she hadn't fully grasped that she'd never see them again. When people were desperate and salvation was nigh, they often glossed over the details, and Sam had only been nineteen. Jesus.

Jillian didn't have time to think about it. She looked for a parking spot as they cruised by the learning centre, then spotted a sign for an underground parking garage. Five minutes later, she and Ruth stood in the learning centre's lobby and smiled at an approaching Andy.

"Welcome, welcome." His eyes settled on Ruth.

"This is Andy. I've told you about him," Jillian said. "Andy, this is my mother."

He shook Ruth's hand. "I've been looking forward to meeting you since Jillian suggested bringing you along with her today."

"He's quite the charmer, isn't he?" Ruth said. Then, out loud, "I like to keep up with what my daughter is doing, especially when she's considering leaving a steady job."

Jillian sighed. "I thought—"

"I'm not complaining, dear. I don't like to see you unhappy. You've been trying to put on a brave face, but a mother knows." She touched Andy's arm. "It's been a while since she's sounded enthusiastic about anything. You're too young to be fed up with life, Jillian."

"I know," Jillian mumbled.

"What exactly is it that you do here?" Ruth asked.

"This is a drop-in centre. Those who feel the need for guidance or want a sympathetic ear can come inside, rest, and unburden themselves." Andy gestured toward the two twenty-somethings lingering near the lobby doors. "But if someone just wants to take the weight off their feet, that's fine, too."

Jillian eyed the comfy chairs ringing the lobby. Only one was occupied. A woman with a bunch of shopping bags at her feet sat talking to a recruiter, only she didn't know that. Sure, everyone could come in and relax, unaware that they were fish in a fishing hole.

"For those truly in distress, we have private counselling rooms." Andy led them down a corridor and swung open a door that stood ajar. The cheerful decor and plush chairs gave the room an inviting air. Stacks of literature filled a bookcase, and a box of tissues sat on a table.

"Is everyone here a trained counsellor?" Ruth asked.

"We have our own intensive training course, and everyone has gone through our counselling program."

Jillian nudged Ruth's arm. "The program I was telling you about. The one that puts you back onto the right path."

Andy nodded. "Many of those who complete our program are so excited by their transformed lives that they want to help others achieve the same. Matthew used to be a financial advisor. Now he counsels those who are drowning in debt. Jessica was a real estate agent. She likes to say that she'd rather save lives than sell houses."

Ruth's brows shot up. "So they gave up their jobs."

"Yes. In fact, some go further than that. They join the community, live among those who now serve God by serving others." Andy pointed upward. "Many live on the upper floors of this building."

They rounded a corner farther down the corridor and a few steps later, Andy pushed through a pair of swinging doors. Jillian and Ruth followed him into a modern kitchen in which several people were slicing and dicing, and stirring boiling pots of water or soup. "This is where we prepare the meals for the residents," Andy said.

"Do you have any type of meal program for the needy?" Jillian asked.

"No. We ran a pilot program once. We invited the less fortunate in the neighbourhood to have a meal, but too many arrived intoxicated or stoned, or behaved inappropriately. We had to decide who we want to serve. There are already plenty of programs and shelters for those in need, but we're the only organization that counsels those who've recognized that they've lost their way, that they must heal their souls and discover God's purpose for their lives."

Ruth's brows knitted. "What about the church?"

"The church has lost its way," Andy said, with a regretful shake of his head. "There's no accountability, no commitment, no consequences when someone transgresses."

"I agree," Jillian said, wondering what consequences those in the cult faced. According to the Fellowship's earlier investigation, humiliation in front of one's peers and menial work were common. Had Lancaster Jr. added death as a punishment for those who fled? "Before I met you, I was wondering whether I should talk to a local pastor, but he would have told me to persevere at work and not worry about it."

"The churches are part of the problem," Andy said. "Your instincts were right."

She smiled at him. "They led me here."

He grinned back at her. "Yes, they did!"

They returned to the lobby and proceeded down another corridor. As Andy guided them through his chosen stops, Jillian silently congratulated the soul healers for putting on a wonderful show. Anyone seeking a way to help those in need would be impressed. In addition to counselling, the group offered adult literacy classes, the coaching centre Jillian had visited, and several other programs for lost souls, each targeted to those with a particular interest. All were recruitment vehicles. No daycare or programs geared to parents, though. Children were inconvenient.

Everyone they met extolled the virtues of working and living at the centre. They all loved bunking with their fellow kindred spirits, the food was great, they fell into bed at night satisfied that they'd spent that day helping others, and they were happier than they'd ever been.

"That's a taste of what we do here," Andy said as they re-entered the lobby. "As you can see, Jillian, there's plenty here for someone who wants to spend her time making a difference." He beamed at Ruth. "I'm sure your mother would be proud to see you teaching someone to read."

"I certainly would." Ruth turned to Jillian. "But you don't want to lose your accounting skills. I didn't see anything here that suits your talents."

Jillian rolled her eyes. "I'm tired of sitting at a desk, pushing paper and helping nobody. I can do more."

Ruth gave her a long look. "But you like accounting. It plays to your natural aptitudes."

"I want to do more. Mom." *Jesus, don't call her Ruth.*

"Someone has to keep the books." Ruth gazed at Andy. "You must have an accounting department."

"Mom—"

Ruth whirled back to her. "Jillian, you said yourself that it's not the work, it's the fact that you don't feel what you're doing makes a difference. You told me you'd love to do the books for a non-profit, or another organization where you can see a direct relationship between what you do and having an impact on others." She sighed. "I understand what you want. You can do that *and* accounting. It doesn't have to be one or the other. Speaking of money . . ." She shifted her attention to Andy. "I don't mean to be crass, but do you accept donations?"

Andy's voice lifted. "Of course. The community's support is very important to us."

Jillian couldn't help but give him a point for not pretending that he wouldn't take Ruth's money, or would do so only by necessity.

"Is there somewhere I can write you a cheque?" Ruth asked.

Andy took them to the first counselling room he'd shown them. Ruth slipped her purse off her shoulder and rummaged through it. Jillian stifled a chuckle. What had Ruth thrown into the purse she'd first set eyes on a couple of hours ago?

"Here we are," Ruth said, finally fishing out a chequebook and pen. "Who do I make the cheque out to?"

"Make it out to 'The Christian Literacy and Nourishment Foundation.'" Andy went to the bookcase, lifted a paper from a stack, and set it on the table. "That's the name of our charitable foundation." He underlined the name on the flyer with his finger.

So that was the name the soul healers were using for this particular setup. It was on the list of companies in the Fellowship's file on the cult. Jillian forced her mind back to the stuffy room and tried not to show too much interest in the cheque Ruth was writing. Ruth ripped the cheque from the chequebook and handed it to Andy, whose eyes slightly widened. "Thank you. That's very generous of you."

"You obviously do good work here," Ruth said, sounding absolutely sincere. "My late husband left me very comfortable, and right now the money's sitting around doing nothing. I'd much rather put it to use. I'll have to be honest, I didn't know what to expect, given your recent troubles."

Andy frowned. "Recent troubles?"

Ruth nodded. "That woman who was on the news a while back . . . something about her sister." Her brow furrowed. "Oh, yes, her sister had," she looked at Jillian, "she'd committed suicide, hadn't she? For some reason, her family blamed the soul healers."

"Mom!" Jillian tutted. "Don't believe everything you hear on the news. The poor woman just couldn't accept that her sister had died so young."

Ruth's mouth pinched. "I know, I know, and that's what I'm trying to say. It's obvious these people do good work. They can't save everyone."

"No, we can't," Andy said mournfully. "I'm not sure which woman you're referring to, because it's not unusual for us to be accused of ruining someone's life. When you work with people to transform their lives, as we do, you'd be surprised at how spitefully family and friends can react to positive change. You'd think they'd be supportive and encouraging, but that's often not the case."

"They're envious," Ruth said.

"Yes. So they lash out, rather than examining their own lives. Look at what happened to Jesus."

Oh, please. Regardless of what one thought of Christianity, there was no denying that Jesus had challenged the status quo and gotten under the skin of powerful people. That was quite different to chucking one's job to become a mindless cog in a corrupt wheel.

"I have to admit, when Jillian said she was going to leave her job to work with you, my first reaction was to tell her not to do it. But if she can use her accounting skills to help an organization that helps others, I say do it." She gripped Jillian's arm. "I want you to be happy."

Andy failed to mask his surprise at the news that Jillian had made the decision to quit her job and work with the group. "That's fantastic news! You'll have time to undergo our intensive program and do some accounting for us. I'll speak to our accounting team."

"Great!" Jillian said.

"Don't get too excited. You won't get anywhere near the real books until they completely trust you," Ruth said.

"Hopefully your generosity and interest in your daughter will get me there faster," Jillian replied. "I was sort of hedging about it. After all, we're talking about leaving a full-time job I've had for years. But after coming here . . . and with your support, which really means a lot to me," she said to Ruth, "I think I'll do it. I'm going to hand in my notice. What's the worst that can happen?"

"I'll call you later to discuss the details," Andy said. "You'll see a familiar face around here, Jillian. Christine is taking a break from her studies to join us. In fact, she's moving into one of the rooms upstairs."

Wonderful. Just wonderful.

"We should go," Ruth said. "We have shopping to do."

"Don't let me keep you." Andy beamed at them. "Thank you for visiting, and thank you so much for your generous donation. Jillian, I'll phone you later."

Ruth patted his arm. "Bye, Andy."

"Let me walk you out," he said, sweeping his arm toward the lobby doors.

Jillian resisted the urge to glance at Ruth. They weren't even allowed ten seconds alone to go to the exit.

After saying their good-byes, Jillian and Ruth strolled along the sidewalk and waited until they were in the parking garage before speaking. "How much did you give him?" Jillian asked.

"A thousand dollars. He knows there's more where that came from." Ruth took Jillian's arm. "Typical cult. I've seen the blank looks and heard the regurgitated sound bites before. And Andy was lying. When I alluded to Jane," she said, in response to Jillian's puzzled glance. "He knew exactly who I was referring to. That doesn't mean he knows about a murder, though."

"He matches the description of the man who visited Amanda."

"That doesn't mean it was him."

They'd reached the car. Jillian unlocked the doors and slipped into the driver's seat. "How long do you think it'll take me to get access to Lancaster Jr. or someone close to him?"

"It's difficult to say." Ruth grimaced as she pulled on her seatbelt. "You'll have to move in with them. You'll want to be the most dedicated worker they've ever had."

Yep, she'd increase her hours until she stayed overnight. Then she'd give up her apartment.

"I doubt anyone at the higher levels bunks at the learning centre, but you never know what you'll pick up. I'll do what I can to get a meeting with someone important. I can't dangle a huge donation in front of them too soon, though."

"Weeks or months, then," Jillian said, keeping her voice light.

Ruth gave her a sympathetic smile. "We'll move as quickly as we can."

Fear tightened her throat. Once she'd moved into the centre, would she ever leave it, or would she be a prisoner with an indefinite sentence?

Chapter Fourteen

JILLIAN JERKED AWAKE when someone nudged her arm. "Don't let them catch you dozing," Cathy whispered.

Her surroundings came into focus. What time was it? How long had she sat here listening to Lancaster Jr. drone on, her muscles sore, her bum aching, and her bladder bursting? She stretched out her legs, careful not to kick the person in front of her. The faces around her were etched with weariness, but everyone's eyes remained on Junior, seated at the front of the room like a king upon a throne. He was the master and they were his children, gathered at his feet. She wanted to march up to him and rip off the black robe he wore. The man wasn't ordained. He hadn't even gone to college.

Stifling a yawn, she pondered whether to approach the grand poobah tonight, then decided against it. Since this was her first cleansing session with Junior, it was too soon to make a move. After working long hours for the cult for almost a month, she'd recently moved into the centre. She was still a lackey, albeit one who was permitted to handle trivial transactions at the bank. Of course, she never went alone. Someone always accompanied her, for her protection. Uh-huh.

The intensive counselling program had turned out to be exactly what she'd expected it to be—intensive mind control. Add to that the long hours, the lack of privacy, the sometimes long gaps between meals, and these rambling lectures, and it was no wonder the brains of everyone around her had turned to mush. If not for centering herself regularly throughout the day, she'd be right there with them. She'd felt the magnetic pull to agree, to belong, to stop fighting it and give in. But she'd resisted. Her reward: knowing she was trapped, and cringing at the lost souls around her. She sometimes felt as she had when she'd been the only sober person in a roomful of drunks, watching everyone thinking they were oh-so-wonderful and fun, when all they were doing was making asses of themselves. At least those gathered here thought they were doing something useful with their lives. But that was the tragedy.

She focused on Junior and wondered how often he showed up to guide his flock. Fatigue had prevented those at the centre from showing much excitement about the scheduled seven o'clock meeting, but anticipation had been in the air all day. There were some unfamiliar faces here, and a few familiar ones who didn't live at the centre. Bob and Carol had arrived and waved to her, but now that she was one of them, they apparently didn't need to sit with her.

How many of these meetings would she have to endure? When she'd managed to speak with Sam a few days ago, she'd learned that Ruth was dangling her carrot, so hopefully Jillian would be moving up soon. A private room and untimed shower would be nice, though she suspected that those would be out of her reach until she was out.

"Now, my brothers and sisters, sometimes new souls who come to us need our support," Junior thundered. "I see a new face here."

Blood rushed to Jillian's cheeks. He wasn't looking at her, but everyone knew who the newbie was. She hugged her legs to her chest.

To her relief, Junior raised a finger and started to ramble again. "Physical irritations. That's one of the signs. Physical irritations." He surveyed his flock, then continued. "It's an industry now. Go into any pharmacy and walk the aisles packed with pills, oils, ointments, patches, something to ease every ailment, to treat the symptoms." His mouth twisted. "Stress. Worry. Stubbornly walking the wrong path while the soul weeps. Is it no wonder that so many find comfort in a pharmacy? Is it no wonder that a sick soul leads to a sick body? That an unbalanced soul leads to an unbalanced physiology? The pharmacy has become the new church, where there's a quick fix for every ailment. We know better, my brothers and sisters. We're walking the path of light. Our souls rejoice. We don't have need of the placebos on pharmacy shelves that treat the body, but not the soul." He held out his arms. "Christine, please come forward."

Jillian's horror grew as Christine leaped to her feet and picked her way through the gathering to Junior. Her face glowed; you'd think she was about to meet Jesus freaking Christ Himself. Jillian couldn't bear to watch, but she kept her gaze forward and hoped that Christine wasn't about to be publicly humiliated. It was bad enough that Jillian had stood by and allowed her to withdraw from university and shut out her family and moronic friends.

"Christine." Beaming at her, Junior took the girl's hands. "Christine. You're blossoming, Christine. Your soul's light is shining brighter."

"Thank you," Christine said breathily. Jillian was surprised she didn't genuflect.

"You came to us distressed. You were in pain. In here." Junior let go of one of Christine's hands and pressed his hand against her chest. Yeah, her chest! Didn't anyone else notice that he was touching her breast? "But now you're among people who care, people who want the best for you, who recognize that you're special, that you have potential."

Jillian was still staring at the position of Junior's hand. If he called her up and did the same thing, it would take all her willpower not to deck the guy.

"Rebecca has brought your condition to my attention," Junior said smoothly. He finally removed his hand from Christine's breast and beckoned for someone else to come forward. Rebecca rose, moved to Christine's side, and handed Junior a plastic bottle. Then she moved aside and clapped. Now everyone was pushing to their feet. Jillian rose with a groan; her legs were killing her. A group on the other side of the room broke into an enthusiastic rendition of *He's Got the Whole World in His Hands*. Others clapped along. Anticipation charged the air. Jillian glanced at Cathy for a clue of what was about to happen, but Cathy's eyes were fixed on Junior and Christine. Jillian joined those punctuating the beat with their hands.

As the end of the song drew near, two men in suits hovered near Christine. Junior led the assembly in applauding the singers, then motioned for quiet. Everyone remained on their feet. Jillian took a step to her left to gain a clear view of Junior and Christine.

He lifted the plastic bottle. "I'm told that you use this medicated shampoo, that when we wanted to take it from you, you insisted that you need it."

Christine nodded.

"Does Christine need this shampoo?" Junior asked the assembly.

"No!"

"Is Christine's ailment a sign that her soul still suffers?"

"Yes!"

"Can we help Christine?"

"Yes!"

"Will the Lord work through me to help Christine and heal the sickness blemishing her soul?"

"Yes!"

Junior handed the bottle to Rebecca and softened his voice. "Christine, you don't need that shampoo. Your problem is a symptom, a sign that you'd veered off the true path. But the Lord reached out to you and brought you to me. I will guide you back to the light. You are already on your way." He stood. "Face me, Christine. Look into my eyes."

Christine shifted position to face Junior head on and gazed at him. When the two suits moved behind her, Jillian knew what was coming. Even when she'd believed, sincerely prayed, and meant the words she'd sung, she'd never swallowed the charade that was about to take place.

Junior took Christine's face in his hands. Jillian's jaw clenched. Suddenly she was staring into Lilibeth's cold eyes. The sick party. Her arrogance. The choice. With a shudder, Jillian forced herself back to the present. Junior wasn't a Beguiler. He couldn't directly manipulate Christine's mind, but the effect would be the same: she'd believe an event had taken place, but it hadn't. Jillian had returned to reality when Lilibeth had released her. How long would it take for Christine to realize that she'd accepted a lie?

"In the name of Jesus, I drive away the sickness infecting your soul," Junior boomed. "You have returned to the true path. You have rejoined God's family." He released Christine, who fell backwards into the arms of the two suits.

"Praise, Jesus! Thank you, Lord!" echoed around Jillian. Eyes welled with tears. Cheeks grew wet. A few went into a frenzy, dancing wildly and shouting exhortations.

As she had when she was younger, Jillian wondered why people played along or willingly fooled themselves. Why did every single person fall backwards? Did people instantly know but didn't want to disappoint the audience? When they knew, for a fact, that they weren't healed, why did they keep returning and handing over money? Was it a matter of not wanting to admit that they'd made an ass of themselves? A need to belong? She hadn't understood it then, and she didn't get it now. Then again, she'd returned and watched, even though she'd seen through the healing shtick. *Why?*

Now Christine was bouncing around with her arms lifted to the Lord. One of the suits had left the room; the other grinned at Junior. Jillian couldn't tell if he was laughing at Christine or overjoyed that Junior had healed her.

The second suit returned, holding a bowl. Junior motioned for everyone to calm down. "Christine," he said. "Christine." Christine stopped bouncing and returned to him. "Show everyone where you stand. Show *Satan* where you stand." He motioned to Rebecca, who handed the shampoo to Christine. The suit held out the bowl. "Go ahead," Junior said to Christine. He sat down and shifted his attention to those gathered. "Give her your energy, brothers and sisters."

Everyone pumped their fists into the air and chanted. Jillian eventually caught the words and forced herself to join in. "Say good-bye to Satan. Say good-bye to Satan."

Christine held up the medicated shampoo and screwed off the cap. She poured her relief from whatever scalp condition she suffered into the bowl. When the bottle was empty, she held it upside down, made a face at it, and handed it to one of the suits. The assembly went wild. Christine's face glowed; beatific was the word that came to mind.

Junior leaped to his feet and threw his arm around Christine's shoulders. "Let us pray."

Jillian bowed her head but didn't listen. Guilt didn't begin to cover it. She'd stood by and let the soul healers reel in Christine, who'd thrown away her education without a second thought, just as she had her shampoo. And what about Cathy? Dan. Rebecca. Ryan. All the others standing in this stifling prison. If the windows were the eyes to the soul, their souls weren't unblemished and free and joyful; they were sick and chained and dull. She wanted out of this place, but she was stuck here until she either found out what had happened to Jane, or was convinced that the cult had nothing to do with her disappearance. Right now, Jillian was at the bottom of the totem pole. She needed to move higher, and the sooner, the better. *Come on, Ruth!*

When she heard rustling, she raised her head. "Praise God!" Junior, his arm still around Christine, bellowed. He murmured something to Christine and lifted his arm. Smiling, she went back to her place. Junior's eyes searched the assembly. "In Christine, we have a beautiful sister," he intoned. "If only all of you were like that. But you're not! Bring the whore forward."

Everyone froze. The mood instantly changed. Jillian wanted to shrink into the floor. He wasn't referring to her, was he? She was the only newbie. She let out her pent breath when the two suits jostled into the audience and grabbed someone's arms. "What?" Pat shrieked as they pulled her to Junior. A palpable sense of relief rippled through the room. The pack turned on the victim. First it was a low rumble . . . "Whore, whore, whore . . ." Then the voices grew louder and fists pumped. "Whore! Whore! Whore!"

Pat's faced flushed. She lowered her head. Junior raised his hands and waited for the chanting to stop, then grasped Pat's chin and jerked her head up. "Did you think nobody would notice your weakness? We all have to be vigilant. Satan is always looking for a way in. When you succumb, you endanger all of us."

"I'm sorry," Pat mumbled.

"You're sorry?" Junior turned to the audience. "She's sorry," he said, evoking boos and jeers. "You know the rules, Pat. You do not enter into a relationship without my permission."

A voice rose from the assembly. "It wasn't her fault." Kevin raised his hand. "It was my fault. I shouldn't have kissed her."

Junior glared at him. "Silence! The woman is always the temptress. Satan always works through the weaker sex."

Jillian wanted to roll her eyes, then a shot of adrenalin revitalized her. Jane had said that romantic relationships weren't forbidden or discouraged. Jillian could be grasping at straws, but she'd finally learned something worth reporting to Sam.

"I'm sorry," Pat said again.

Junior beckoned to Kevin. "Come here." Nobody spoke, not even a whisper, as Kevin threaded his way to the front. "I'm disappointed that you gave in so easily. Why didn't you report her? Why didn't you resist?"

"I—I don't know," Kevin said. "It happened quickly. I—"

"Hit her."

Kevin gulped. "What?"

"Slap her."

Pat covered her mouth with her hands.

"She led you astray. Slap her."

"No, I—"

"Slap her!"

Kevin lifted his hand.

"Slap her!"

Pat stepped back and cringed. "Kevin, please."

Kevin half-heartedly slapped her. Pat's eyes teared up, but Jillian could tell it hadn't hurt, at least not physically. So could Junior. "Maybe I was wrong," he shouted. "Maybe you should no longer be among us, Kevin. You've lost your way."

Kevin's eyes widened. "No! It *was* wrong. I won't do it again."

"You should be furious that this woman led you astray. You should want to teach her a lesson, to make an example of her, to make sure she knows that you are not vulnerable to Satan," Junior said, ticking off each item with a jerk of his hand. "Slap her."

Kevin raised his hand again.

"Slap her!"

This time the crack of his slap could be heard around the room. Pat openly sobbed and rubbed her cheek. Disgusted by what she'd just witnessed, Jillian forced herself to cheer along with the others. So, Junior was a piece of work. What a surprise! Things *had* changed under him. Jane hadn't mentioned physical punishment, or the cruelty of forcing cult members to carry out the sentence. One thing was certain: Kevin and Pat wouldn't be kissing again; in fact, Pat might not kiss anyone for the rest of her life.

"You did well," Junior said, pumping Kevin's hand and slapping his back. "What will you do if she wants to kiss you again?"

"I'll hit her."

"What did you say?"

"I'll hit her," Kevin roared, then he turned to Pat and spat at her. Jillian seethed; it didn't matter that he'd missed or that he was under Junior's spell and unable to think for himself. From now on, Kevin could go screw himself.

"Join your brothers and sisters and be proud of what you did here tonight."

When Kevin returned to his spot, those around him gave him a hero's welcome, clapping, praising the Lord, and patting his back.

Poor Pat still stood in the spotlight, her cheeks stained with tears.

"What do you have to say for yourself?" Junior asked.

"I'm sorry."

"Do you repent?"

Pat's voice quavered. "Yes, I repent."

"What?"

"I repent! I repent!"

"I'll be keeping an eye on you." Junior sat back down. "Go!"

Her eyes downcast, Pat shuffled toward the audience. Everyone parted as if she were a leper and gave her a wide berth when she gave those around her a guarded look.

"Let Pat's transgression be a lesson to all of you, and learn from Kevin." Junior closed his eyes and lifted one hand. "I bless all the souls gathered here, the souls who are on the true path and will light the way for those stumbling in the darkness."

"Amen," everyone said.

"I'll see you again soon. Remember to be on your guard and report all transgressions. Satan will not enter here!"

Since they were all still on their feet, Junior received a standing ovation. Nobody chattered on their way out; only whispers reached Jillian's ears. She glimpsed Cathy's wan face before Cathy silently turned to join those filing from the room. All right, then. No discussion. Pretend it had never happened. Not looking forward to Junior's next visit, Jillian trailed after Cathy, then almost jumped out of her skin when someone grabbed her arm from behind. She spun around; her brain took a second to place the man smiling at her. "Tom! I didn't know you were here."

"I was standing in the back." Still holding her arm, Tom said, "The Soul Master would like to meet you."

Jillian's answering smile was genuine. "Really?" This was too easy.

"Really. Come on." He relaxed his grip on her arm but didn't let it go. They walked against the flow and broke from the fleeing crowd.

Junior was sitting on his throne. When he spotted them, he broke into a grin and stood. "This must be Jillian."

Tom finally released her. Junior took both her hands and stroked their backs with his thumbs. She fought her revulsion and concentrated on smiling. "I've heard good things about you." Junior's eyes slid shut. "You have a strong soul, but also a troubled one. God led you to us."

"I can sense that Jillian's soul is recovering, rejuvenating. Her aura is calmer than it was at the retreat," Tom said.

Irritation flickered across Junior's face. "You've started down the path of light. I see you making a difference. You will be a pillar." He opened his eyes. "You will serve God well."

Jillian gazed into his brown eyes and mustered as much innocence and faux admiration as she could. "I hope so."

He stared at her. If he expected her to kiss his hands or anything ridiculous like that, they'd stand here all night. "We'll speak again," he said, squeezing her hands. "Go join your brothers and sisters."

"Thank you." She slowly turned; her face flushed when she realized that several of her peers had lingered behind and witnessed her encounter with Junior. Nobody liked the newbie who breezed in and became the pet. She wasn't trying to win a popularity contest, but she was stuck living with these people.

Hoping her embarrassment would buy her sympathy, she sheepishly left the room and climbed the stairs to the fourth floor. There was already a lineup outside both bathrooms. Jillian went into the cramped room she shared with Cathy and collected her pajamas, then decided to hang around in the room instead of standing in line. Cathy could fill her in on the queuing situation when she returned. Jillian wanted to savour this unexpected private time. She could hear the voices in the hallway, but nobody was breathing down her neck. After dropping her pajamas onto her bed, she opened the bedroom window, leaned out, and stared down at the alley that separated this building from the one next door. Several SUVs were parked in a neat line. Junior's convoy? Yeah, he'd probably return to his private gated estate and relax in the Jacuzzi in his ensuite, while she waited for her three minutes in a bathroom she shared with everyone on this floor. The soul healing business paid well.

Goosebumps dotted her arms and the light breeze made her shiver, but she wasn't ready to close her cage door. She rubbed her arms, then frowned when she heard male voices. This floor was for women only. No, wait. The men were outside, their voices travelling far in the night air. A flash of white caught her eye. One of the suits had removed his jacket. Junior's entourage was preparing to leave.

"I'm so glad you're not angry," a woman said. "I want to make amends, I really do."

Jillian turned around, peered at the empty room and doorway, then leaned out the window again. There was a woman with Junior's group. Jillian sprinted to the light and turned it off, then returned to the window and squinted into the darkness. An SUV's interior light came to life when someone opened the driver's door. Jillian caught the face of the woman climbing into the backseat. Her heart thudded. Pat? What the hell was she doing with Junior's gang? A door slammed shut. Several others followed. Engines roared to life. The convoy slowly rolled forward.

Jillian watched until she could no longer see the taillights of the trailing SUV, then slid the window shut and turned the light back on. Her mind racing, she sank onto her bed. Best not to let anyone know that she'd just witnessed Pat leaving with Junior. Was he going to kill her? No, Pat hadn't shown any signs of wanting to leave the cult. It sounded like tonight's spectacle hadn't changed her mind, and if it had, it would be too early for Junior to know. That left either some weird cleansing ritual, or Pat was about to make amends to Junior, all right. Jillian had read about too many instances of cult leaders using some of the women in their flock as a personal harem. Well, if Junior made any moves on her, he'd get a good swift kick to the balls, investigation be damned. But what about Pat? God, this situation sucked.

Cathy shuffled into the room. "There you are!"

"I didn't feel like waiting in line."

"Well, go now. And when you get back, the light will be out. We need to be up early tomorrow."

"Yeah, fine," Jillian said, wishing she could speed things up by asking Cathy about Amanda. But Jillian wasn't supposed to know her, let alone care about her. She didn't even know if Amanda had lived here. "Good night." She went into the hallway to join one of the lines. She hated it here, but she was lucky. She could be Pat.

JILLIAN ACCEPTED THE deposit slip from the bank teller and dropped it into the empty deposit bag. "Let's head home," she said to Will, her escort for today's trip. Outside, they strolled along the sidewalk in silence. Was he thinking about last night, too? Nobody had said a word at breakfast—not about Pat, anyway. Everyone had apparently erased that part of the evening from their memories.

They stopped at a traffic light. *"How are you doing?"*

Jillian didn't look around for Sam. *"I met Junior last night. We had a group session with him. He made a guy hit a woman, and then I saw her get into an SUV with him. I haven't seen her since. She wasn't at breakfast."*

"What's her name?"

"Pat. I don't know her last name. We don't use them."

"We?" Sam sounded surprised.

"Don't worry, I'm not falling for it. In fact, I'm going berserk. What's happening with Ruth?"

"There's movement on that front. Expect to be invited out for dinner with Junior soon."

It wouldn't be soon enough. *"Christine gave up her medicated shampoo."*

"We'll get her out." Sam paused. *"You're holding up all right?"*

"Jillian, come on." Will, who'd started to cross the street, beckoned to her.

"Sorry." She hurried after him. *"I'm fine."* But she wasn't doing her job. It would help if she got more than four to five hours of sleep at night. *"Something's changed. Jane said the soul healers didn't discourage relationships, but Junior was upset because Pat kissed someone."*

"The guy who hit her?"

"Yes."

"Interesting," Sam drawled. *"You're doing good. Anything else?"*

"No. I'm wasting my time at the learning centre. Jane isn't there, and nobody knows anything."

"You're not wasting your time. You have to go through this part to get to Junior."

"I know." But for how long? And damn it, they were only a couple of blocks from her prison. She'd have to say good-bye to Sam. *"I don't know if I'll be going to the bank tomorrow."* She rarely went two days in a row, and her heart sank when she realized that the day after next would be Saturday. She hated weekends. The bank was open on Saturdays, but the centre was busy, so it was all hands on deck. Fortunately she

spent her time in the kitchen. She'd never thought that she'd volunteer to cook for a large group, but it was that or "counselling" the victims who came into the centre to rest their feet. She'd rather chop veggies, stir soup, make toast, wipe counters, load the dishwasher, and whatever else Josie, the kitchen's sergeant, assigned to her.

"I'm here every day. We won't miss each other," Sam said.

Maybe not in the sense that they'd fail to rendezvous, but Jillian missed Sam—someone sane. She inwardly snorted. She wouldn't have described Sam that way soon after meeting her; she'd thought Sam was loco. Jillian wanted to turn around and look at her, though Sam could be on the other side of the road. Gritting her teeth, she kept her eyes forward. She felt fragile today; she needed to get a grip. She might not be succumbing to the soul healers' madness, but she was going freaking stir crazy. A hot shower that lasted longer than a minute, a decent night's sleep, five freaking seconds to herself . . . she'd never take any of it for granted again. She wouldn't think about the possibility that this would be her first cult infiltration of many. Nope. Not going there.

"You're not alone in there. Ruth and I are with you." Sam's voice was gentle.

Jesus, where was she? *Can she see my face?* Jillian's throat tightened. *"I'm okay. I'll talk to you soon."*

"Yes, you will."

Silence. "Jason has asked me to help him prepare for our next tax payment," she said, to fill it. "What will you be doing?"

"Counselling." Will smiled. "I know Satan prevents most people from hearing the message, but if I reach even one person, it'll be a wonderful day."

"Yeah," she murmured, wondering how someone could be so deluded. Living at the centre wasn't exactly hell, but why would anyone encourage others to join the soul healers? You gave up your home, your freedom, your life, and for what? There was no pot of gold at the end of the rainbow. The intensive program transformed lives, all right . . . it ensnared minds and spat out people blindly dedicated to Junior and his mumbo-jumbo. But didn't any of them have moments of clarity, when they realized that they'd thrown away their lives, families, and friends, and weren't going anywhere? Were they too invested to get out? Afraid? Ashamed?

She'd read the books and watched the documentaries, but the closest experience she'd had was when she'd been a devout Christian. No way did she think that organized religion was a cult, but for the longest time, she'd willfully ignored her questions and doubts. Did Sam do that? She'd said her faith wasn't rational. What exactly had she meant?

"After you," Will said, swinging open one of the learning centre's lobby doors and sweeping out his arm.

Jillian shook herself. "Thanks." She squared her shoulders and strode into the land of the dead.

Chapter Fifteen

Jillian unbuckled her seatbelt, climbed out of the sedan, and shot Andy a smile. "I hope my mother hasn't done anything silly."

"No, no, I told you I'd keep an eye on her while you were undergoing the isolation phase of the program."

Yeah, no contact with family and friends allowed, with the goal that by the time the isolation month had ended, the new and indoctrinated soul healer wouldn't want to communicate with anyone on the outside. After all, Satan was everywhere, and he loved to use those closest to you to get past the defences of unsuspecting souls. Plus, the program's initial phase was only the first of many. If Mom wasn't loaded, Andy wouldn't have surprised her an hour ago with the news that he was taking her out to dinner with her mother. Since Sam hadn't mentioned the meeting when they'd met a couple of days ago, the details must have been finalized since then.

Walking through the parking lot, Jillian shielded her eyes with her hand and scanned the area around the mall's doors. "Why did she tell you to pick her up here?"

"She said it would save her a taxi home." Andy pointed. "There she is."

"Mom!" Jillian waved, then waited for a car to pass by before crossing over to the doors.

Ruth held out her arms; a shopping bag dangled from one and a purse was slung over her other shoulder. "Hello, sweetheart."

As they embraced, Jillian remembered her real mom, whose birthday was next month. Mom wouldn't get the obligatory card and guilt money this year, as she had all those times when Jillian had been too busy to drive over and deliver her gift in person. Instead, she'd phoned: "Hi, Mom, just calling to wish you a happy birthday. Sorry I can't be there. Maybe next year." Okay, most years, she'd been away working a case, but she'd had a million excuses at the ready for those times when she wasn't. Each year, she'd grudgingly managed Christmas and a quick two-day visit squeezed between assignments. Every other holiday and occasion, she'd sat in her apartment, watched TV, and blamed Mom for the emotional void between them.

"You look tired." Ruth had drawn back and was holding Jillian at arm's length.

"I am tired. But I'm okay."

"Nice to see you again, Andy. He took me out to lunch, you know." *"We should be meeting with Junior."*

"No, I didn't know." *"Good. I'm not going to discover anything at the centre."* "Thank you," she said to Andy. *"Have you located Pat?"* During their last rendezvous, Sam had told her that the Fellowship had found out Pat's last name from the ex-cult group.

"No."

At least she hadn't turned up dead.

Andy grinned. "I enjoy your mother's company." He extended his hand toward Ruth. "Can I carry your bag?"

Ruth chuckled. "No, it hardly weighs a thing, and it's for Jillian. I bought you your favourite sweets."

Her favourite sweets? When she was a kid, she'd loved Sweet Tarts, but she hadn't eaten any in years.

Ruth slipped the plastic bag off her arm and handed it to her. *"Don't bother checking for a message. There isn't one. Hand them out to everyone when you get back. Brighten their day."*

Jillian peered into the bag and blinked. Sweet Tarts. If anyone else had given them to her, she would have been surprised. Still, the bag of treats unnerved her. She'd spent an interesting and illuminating evening reading her own file, and it hadn't mentioned Sweet Tarts—or anything about her sexual orientation, other than stating it. "I can't eat all these by myself. I'll share them with everyone at the centre . . . if that's okay," she said to Andy.

"Why wouldn't it be?" Andy asked, opening the sedan's back door for Ruth.

Because simple pleasures weren't high on the soul healers' list of priorities. "I don't know, I just don't want to break any rules."

"By sharing a gift?"

"You're right, I'm being silly," she said, slipping into the passenger seat. Actually, she'd hoped to convey that she was a good little obedient soul healer. *"I assume Sam is nearby."*

"Yes, and she knows where we're going."

"I won't ask how you knew about the Sweet Tarts."

"Lucky guess," Ruth said.

"Yeah, I'm sure it was." She wondered whether Ruth was chuckling to herself. They drove from the parking lot.

"Oh, I used to go to dances there," Ruth said, pointing out the window at an old movie theatre. "That building has an interesting history." She proceeded to tell them about it, and continued to chatter until they pulled into a family restaurant's parking lot. Jillian congratulated whoever had chosen the place. They couldn't invite a potential financial windfall to a fast food joint, but a swanky restaurant wouldn't have been appropriate, either. Asking for money while dining on fine cuisine and drinking expensive wine would be a hard sell.

The greeter led them to a table already occupied by Junior, Tom, and a man and woman Jillian didn't recognize. Tom leaped to his feet and pulled out a chair for Ruth. "Thank you so much," she said, as Jillian sat next to her. Andy chose the chair to Jillian's right. The three of them smiled at the four soul healers across from them. Jillian felt as if she was at a negotiating table, but that would come later.

Junior beamed at them. "I've heard so much about you," he said to Ruth. Jillian inwardly snorted. Not from her. "Let me introduce everyone. I'm Anthony Lancaster, Jr. This is Tom Clark, Maggie Sanders, and Jackson Peters." He turned to them. "And this is Ruth Harwick."

As everyone murmured greetings, Jillian noted that Junior hadn't introduced her. Well, she was just a means to an end, here.

"We know that Peters and Sanders are in Junior's inner circle," Ruth said. *"Andy's here to make us both feel comfortable. Is Tom the same Tom you met at the retreat?"*

"Yes."

"Then he's here for you, too."

"I have the impression he's higher up than Andy is."

The waiter arrived to take their drink orders. Afterward, and throughout the meal, the soul healers stuck to neutral topics, laughed in all the right places, and subtly flattered Ruth. They included Jillian in the conversation, but she let Ruth do most of the talking. When everyone was pleasantly stuffed and relaxing over coffee and tea, Tom opened the conversation they were all waiting for. "We were humbled when Andy told us you were considering a donation to our organization. We wanted to meet with you, so we can answer any questions you might have about what we do."

Ruth sipped her tea. "Andy already took me on a tour of your learning centre. I was impressed by what I saw. And now, with Jillian living and working there, I feel as if I'm a part of it, too. If I was younger, I might consider joining her, but I don't have the energy to work the hours she does." She turned to Jillian. "I've missed you. I understand why you haven't been able to speak with me. Andy explained it. I hope we can see each other now."

"Jillian is about to enter the second phase of the program," Andy said. "We're sort of breaking the rules by inviting her along."

The others chuckled.

"To be honest, I was a little irritated when they told me," Jillian said. "I'm missing a session tonight." She patted Ruth's arm. "But I'm glad I came."

Ruth smiled at her. "How are you doing at the centre? Andy says you're enjoying it." *"Agree, but give me something to work with."*

"Yeah, I am. For the first time in ages, I feel as if my life has purpose. I'm not just pushing paper for some corporation's bottom line. I don't feel like a zombie." Even though she was surrounded by them. "But I feel a bit frustrated. We're doing such important work, but I feel underutilized."

"What do you mean?" Tom asked. She could tell the others were holding their breath.

"I'm an accountant, and a good one, if I believe the performance reviews I received when I was working. They bumped me into management because I was exceeding expectations. I want to use my skills to help the centre," Jillian glanced at those across the table, "and to further everything we do, but I'm tallying up receipts, doling out petty cash, making bank runs, and double-checking someone else's work to make sure we're dotting our i's and crossing our t's for tax purposes. I could be doing so much more. I *want* to do more. When reviewing the work, I've noticed a few places where we could be reinvesting the money in ways that will reduce our taxes, and there are a couple of inefficiencies that I'd investigate . . . if it were up to me."

Ruth's forehead puckered. "You've always been good at making sure everything runs smoothly and efficiently." She shifted her attention to those opposite her. "You know, when you're in my position, the phone's ringing off the hook and the mail keeps on coming." She scowled. "All asking for money, of course. But you don't know how much they actually put toward their programs. I've read horrible things in the newspaper about some charities."

"I've seen some of the books, Mom." Yeah, for smaller accounts they used for the learning centre. "Just about every cent goes back into the centre."

Ruth grasped her wrist. "I'm sure it does, sweetheart. That's what I'm trying to say. Having you more involved in the accounting, uh, area, would make me feel so much more comfortable about making a sizable donation, and perhaps supporting your work on an ongoing basis."

Several of those across the table raised their cups to their lips, leaving Sanders to respond. "Of course, Jillian *will* be more involved in doing our books. We've been impatiently waiting for her to finish the first phase of her program, so she can take on more responsibility."

"In fact, we're holding our monthly review next week. On our way out, I was going to invite you to attend," Junior said to Jillian.

"I'd love that," Jillian said, meaning it. "I want to do everything I can, use the talents God gave me to make a difference."

Murmurs of agreement rumbled around the table.

"I haven't seen you this determined in a while," Ruth said. "It's good to see it."

"You mentioned perhaps joining her," Peters said.

Ruth nodded. "If I was younger, I'd jump at the chance. I've never seen Jillian more peaceful." She smiled sheepishly. "But you don't want me. I'd only slow you down."

"Actually, we might have a program for you," Tom said smoothly, "but let's focus on Jillian for now. Maggie's right, we've been anxiously waiting for you to complete phase one. I hope you'll agree to come to the meeting."

As if she had a choice. "Of course I will." She grinned at Ruth. "This is exactly what I want to do, Mom. When I was working, it wasn't the accounting that was depressing me. It was the company, the environment, not feeling as if I was doing anything meaningful with my life. This is it. I haven't felt this excited about anything in a while."

Her eyes bright, Ruth smiled. "I couldn't be more pleased." She drank the rest of her tea. "You won't complain if I make another donation, will you?"

Jillian rolled her eyes. "I only complained because you were giving money to anyone who asked, without researching the organization. This is different. We know this is a worthy cause."

"It's certainly done wonders for you." Ruth reached into the purse she'd slung over the chair and slapped her chequebook onto the table. She uncapped her pen. "Let me write you another cheque," she said to Junior.

Junior raised his brows. "That's very generous of you." The others made the appropriate noises about Ruth's generosity and selflessness.

Jillian figured it would be strange if she didn't eye the amount Ruth was donating. Ten grand. No matter what happened, the Fellowship wouldn't recoup the money it was throwing at the soul healers. Now those were books she'd love to get a look at. Sam claimed not to know the details about where the money came from and who managed it, but it had to be Supporters. A particular family or families, maybe? The money had to be passed down from generation to generation. She could try to find out who owned the island, but she'd have to visit the local records office. What were the chances that an investigation would take her to the nearest city—alone? Would Sam go along with it? Maybe she already knew whose name was on the deed; that was one question Jillian hadn't asked.

Now that everyone had gotten what they came for, they made small talk and finished their coffees and teas. *"Good work,"* Ruth said as they left the restaurant. *"Let's hope the meeting is off-site."*

"We've already checked Junior's estate." Or rather, Sam and Ruth had, while she was stuck playing nice little soul healer.

"If they have Jane, they wouldn't keep her there, and I doubt that's where you'll meet," Ruth said.

"They won't tell me where I'm going in advance. They'll just take me there."

"Depending on when and which route you take, we might not be able

to follow you. But don't worry. You're extremely valuable to them alive right now."

But for how long?

WORKING IN THE network room, where those on the outreach team chatted online with potential victims and worked on the group's websites, Jillian tried to decipher the spreadsheet macro someone had set up. Judy, one of her contacts regarding the accounts, had her reviewing the centre's numbers from three years ago. They were keeping her busy with nonsense work. How were they planning to occupy her for years? Maybe the monthly review meeting would provide a hint at the answer, but she hadn't heard another word about it since the dinner last week.

"Hi."

She jumped.

"Sorry, I didn't mean to frighten you," Andy said. "Are you in the middle of something?"

Jillian twisted in her chair to look at him. "Nothing I can't break from."

"Good. The meeting the Soul Master referred to is tonight. I thought we could grab dinner somewhere and then go together."

"Sure," she said, struggling to keep her voice even. She'd hoped to get advance warning so she could let Sam know when the meeting would take place, and Andy's invitation to dinner surprised her. Maybe it was part of softening her up, so she'd go along with the idea of bilking Mom out of her money. "Are we leaving now?"

He nodded.

"Okay." She signed out of the account that allowed her access to the books, and nothing more. The web was off limits. "Where are you parked?" she asked when Andy pivoted in the corridor and strolled away from the lobby.

"Out back. Nobody cares if you park there for a few minutes." He led her to the same blue sedan he'd used to drive her to meet Ruth; it was the same model as Derek's, the guy who'd driven them to the retreat and who Jillian hadn't seen since. Maybe the soul healers had an arrangement with a local dealership.

To hide her dismay, she gazed out the passenger window when Andy drove out onto a side road. If Sam was around, she could be parked nearby, but Jillian doubted it. She was on her own. "Where's the meeting?"

"At Jackson's house. You met him at dinner last week."

That didn't tell her anything. "Thanks for checking in on my mother while I'm focusing on my program."

"No problem. In fact, I want to talk to you about your mother."

I bet you do. But then he asked whether she was happy at the centre, and a bunch of other questions that she answered by telling him what she hoped he wanted to hear. He didn't speak about Mom again until they were waiting for their desserts at another family restaurant.

Andy dabbed at his mouth with his napkin, which he then neatly folded and set on the table. "I can tell you love your mother."

Unexpectedly, her vision blurred. *Mom*—her real mom—a wave of grief washed over her. She didn't fight it. Andy would think she was tearing up over Ruth. "I do. That's the only downside to my experience so far. Worrying about her. Oh, she's fit, but she's by herself." She let out a long, heartfelt sigh. At least Mom had Danny.

Andy's forehead creased. "Did you notice that your mother is sometimes forgetful?"

"No," Jillian said, not bothering to hide her shock.

"I'm afraid she is," Andy said mournfully. "Also, I took her shopping yesterday, and she got confused when she was at the cash."

"Well, she's never been good at math."

"No, it was more than that. I had to help her."

Jillian stared at him. She was astounded that he was moving in for the kill so soon, not that Ruth might be addled. No, Ruth was as sharp as a tack. Did Andy believe his bullshit? Had the higher-ups told him that his lies were in Ruth's best interest? The waitress arrived with their cake. Jillian murmured a thanks and lifted her fork. She wouldn't help Andy along.

"At the dinner last week, we mentioned that we might have a program for her. We were thinking about our senior phoenix program, but given your mother's, uh, condition, we were wondering if you'd consider our senior care program."

Those bastards wanted to put Ruth into a home, and guess where all her money and assets would go? "What's the senior care program?" she asked, wanting him to spell it out.

He ate a bit of cake before answering. "It's an exclusive care program that's only available to the senior relatives of those with cleansed souls. Your mother would move into a state of the art care facility, where she'd be monitored twenty-four hours around the clock. The staff, which is top-notch, caters each senior's daily program to each individual's needs. Your mother would be among friends, be intellectually stimulated, remain physically fit. You wouldn't have to worry about her."

Thank god her mouth was full, because she couldn't stand people who took advantage of seniors. How many cult members had stuck their relatives into what was probably a group residence with none of the services Andy had described?

"I know this is a difficult subject," Andy said gently.

"It sounds expensive. I have some savings, but I was hoping to eventually donate the bulk of them to our work."

"Your mother would have to sell her home. Given her condition, I'm sure you'll have to take over her finances. Do you have her power of attorney?"

He made the question sound so innocent. "Yes, I do."

"You may have to use it."

Jillian grimaced and put down her fork. "This whole thing has come as a bit of a shock. I'll have to talk to her about it."

"So you'll consider it."

"If what you're saying is true, I can't ignore it. I'm not saying I'll put her into the program, but . . ." She lowered her head.

"I'm sorry to be the bearer of distressing news. Think about what I've said. Let's talk about something else."

Jillian lifted her head and gave him a wan smile. She picked up her fork but had to force down the rest of her cake. The conversation and Andy's glibness made her sick, and there was still a meeting with the Soul Master himself to come.

Chapter Sixteen

As Jillian listened to Junior ramble, the realization sank in that they wouldn't discuss anything related to finances at this meeting. Ten people sat in the spacious living room, but nobody was discussing business. Junior was holding court. She was here because the soul healers wanted to get their hands on her mother's money and thought she was too devoted to see it. But no matter. Andy had driven her to a home that wasn't on the Fellowship's list of soul healer assets and therefore hadn't been searched. Jane could be here, and Jillian had a plan to look for her.

"It's me they want!" Junior thumped the arm of his chair, bringing Jillian back to her surroundings. "They don't give a damn about anything but getting their hands on me. They're instruments of Satan, especially the government. They have a whole department looking into my affairs."

Jillian coughed into her hand. Junior was obviously paranoid and not making sense most of the time, and she was convinced that he was on something. She'd learned to recognize the signs during her agency days, when suits had disappeared into the bathroom too often, or openly used. No wonder a posse had tagged along to the dinner with Ruth. They'd wanted to keep him in check. Whoever was supplying Junior, and maybe Jackson, because he struck her as a user too, might have provided the murder weapon to take out Amanda and Janet Bailey. Hell, the dealer might have done the deeds himself, or instructed one of his lackeys to do it. She'd wager that the soul healers were a preferred client.

"I have a man inside." Junior waved his finger in the air. "I know what they're up to. They're just waiting for the right time. But God will warn me. Satan will not prevail." He grabbed his glass from an end table, swilled the gin around, and downed the drink in one shot. Sitting next to him, Andy lifted the bottle and refilled Junior's glass. Jesus, she'd sort of liked Andy, but tonight he came across as a snivelling sycophant who would probably kill himself—or ex-cult members!—if Junior ordered him to. Several mass suicides she'd read about came rushing back. No, the soul healers weren't that type of cult—before Junior took over. Now . . . no. Junior's paranoia hadn't spread to the rank and file yet, but she'd gathered that the atmosphere was tenser since Senior had passed away.

She froze when Junior pointed at her. "You'll protect me. You'll tell them we pay our taxes. We tithe to the greedy government." Another shot of gin went down the hatch. "I see good things for you."

"If they try anything, we can keep them tied up for years," Jillian said. "I assume you have decent counsel."

He roared with laughter and thrust his arm toward Jackson. "Right there."

Great.

"We put him through law school."

Which meant Jackson had been a soul healer for at least twenty years, she'd estimate. She glanced at her watch. If she was going to search for Jane, she'd better get on with it. "Do you mind if I use the washroom?"

"Not at all," Jackson said. "It's just up the hall, on your left."

"Thank you." She rose and followed Jackson's directions.

Good, the door had a sturdy lock and the bathroom wasn't cramped. She sat in a spot where she wouldn't hit her head on anything if she slumped sideways, leaned back against the wall, and closed her eyes. Unfortunately, she didn't have a good sense of time while projecting, so she'd need to move quickly and hope that she wasn't taking too long.

The familiar nausea passed as quickly as it came. She floated into the hallway and through the ceiling into the upper floor. While not sitting on acres of landscaped property, Jackson's lavish home was located in a gated community in the posh area of town. No kids, but his wife was watching TV in a rec room that housed pool and air hockey tables. She'd greeted their guests and then made herself scarce, but her deference to Junior had told Jillian that Mrs. Peters had undergone "the program." The master bedroom was empty, and so were the guest bedroom and its luxury ensuite.

Into the next bedroom—shit! Jane! Right there, on the bed. A hum echoed in Jillian's ears. Jane's lips weren't moving, but she was murmuring. Jillian concentrated and picked up bits and pieces, all nonsense. Jane's eyes were unfocused; track marks were visible on her extended right arm. The bastards were keeping her high, and she'd lost weight. A bowl with dried soup stood on the night stand, so they weren't starving—

A bang reverberated around Jillian's consciousness. What the hell? Another bang. *Oh, shit!*

She slammed into her body with a gasp and quickly got her bearings. Too quickly. She lifted the toilet seat and bent over the bowl, gagging. Nothing came. Another knock at the door. "Just a minute," she shouted, then staggered to her feet and flushed the toilet. Damn it, she'd wanted to see if Pat was here. Did Jackson's wife know about Jane? She must. *Bitch.*

Jillian washed her hands, then opened the door and smiled sheepishly. "Sorry," she said to Andy. "Something at dinner didn't agree with me."

"You'd been gone for almost five minutes, so I thought I'd better make sure you're okay."

Five minutes? If he was anyone else, she'd wonder about him. And five minutes was generous. At the centre, people pounded on the door after three. "I'm fine."

Andy grimaced. "We should go soon."

Jillian feigned disappointment. "Already?"

"The Soul Master invited you tonight to introduce you to those who don't know you. The next meeting won't be so relaxed."

"I'm looking forward to working with everyone," she said, a sudden burst of elation making her grin. Now that she'd found Jane, she might be getting out! Okay, they still didn't know whether the cult was responsible for Amanda and Bailey's deaths, but she'd come inside to find Jane. If the Fellowship wanted her to remain undercover, it had better have a damn good reason. The soul healers had kidnapped Jane and were drugging her. Surely that should be enough for the Fellowship to at least depose Junior, if not shut the cult down. All Jillian had to do now was make contact with Sam. Mission accomplished.

JILLIAN TRIED NOT to fidget as she waited for Will to arrive. She was supposed to be serene, fulfilled, and pleased as punch to be a slave—not desperate to get outside, so she could hopefully relay the news about Jane to Sam. Junior and gang might have moved Jane since Jillian had stumbled across her two days ago, but since they had no reason to suspect that she was about to be rescued, Jillian doubted they had. She wanted out of here! She could hardly concentrate now.

She sighed with relief when she spotted Will. "There you are," she said with a grin.

"I ran into Tom," he said. "He—"

Tom, here? "Let's go," she barked, her stomach churning.

"Jillian!" a voice rang out behind her.

Damn it. She turned around.

Tom strode toward her. "Where are you going? I told Will to find Cindy. You don't do bank runs anymore." When he held out his hand for the deposit bag, she reluctantly handed it over. "Go find Cindy," he said to Will, who dutifully trotted off.

"I really don't mind going to the bank," Jillian said.

"Don't be silly. You're on the finance team now. Your time's too valuable to be doing bank runs. Do you remember Oliver? You met him at Jackson's."

"Yes, I do."

"He's waiting for you in the network room. I believe he has a new set of books for you to examine."

Woo-hoo! "I'll go see him."

"Good."

Her answering smile was strained. Anyone watching her march to the network room wouldn't see a joyous soul. How was she going to get a message to Sam?

An hour later, she sat reviewing one of the files Oliver had given her permission to access, but her mind was working on the communication problem. Here she was, in a room filled with computers connected to the Net. But they were rigged so that only certain sites could be reached, and every keystroke was logged. If she tried to send an email, she could be found out before the Fellowship got its hands on Jane. Jillian swallowed. What would the soul healers do to her if they discovered she was spying on them? Would Sam find her dead from a drug overdose? Maybe not. Jillian wasn't a helpless damsel in distress, but she needed to stay on her toes.

Her stomach grumbled; it was almost time for lunch. She managed to absorb the records on the screen, then rose along with everyone else when all the computers sounded the lunch alarm. As she walked through the lobby on her way to the dining room, she practically salivated at the sight of people's cell phones. How she'd love to grab one from someone's hand and quickly call Sam!

An idea almost made her stop short. She already had the key to getting in touch with the Fellowship. Now she couldn't walk fast enough, and wolfed down her lunch while half-listening to the chatter around her. Her eyes were on Rick, who sat at the top of the learning centre's pyramid. The moment he pushed away his plate and stood, she did the same. "Rick," she called, hustling toward him.

He turned to her.

"I need to get in touch with Andy."

His eyes narrowed. "Why?"

"Tell him that I've thought about my mother, and I want to talk to him about it. He's been waiting to hear from me."

"I don't like to disturb anyone unless it's necessary."

"Trust me, he's been waiting for an answer from me."

"Then why hasn't he come to see you?"

Good question. "Because it's a difficult subject." She moved closer to him and lowered her voice. "It concerns my mother . . . her mental state. When he discussed it with me, I got upset, so he told me to take my time, and to let you know when I was ready to talk to him." Jillian didn't think it would matter if Rick told Andy the lie. She'd admit to him that she'd fibbed because she didn't want to wait until Andy next visited the centre.

"I see," Rick said. "So Andy insisted that you speak to me." She could hear his wheels turning. Rick might be the top dog here, but Andy was closer to Junior. "I'll pass along your message. That's all I can do."

"That's all I ask. Thank you." Now all she had to do was wait.

WHEN ANDY PEERED into the network room a couple of hours later and beckoned to her, she couldn't help but grin at him. Anytime she wanted something, all she had to do was dangle Mom and the soul healers bit.

"I want to talk to you about my mother," she said as soon as she stepped into the corridor. "Ever since our talk over dinner, I've worried about her." She met his eyes. "You were right. Knowing that we're taking care of her will give me peace of mind. Honestly, I've just found what I've been looking for all my life, and now I'm anxious again."

Andy eyed her sympathetically. "Maybe you knew your mother was having difficulties, but you wouldn't admit it to yourself."

Bastard. "Maybe."

"You realizing it—that's a sign that you're reconnecting with your inner self. The soul is honest, pure. You can't lie to yourself when you're in harmony with your true purpose."

Oh, please.

"Let me talk to your—"

"No. I have to do it. She won't give up her home easily. She's fond of you, but I'm her daughter. I need to make her understand that it's for her own good." Jillian softened her voice. "But I want you there when I speak to her," she said, in barely a whisper. "Will you do that? Be there with me?"

His Adam's apple bobbed. "Of course I will."

For a moment, she thought he was going to hug her, but they were standing in a main corridor. Someone would report them to Junior.

Hating what she had to do next, she thought back to the weeks following Dad's suicide. One afternoon, she'd left school early after visiting the nurse with a stomach ache that was more about her nerves than anything else. When she stepped into the entryway at home, her shout to Mom died in her throat. Her heart pounded; she wanted to clap her hands over her ears to shut out the piercing wail coming from the direction of the bedrooms. Trembling, she'd crept down the hallway and hesitated outside Mom's door. It was ajar; she pushed it open. Mom sat on the bed, rocking back and forth with one of Dad's shirts clutched to her chest. Her tears flowed freely, each sob pummelling Jillian's protective bubble. Mom didn't cry, not like this. Mom was strong and stoic and a survivor. She wouldn't do what Dad had done. She wouldn't!

Not wanting Mom to know that she'd seen—she'd seen!—Jillian had backed away, stumbled down the hallway, and raced outside. She'd run, and run, and run, tears streaming down her face, telling herself that Mom wouldn't do it; Mom would never do it. But maybe she shouldn't depend on Mom so much, shouldn't count on Mom being there. Maybe she should rely on herself from now on.

Good, tears were prickling at her eyelashes. Thinking about that afternoon never failed. "Can I phone her to set up the meeting?" she whispered to Andy. "I feel I have to do this."

He gulped and touched her arm. "Let's go to one of the counselling rooms."

"Okay." She blinked back her tears as they looked for an empty one. When he pulled out his phone, she wanted to grab it and punch in her real mother's number, and say she was sorry—sorry for not being there, sorry for shutting her out, sorry for protecting herself. Had Mom done the same? Was that why they'd grown apart, couldn't relate to each other emotionally, had left so many things unsaid? What a waste.

She stifled a snort when Andy dialed the number for her and handed her the phone. "Take your time. I know this is difficult," Andy murmured.

A click. "Hello, Andy. What a pleasure!" Ruth said.

"It's me, Mom," Jillian said. "I'm using Andy's phone."

"Jillian?"

She gave Ruth a couple of seconds to get over her surprise and perhaps start to record the call. Since Andy's phone might be monitored, she'd have to be careful. "Yes. I'm calling because Andy and I want to talk to you about something important. Well, *I* want to talk to you, and I want him with me."

"You like him."

"Yes, I do," she said, wishing telepathy worked over the phone.

"Are you all right?"

"Oh, yeah. In fact, you know the talk we had before I decided to quit my job? I said I was looking for something, and I was optimistic that working with Andy and his group would help me find it. Well, I was right. I've found what I was looking for."

"You did," Ruth said, her voice even.

"Yes. I realized it at the meeting with the finance team, the one the

Soul Master spoke about at the dinner."

"Oh, so you went to that meeting?"

"Yes, and I'm taking on more responsibility now. No more bank runs for me. I'm too busy with other things."

"That's good to hear, Jillian. Now, what do you want to talk to me about?"

"Not on the phone, Mom. Can we meet? Maybe tomorrow?" She glanced at Andy, who nodded.

"I've love to see you, and Andy. Why don't you take me to lunch?"

Jillian chuckled. "All right." They arranged a time to pick up Ruth from her home, then said good-bye and hung up. Jillian blew out a sigh. "Well, that's done." She handed the phone to Andy and edged toward the door. "I can't pretend I'm pleased. I know I'm doing the right thing, but . . ." To discourage Andy from comforting her, she opened the door.

Following her, he put his hand on her shoulder. "I understand."

"I'd better go back to the network room. I want to finish something up before dinner. I want a clear mind for the session with the Soul Master tonight." If only she could sleep with her eyes open.

"I'll pick you up tomorrow at 11:45. Wait for me in the lobby."

"Thank you, Andy. I really appreciate it." Rubbing her eye, she forced herself to slowly walk away. Bounding down the corridor would raise Andy's eyebrows, so she'd have to quietly celebrate contacting Ruth and control her exultation that she'd soon be out of this place.

LEANING AGAINST THE kitchen counter with her head lowered, Sam chewed her lip as she listened to Ruth's conversation with Jillian.

"See you tomorrow at noon. Bye," Jillian said.

"Bye." They hung up.

Sam slowly exhaled.

"I told you she was all right," Ruth said. "She looked fine when you projected into the learning centre."

Sam tensed. "Someone else was doing the bank runs. They've been holding her prisoner," she said through gritted teeth.

Silence, then, "She knows where Jane is."

It certainly sounded like it. Sam lifted her head. "Jane is wherever that meeting was held. We need the location." They'd either met in the middle of the night—doubtful, or Jillian had departed using an exit Sam wasn't watching. Sitting on her behind in her car was a stupid use of her time. She should be doing something!

Ruth nodded. "I'll get that information tomorrow. How do you want to proceed?"

Carefully. "We have to get Jillian and Jane out at the same time. If we pull Jillian first, they might move Jane. If we extract Jane before Jillian, it will cast suspicion on her. She went to a meeting where Jane is being held, and the next thing they know, Jane's gone."

"While you take a team to get Jane, I'll go to the learning centre and demand to see my daughter. We'll walk out. They won't be able to stop us."

"No. We'll both get Jillian."

"Sam!"

"She's my responsibility, Ruth," Sam said quietly.

Ruth scowled. "She's perfectly capable of taking care of herself, and so am I, for that matter."

"I've been sitting around for months precisely because I'm supposed to have her back." For how long? She'd never felt this useless. "I hope our next investigation won't involve her going undercover while I twiddle my thumbs, and that's after months of training her."

"It's not Jillian's fault."

"No, it's Roberta's. I could have been doing something useful, but no, Roberta wants us to be a team."

"You needed a period of relatively quiet time," Ruth said. "For the past twenty years, you've worked non-stop, except for a few days here and there on the island."

"Is that why Roberta is insisting that we work together for a while? I can understand it for this investigation, though I wish I'd had a more active role. But since Jillian can take care of herself, as you pointed out, why do we have to keep working together?" Sam shook her head. "If Roberta wants me to take a week off, she can just tell me to do it."

Ruth snorted. "You needed more than a week, and I'm sure she has her reasons for having you team with Jillian for a while."

Sam studied her. What was Ruth holding back?

"Is she that horrible to work with?" Ruth asked.

"No. Well, sometimes she gets on my nerves." When Jillian was deliberately trying to get a rise out of her. "But most of the time, she's okay."

"Is it because she's an atheist?"

"No." Sam paused. "But it's a bit odd, don't you think?"

Ruth cocked her head to one side. "I'm sure our Lord has His reasons. She has the gifts. She's dedicated her life to Him, whether she realizes it or not."

"When we met with Miriam, she brought up boons."

"You hadn't told Jillian about them?"

"I . . . didn't see the point of mentioning them. When Jillian heard that receiving one requires an act of faith, she said herself that she won't get one."

Ruth's eyes flashed. "That's not for her, or *you*, to decide. Our Lord is well aware that she doesn't believe. He might require something else from her, and it could be years before He bestows a boon upon her. Not everyone receives a boon as quickly as you did."

Sam felt her face tighten. She'd only received hers so soon because she'd screwed up. She smoothed her expression, but Ruth had noticed.

"You were an excellent student." Ruth raised a finger. "But the one lesson you've refused to learn is to forgive yourself. He wasn't angry. He gave you the boon. He forgave you. It's time for you to do the same. Then maybe you'll stop driving yourself so hard."

That wasn't why she preferred to be busy, but Ruth could continue to believe that she had it all figured out.

"And maybe you'd trust Jillian more. If something happens to her, it won't be your fault. You've taught her well, and she's a sharp cookie. Case in point, she managed to contact me and convey her message."

"You're right," Sam said, knowing that if anything happened to Jillian, she'd never forgive herself. "Let's get back to our next step. I'm going with you to get Jillian."

"All right," Ruth conceded. "What date should I give her? I'm sure she's eager to leave."

"I'll call Roberta right away. It won't take her long to put a team together. Once they know the location, they can figure out how best to extract Jane. They'll want time to scout out the place. So . . . let's see, tomorrow's Tuesday. Tell her we'll come for her on Thursday morning. You'll go in and walk her out. I'll be in the car—with the engine running."

Chapter Seventeen

JILLIAN CALMED HER racing thoughts when Ruth slipped into the backseat of Andy's sedan. She could pass on her information during lunch. The irrational fear that Ruth would suddenly become inaccessible was just that—irrational.

"It's a lovely day, isn't it?" Ruth said.

"It is," Jillian said brightly, at the same time Andy said, "Beautiful day." They made small talk until they pulled into the parking lot for a restaurant that offered all-day breakfasts and a lunch buffet.

Jillian waited until they were seated, then said, *"I found Jane."*

"Well done," Ruth said, then, "I think I'll have a breakfast. I'm too comfortable to get up." *"Where is she?"*

Jillian gave her the address and added, *"Jackson's house."* "Try the waffles. They're good."

"Mmm. I'm in the mood for maple syrup. Waffles it is." Ruth closed her menu and set it on the table. *"Jeremy checked out the address of everyone who had dinner with us. That one wasn't on the list. It must be a second or third home and in someone else's name."*

"Jane isn't in great shape. They're drugging her. Junior is paranoid, and I think he's using." "I'll have waffles, too. How about you, Andy?"

"I don't like the sounds of that," Ruth said. *"A paranoid cult leader on drugs? That won't end well. It's a good thing we'll be getting you and Jane out on Thursday. I'll come for you sometime in the morning."*

Thank god! Tomorrow would be the longest day of her life. *"Any sign of Pat?"*

"No."

"I'll go along with the majority," Andy said with a smile. "Ah, here comes our waiter. Tea for everyone?"

They both nodded. *"What are we going to do about the cult?"* Jillian asked as Andy ordered.

"First things first. We'll get Jane out and see what she has to say."

If, for some inexplicable reason, the Fellowship decided to let the soul healers live on, Sam had better honour her promise about extracting Christine. Fortunately Jillian didn't have much contact with her, because every time she glimpsed Christine's glazed, tired eyes and heard her spew the cult's garbage, she wanted to puke. She'd stood by while Christine threw away a promising future.

Ruth clasped her hands on the table. "You said you wanted to talk to me about something. I assume it's serious," she glanced at Andy, "since you brought your young man along for moral support."

"He's not my young man, Mom," Jillian said, mortified at Andy's flushed face.

"He'd like to be."

Jillian let it pass. "Let's wait for our food and then we'll have a chat." *"We're going to talk about putting you into a home. Of course, I'll then wave around my power of attorney, sell everything you own, and donate it to the cult."*

"Of course," Ruth said, sounding amused. *"And to think I liked Andy."*

"It's not his fault. He's one of the sincere ones." Exactly the sort who'd follow orders and kill? Jesus.

"I know. I wonder who he was before the soul healers hooked him."

Jillian had never thought to ask him for more than he'd volunteered, and realized that she'd had a dismissive attitude toward her fellow prisoners. They all had former lives, dreams, and families, but she'd viewed them as cult members, deluded pawns, zombies. Yes, she'd understood that anyone could be snared by a cult at vulnerable times in their lives, but she'd quickly forgotten that those she lived, ate, and worked with had once lived on the outside. Maybe it was a defence mechanism. Viewing everyone in the same way she viewed Christine would cripple her. Or maybe it was that she'd never been a people person.

An hour and a half later, Ruth gave her a half-hearted wave and shut her front door. Jillian gazed out the passenger window. "She's not happy, but I suppose it's difficult to accept that you can't live alone anymore." She turned to Andy. "I didn't want to make her cry." She wondered what Ruth thought about when she wanted to provoke tears.

"You were gentle and respectful," Andy said, pulling away from the curb. "It was obvious to me that you care about her very much, and she knows that, too."

They lapsed into silence. When they were a few minutes away from the learning centre, Andy cleared his throat. "Funny remark your mother made, about you being my girl."

Jillian swallowed. "Yeah. I guess since you've been keeping an eye on her, she's put two and two together and come up with five. I'm sorry if she embarrassed you."

"No, that's all right." He paused. "I can't say—I mean, I am rather fond of you."

Oh, shit. "There's no point thinking about it. You know the Soul Master's rules. We'd need his permission. I know he wants me to focus on the finances right now, and I'm still relatively new. I don't want him to think that I'm more interested in finding a boyfriend than I am in serving God."

"Of course, of course," Andy sputtered. "Thank you for reminding me. I shouldn't have said anything."

"No, I'm flattered. For the record, you're a nice guy." If she wasn't a lesbian and she wasn't seeing him at his worst . . . "If circumstances were different . . ." And if he didn't match the description of the guy who'd visited Amanda . . .

She cringed when his cheeks reddened. Thursday morning couldn't come soon enough.

JILLIAN QUIETLY SIGHED into her pillow and rolled over. She'd be on tenterhooks tomorrow, wondering when Ruth would show up and set her free. *Please let it be as soon as the centre's doors open.* Today an hour had felt like five; tomorrow Jillian would struggle to concentrate. She'd have to remember to appear casual as she strolled from the building with Ruth. She wasn't to make a run for it. At this rate, she'd be too tired to do more than walk, anyway. Her excitement was keeping her awake; she'd be exhausted when she dragged herself out of bed at the crack of dawn.

She looked forward to sleeping in her own room tomorrow. She'd love to be on the island, but unfinished business would temper her delight. There was still Christine to free, and ideally everyone else. Still, she'd welcome a few days at home. They'd have to lay the groundwork to topple Junior from his pedestal and ease his bewildered flock back into normal, free-thinking lives.

What felt like five minutes later, she groaned when someone shook her shoulder. Already? Jillian cracked an eye open and squinted into the gloom. The sun wasn't even up. "You okay, Cathy?" she mumbled, her eyelids sliding shut.

"Get up," a male voice said urgently.

Her heart pounded; her eyes snapped open. She squinted at the shadowy figure standing over her. "Andy?" she whispered.

"We have to go."

"What?"

"I'll explain when we're out of here. Get up and get dressed. Hurry!"

"I can't just go," she hissed. "I have work to do."

"Jillian, please. Trust me, you don't want to cause a fuss. Not tonight." He sounded frightened. "Just do what I'm telling you to do. Please."

Her heart sank. If she didn't go along with him, she could scuttle the operation to rescue Jane. "Wait outside while I get dressed."

"Don't take long." He stepped into the hallway and quietly pulled the door shut.

She threw her blanket aside. Shit. He'd better not have decided that they belonged together and should make a run for it. *I'm flattered.* Idiot! She should have told him she wasn't interested, period.

As she pulled her clothes from the bureau she shared with Cathy, she considered the alternatives. If Andy wasn't here so they could run off to a new life together, then what? She zipped up her jeans and froze. Jesus, he wasn't intending to shoot her up, was he? No, she hadn't fled the soul healers, though maybe something she'd said, or the way she'd behaved, had aroused suspicions. No, Andy had seemed fine at the lunch with Ruth, and genuinely embarrassed during their awkward conversation in the car. Jillian was certain that he hadn't been testing her, and since then, she hadn't seen or spoken to anyone who counted.

"Jillian?" a sleepy voice murmured. "What are you doing?"

She was about to tell Cathy to go back to sleep, then changed her mind. "Can you do me a favour?" she whispered. "My mother is coming to see me today. If I'm not here, can you tell her I had to leave with Andy?"

"Andy?" Cathy sat up. "What's going on?"

"I can't tell you. I'm sorry."

"Is everything okay?"

"Yeah. Nothing for you to worry about. Andy isn't doing anything wrong. He's serving the Soul Master." She finished tying her sneaker. "Go back to sleep, or you'll be exhausted tomorrow."

Cathy didn't argue. Jillian joined Andy in the corridor and silently followed him down to the ground floor and through one of the back exits. "Can you tell me what's going on?" she asked.

"I'm not sure," he murmured.

Her eyes instinctively closed when they rounded the building into the alley and a headlight beam hit her full in the face. Andy grasped her arm. They strode to a waiting SUV; another one sat behind it. Jillian slid into the backseat and struggled to contain her shock. Jane was slumped next to her. Andy climbed in next to Jillian and pulled the back door shut.

"Go," Junior growled from the passenger seat. Jillian gulped. So she and Andy weren't riding into the sunset, then. The SUV lurched forward.

"I told you they'd come after me," Junior spat to Jackson, the driver. "But the Lord thwarted them. The Lord has eyes and ears everywhere."

Had he found out about the Fellowship's planned extraction of Jane? How? Jillian turned to Andy. Their eyes met. He didn't know what the hell was going on, either. Jane groaned. "Who's this?" Jillian said, to nobody in particular. "And where are we going?"

"Somewhere they won't find us," Junior said.

Andy jutted his chin toward Jane. "That's a former soul healer who's returned to the fold. Outside influences have corrupted her. She's undergoing a cleansing."

Is that what they called it? "Why are we leaving? What's going on?"

"You'll have to trust me. I am your Soul Master," Junior boomed. "Now be quiet. My head is aching."

Jane groaned again. She turned her head. Unfocused eyes settled on Jillian's face. "I know you," she rasped.

Shit!

"You . . . you're of God."

"We're all of God, Jane," Jackson snapped. "Except you. Be quiet. Somebody give her something."

"It's too soon," Junior said.

"I know you," Jane said again.

"I told you we should have sent her on," Jackson said to Junior. "Give her something."

Sent her on? Did Jackson mean kill her, or were they running some type of human trafficking ring?

"I can't do it from here. I'll do it next time we pull over," Junior muttered. "Let's put some distance between us and the city first."

"The Lord . . . He's answered," Jane said, gazing at Jillian. "He sent you. You've come . . . for me."

Jillian forced a puzzled expression. "She must be hallucinating."

"She must be," Jackson said, looking at Jillian in the rearview mirror.

She stared back and gave him a small smile. Okay, she was in a car with the Soul Master, two dedicated soul healers, and a high woman who was going to blow her cover, and she had no idea why, or where they were going. She closed her eyes and reviewed every gift and tactic Sam had taught her. *I'm going to need them.*

Chapter Eighteen

I N THE CRAMPED WASHROOM at a truck stop, Jillian dabbed at the dried blood on Jane's lip. If there were numerous stalls, she'd wait for another woman to come in and beg to use her phone. But the restaurant, if one could call it that, was filled with grizzly truck drivers consuming their morning dose of cholesterol. This washroom consisted only of a toilet and sink, and could use a good cleaning.

Seated on the toilet, Jane sucked in her breath.

"Sorry," Jillian murmured, wincing. Jane would have a nasty bruise. *Bastard.*

Jane gripped her arm. "I do know you."

Jillian gazed into Jane's bleary eyes. "No, you don't," she said levelly. "I must remind you of someone. I don't know who you are. We've never met." There was no point telling her not to provoke Jackson. Jane didn't know what she was saying half the time. Jackson . . . he'd revealed himself as a brutal man who had Junior's complete trust and used it to bark orders at him. Curiously, Jackson's wife, an occupant of the second SUV, didn't bear any signs of physical abuse. Either Jackson beat her where the bruises wouldn't show, or he used other women as punching bags.

Someone thumped on the door. "Come on." Jillian threw the wet toilet paper into an overflowing garbage can and helped Jane to her feet. She unlocked the door, swung it open, and pushed Jane to stumble ahead of her. "I was cleaning her up," she said to Tom, another passenger in the second SUV. "We don't want to draw attention." Uh-huh. As if nobody had noticed the junkie being dragged into the washroom. A few had raised their heads from their newspapers and plates, but all had minded their business.

She supposed she could shout for help, but she'd noticed the tell-tale bulge under Tom's jacket and figured most of her other companions were armed, too. A paranoid group packing lead was a recipe for disaster. She still wasn't sure what the hell was going on, but she'd gathered that Junior thought the authorities were about to move in on him, so he'd ordered his circle to flee. Her working theory for her presence? They wanted Ruth's money, and Andy had come along because they thought she trusted him. But she didn't know for sure why she was here, and she couldn't risk everyone's lives.

She'd taken Jane to the washroom after they'd eaten and Jackson was settling the bill. Everyone was huddled near the entrance waiting for them, ready to go. Outside, she eyed the pay phone near the ice machine. So close . . . Jane stumbled and almost fell. Tom grabbed her; she tried to pull her arm away. Jillian stopped walking. Tom was distracted, and everyone else's eyes were on Jane. She could shift. They'd all assume she'd run into the restaurant. When they couldn't find her inside, they'd figure she'd escaped into the bush and could be anywhere. Saving their own skins would take priority over capturing her. Once they were gone, she could shift in and use the pay phone.

But she feared for Jane's life. Jackson could explode at any moment. He'd already hit Jane twice and his fuse was growing shorter. Losing their potential cash cow could push him over the edge. What would stop him from killing Jane five minutes away and dumping her body along the highway? What would happen to Andy? Jillian had no clue where they were going. No money, no ID . . . what if the pay phone didn't work and nobody would let her use their phone? They were in the middle of nowhere.

Nope, she had to stay for Jane. If push came to shove, she'd follow Roberta's order and save herself. Right now, she didn't feel threatened. They needed her to get to Ruth . . . or maybe Andy was more important to Junior than she'd thought, and he'd persuaded Junior to take her with them. She'd see how it played out and keep Jane alive.

SAM TAPPED THE steering wheel and gusted a sigh. The extraction team would have Jane by now, and Ruth would return with Jillian at any minute. They'd go back to the island and decide their next move. Sam would corner Roberta and make it clear that she would *not* twiddle her thumbs any longer. If Roberta wanted her to work a few more investigations with Jillian, fine, but next time Jillian could be useless.

She glanced in the rearview mirror. Ruth rounded the corner. Sam's heart leaped into her mouth. "Where's Jillian?" she barked, the moment Ruth opened the passenger door.

"We have a problem," Ruth said. "She's gone."

"Gone? What do you mean, gone?"

"I asked two youngsters, then insisted on speaking to someone higher up the food chain. He told me she's not there today." Ruth met Sam's eyes. "He said he doesn't know where she is."

Sam gripped the steering wheel and shoved aside the worst-case scenario that popped into her mind. "How could he not know where she is? She isn't allowed to step foot outside the centre by herself."

"I couldn't tell if he was lying."

She released her seatbelt. "I'm going in."

"Sam."

Her phone rang. "I just heard from the extraction team," Roberta said without preamble. "It didn't go well. Jane wasn't there. The house was deserted."

"What?"

"There's more. They found three shallow graves on the property."

Her heart raced. "Do we know whose graves they are?" she asked, failing to mask her fear. She felt Ruth's hand on her arm.

"Pat, the woman Jillian told us about . . . one of the graves was hers. We don't know the identity of the other corpses. We'll tip off the authorities. Also—"

There was more?

"We don't know where Junior is."

Sam's free hand went to her forehead.

"Jeremy is combing through traffic camera footage. We caught two SUVs in the vicinity of the learning centre around three this morning."

"They were going to get Jillian."

"What do you mean?"

"She's not at the learning centre. Apparently nobody knows where she is." Silence. "What happened? Why are they running? How could they have known we were coming?"

"They couldn't have," Roberta said firmly. "Something else must have spooked them."

"Well, find out what it was and why we didn't pick up on it," Sam snapped. "Jillian's out there with a paranoid maniac and killer."

Roberta remained calm. "Sam, we're doing everything we can."

She slowly exhaled. "I know. I'm sorry."

"Jillian isn't helpless, or stupid. She'll try to contact us."

If she had time before Junior flipped out. "I'm going into the learning centre to see what I can find out."

"Let's keep each other posted." Roberta paused. "The best thing you can do for Jillian is to remain focused."

"I will. Bye." Sam disconnected and shoved her phone into her pocket before she flung it out the window. When Roberta had summoned her that day months ago and insisted that since Jillian trusted Sam, Sam should train her, she should have pushed back—hard. She'd never wanted that responsibility. Why had Roberta forced her to do what she'd clearly not wanted to do?

"What's happened?" Ruth asked quietly.

Sam blew out another sigh. "The extraction failed. Jackson and Junior are gone, Jane's nowhere to be found, and three bodies were buried on Jackson's property, one of them Pat's."

"Oh, dear," Ruth murmured.

"A couple of SUVs were in this area during the night. We're assuming they picked up Jillian." She turned to Ruth. "Why hasn't she contacted us? She could easily get away. All she'd have to do is shift. They wouldn't know what happened to her. They wouldn't sit around waiting for her to reappear."

"And why did she go with them? She knew we were coming for her today."

"If she'd disappeared from under their noses in the middle of the night, it could have blown the extraction." Jillian hadn't known it would be a bust. "So I get why she went. But why hasn't she contacted us?" Again, Sam pushed away her worst fear. Roberta was right. Jillian wasn't helpless. "There must be a reason she's staying with them."

Ruth nodded. "We don't know, that's the problem."

"I'll see what I can find out. Wait here." Sam popped the trunk. Moments later, she unlocked the briefcase she pulled from underneath her knapsack, opened it, and sorted through the stack of IDs it contained. She grunted when she found the ID she wanted. *Samantha Moore, Detective.* After shoving the pocket folder and a couple of business cards into her back pocket, she pulled off her hoodie, straightened her blouse, and strode up the street and around the corner.

When she entered the learning centre's lobby, the greeter's eye immediately went to her holstered gun. She pulled the folder from her pocket, opened it, and held it up. "Detective Moore, Fraud Investigations. I'd like to speak to Jillian Harwick."

"Jillian?" The greeter glanced at the two other cult members who'd stopped to listen.

"I'll go get Rick," one of them said, wide-eyed.

"Thank you." Sam rocked on her heels and surveyed the blank faces around her. If she could, she'd shut down this hell hole and free everyone here. She felt even more unhappy that she'd sat around while Jillian had lived in the desert. *Please protect Jillian. Please keep her safe until we find her.*

A man exuding self-importance marched into the lobby and approached her. "I'm Richard Flores, director of this centre."

Sam flashed her ID again. "Detective Moore. I'd like to speak to Jillian Harwick. I'm told she lives here."

Flores frowned. "Why don't we go somewhere we can speak privately?"

"All right."

She followed him from the lobby and into a small room where cult members probably brought hot prospects. Flores shut the door. "I'm responsible for those who live under this roof," he said stiffly. "If you don't mind me asking, why do you want to see Jillian? You're a fraud investigator . . ."

"She's not involved in a fraud," Sam said with a chuckle. She wasn't about to get Jillian killed. "Several months ago, she filed a complaint about a charity her mother had donated money to."

"I see," Flores said, visibly relaxing.

"It took us a while to get around to it. We have so many cases, and frankly, Ms. Harwick's is minor. All I'd like to do is clarify a couple of points in Ms. Harwick's complaint. Her mother said she lives here."

Flores clasped his hands in front of him. Sam waited while he weighed his words. "I'm not sure where she is," he finally said. "All I know is that she's working off-site. If anyone tells you that she's run off with her boyfriend, it isn't true."

"Boyfriend?" Sam didn't believe it for a second, but hearing the word 'boyfriend' in relation to Jillian was jarring.

"Yes. According to her roommate, she left in the middle of last night with Andy. They, uh, saw each other sometimes outside the centre."

"I don't care about Ms. Harwick's personal life or what goes on here," Sam said, hoping to convey that she wasn't here to make trouble for the soul healers. "All I care about is clarifying the complaint. Do you mind if I speak with the roommate? After that, I'll leave."

"I don't see why not." Flores yanked the door open and stepped into the corridor. "Can you go get Cathy?" he said to someone. He turned back to Sam. They waited in awkward silence.

A twenty-something woman came into the room. Her eyes flicked to Sam. She flexed her hands and stared at Flores, who shut the door and cleared his throat. "Cathy, this is Detective . . ."

"Moore," Sam said.

"Moore. She'd like to ask you about Jillian."

Cathy gulped and gave Sam a guarded look. There was no point asking Flores to leave; it would only alarm him.

"I'm looking into a complaint Ms. Harwick filed about a charity her mother donated to," Sam said, hoping to put Cathy at ease. "Mr. Flores said that Ms. Harwick left last night."

Cathy nodded.

"Did she say where she was going?"

She hesitated, then spoke when Flores nodded. "No. She just said to tell her mother that she was leaving with Andy. I haven't seen her mother, though. I—I work on the—"

"The detective isn't interested in you, Cathy," Flores said.

"Sorry."

"Did Ms. Harwick say anything else?" Sam asked.

"No. Well, she said Andy was serving the Soul Master, that he wasn't doing anything wrong. I mean, he was on the women's floor and—"

"Focus, Cathy," Flores barked.

Cathy flinched. "Sorry."

"Do you know what time it was?" Sam asked.

"Around 3:00, maybe? When I looked at the clock, she'd already been gone a few minutes. I had trouble falling back to sleep."

"Is there anything else you can tell me that will help me locate Ms. Harwick? She's not in any trouble. I'd just like to file a report and move on to my next case."

"No. Sorry."

Flores swung the door open. "I'll walk you to the exit, Detective."

"Thank you," she said to Cathy.

"Jillian—Ms. Harwick—she's a conscientious woman," Flores said as he walked Sam back to the lobby at a brisk pace. "She'll return when she's completed her work for our CEO."

Sam wanted to roll her eyes. "When she does, please have her call me." She handed him a business card. Since she was supposed to be working on a routine, minor case, she wouldn't ask him whether he could contact Junior. She also wouldn't ask him whether it was usual for the CEO's lackey to pull people out of bed in the middle of the night. "Have a good day."

She left the centre, strolled around the corner, and pulled out her phone. "You might get a call for Detective Moore," she said to Jeremy. "Also, if a Richard Flores with the learning centre's address has a cell phone, monitor it."

"Will do . . . Detective."

If Sam wasn't worried, she would have chuckled. "Have you picked up the SUVs anywhere?"

"They were going west on Highway 19. Then we lost them."

"Keep looking," she said, knowing that finding them again was a long shot. She hung up and slid into the sedan's driver's seat. "She left with Andy. That's the only message she left for us."

"She probably didn't know where they were going," Ruth said. "But that could be a promising sign. Andy tends to get involved when they want her to contact me about money—or putting me into a home."

"Maybe that's the reason they took her with them. They need money. If Junior is paranoid and feels as if the noose is tightening around his neck, he won't want to touch their bank accounts."

"If we're right, it's only a matter of time before I get a phone call."

Sam called Roberta. "Have we found out why Junior ran?"

"No, but you know how these things go. He might have misinterpreted a harmless comment. We also don't know who killed Pat and the other women. Even if it wasn't him, a murder investigation would see the authorities poking around in the soul healers' affairs again."

"But nobody had found the bodies until we did. They had time to move them." *I'm sorry. I hate conversations like this. I shouldn't think like them.* But she did. Nietzsche was right.

"It doesn't matter. Jillian told us he was paranoid. Whatever he's running from could be in his mind."

"We think they'll eventually contact Ruth about money." They'd play a waiting game while Jillian was in the clutches of a lunatic. If anything happened to her . . . "What can Ruth and I do?"

Silence, then, "You can pray."

Sam wasn't big on prayer—not the "on your knees" kind, anyway. "Call us the moment you know anything." She disconnected and relayed the conversation to Ruth.

Ruth frowned. "A paranoid and spooked Soul Master . . ." She grimaced at Sam. "This isn't going to end well."

No, it wasn't.

Chapter Nineteen

Jillian walked into the convenience store with Andy and scanned her surroundings. They were in a small town—population 1,600—picking up drinks and snacks at what would be their last stop until they arrived at what Jackson described as a well-stocked cabin. She didn't remember a cabin in the bush being on the Fellowship's list of cult assets. Just how provisioned was the cabin? Could they hide there for months without having to pick up supplies? What about clothes? Had Sam and Ruth discovered yet that she wasn't at the learning centre and Junior had flown the coop?

They'd never find her. Everyone with cell phones had turned them off and knew not to use them, and cell coverage would be sketchy in the bush, anyway. How long would it be before they needed money?

Andy surveyed the shelves. "I'll get the drinks. Why don't you pick up the chips and chocolate bars?"

"Sure." She spotted the chips and wandered down the aisle containing them, then stopped. For the first time, she could speak to Andy away from everyone else. Should she try to find out if he knew the location of the cabin? She watched him open a refrigerator at the end of the aisle. No, she didn't want to raise any red flags with him until they'd reached their destination. He was loyal to Junior; he believed all the crap. She didn't want them to leave her behind here, or worse. Jane would only be next.

She grabbed several bags of BBQ chips, then strolled to the counter, where she suspected she'd find chocolate bars. The cashier was serving someone and a woman stood in line, holding a bottle of water and a loaf of bread. A frisson of excitement ran through Jillian. The cashier had a cell phone attached to his belt. If she could quietly ask to use it . . . she glanced toward the back of the store. Andy had picked up a basket from somewhere and was loading it with drinks. The customer at the cash left. The woman moved to the counter. With only two items, she shouldn't be long.

Her heart racing, Jillian stood behind her and willed the cashier to quickly deal with the woman. She didn't want to draw Andy's attention by pushing in. Why was the cashier moving in slow motion? Come on, come on! The woman accepted her change and moved away. Jillian smiled and opened her mouth.

"I think you gave me an extra dollar," the woman said, turning back to the cash.

No! Normally Jillian would applaud such honesty, but not now!

The woman dropped a loonie back into the cashier's hand. "You should only have given me two dollars."

"Thank you," the relieved man said. "If the cash doesn't balance at the end of the day, it comes out of my pay."

"Even if it's only a dollar?" the woman said.

The cashier nodded.

Come on!

The woman frowned. "Honest mistakes happen."

Jillian couldn't bear it any longer. "Excuse me. I—" She felt a hand on her shoulder. Damn it. "I'd just like to look at the chocolate bars."

"Sorry." The woman waved at the cashier. "Have a good day."

"You too," the cashier said. "Thanks again." The door's bell jingled as the woman left. "Wasn't that nice?" he said to Jillian.

Yeah, really nice. Give the woman a freaking gold star. She forced a smile, picked up a few chocolate bars, and twisted to look at Andy. "Ready?"

"Yes."

When he opened his wallet, she tried to glimpse how much money he had. A stack of bills sat behind a twenty. If they were all twenties, he had at least a couple of hundred. Deflated, she strolled back to the SUV with him. Damn that woman. It would have taken Jillian ten seconds to punch in Jeremy or Sam's number, wait until they answered, shake her head, and hang up. They would have suspected it was her. That had probably been her last chance to make contact for at least a few days, maybe more. Given Junior's paranoia, the cabin could be a bunker stocked with enough food and water for years.

JILLIAN STEPPED OUT onto the cabin's porch and breathed in the crisp air. Any other time, she'd try to relax, listen to the chirping, force herself to appreciate the natural beauty surrounding her—and count the hours until she could return to civilization. Communing with nature for more than a few hours at a time wasn't her thing; she'd never dreamed of retiring to the country. Fortunately, the island was private and picturesque, and had all the comforts of a city resort.

Trevor, one of Junior's bodyguards, stood guard next to the door, a submachine gun slung over his shoulder. She could kick herself now for not realizing that the cabin's provisions might include arms. The armoury in the locked shed out back rivalled those in the Fellowship's safe houses and contained additional materials that had frightened her when she'd glimpsed them through the doorway—everything one needed to build explosive devices. Yep, she was in a cabin in the middle of nowhere with a paranoid megalomaniac and enough explosives to blow them all to kingdom come.

She could take out Trevor, but then what? She didn't have keys to either SUV, and it would be one hell of a walk to the nearest town. The cabin would be empty and Jane potentially dead before she could lead the Fellowship here. "Where's Andy?" she asked Trevor, knowing Andy had gone outside a few minutes earlier.

Trevor pointed around the side of the cabin. "Taking a look at the propane tank."

"I'll see if he needs a hand." When Trevor didn't protest, she clomped down the wooden steps and rounded the cabin. Andy was staring at the tank. "Hi," she said, not wanting to frighten him.

His head jerked up. "Hi."

Could anyone hear them here? She didn't think Trevor could, and the cabin's downstairs window was closed. "I didn't expect something this big," she said, sweeping her arm toward the two-story cabin that could comfortably sleep them all in its four bedrooms and the two sleeper couches downstairs. Junior, or perhaps his father, had invested in this place over the years. "We could stay here for a while." Especially since they had enough food and water to last them at least a month. As for clothes . . . Maggie had collected everyone's sizes. Later today, she and Trevor would go on a shopping expedition. Fresh fruits and veggies were also on the list.

Andy grunted. "I don't know how long we'll be here."

"Why is Jane with us? You said she used to be one of us. What happened?" Jillian asked. He didn't know why they'd fled, but that didn't mean he knew nothing about their predicament.

"She used to be on the true path, but then she strayed." Andy wiped his forearm across his forehead. "She was away for years, but I guess the Lord reached out to her. She came back to us, begging for the Soul Master's help. He's trying to bring her back into the light, but Satan is strong."

Jillian struggled not to gape. So that was the yarn Junior had spun. Andy appeared to believe it, but that didn't mean anything with this crowd. "Nothing I've learned since joining the community has discussed or condoned beatings," she said carefully. When he didn't react, she added, "Administering drugs isn't part of the program, either."

He shifted his weight. She could hear the wheels of rationalization turning. When he finally opened his mouth, he didn't disappoint. "Drugs are only used in extreme circumstances, when it's obvious that Satan has taken over most of the soul." His voice dropped. "It breaks down his defences, allows the Soul Master to reach the true person that Satan has imprisoned. When Jackson hits her . . ." Andy moistened his lips. "I don't like it, but desperate times call for desperate measures. Surely you understand that we have to do everything we can to reach her."

"I know, but she seems fragile." And Jackson was a little too enthusiastic about beating Satan out of her. "If she's always high, how will the Soul Master know whether he's winning?"

Andy's eyes widened. "You don't think he can trust anything that comes out of her mouth, do you?" She didn't answer the obviously rhetorical question. "He can tell from her aura. He knows who's true and who isn't."

If that were the case, she wouldn't be here. "Does he have to use drugs often?"

"Only in extreme cases, and sometimes at the request of the troubled soul. Not long ago, one of our members asked that we help her. After leaving us, it didn't take her long to realize that she'd made a terrible mistake. She begged us to help her. I . . . I had been friends with her, so I helped. Unfortunately, Satan was too strong."

"What happened?"

Andy's Adam's apple bobbed. "She didn't make it."

"You mean she died?" Jillian breathed.

He nodded. "I—I wasn't there. I delivered what the Soul Master needed, then left them."

"Did he tell you what happened?"

"No. When I tried asking him about it, he . . . he cried. Amanda was one of his favourites."

Bingo! Did Andy know Jane was Amanda's sister? She'd bet he did, but she had more pressing questions. Okay, so he'd taken the drugs to Junior, who'd entered Amanda's room without being seen. Had Junior meant to kill her, or did he believe the crap he told everyone else about breaking down Satan's resistance? He might have thought that Satan would mitigate the high dose. The man *was* delusional.

She shoved her hands into her pockets. "His favourites?"

"The Soul Master often invited her to commune with him."

Jillian wanted to snort. Then her mind went to Janet Bailey, and Pat, whom she'd last seen leaving the learning centre with Junior. "If Amanda was close to the Soul Master, why did she leave?"

"Satan tries to reach the Soul Master by taking away what's dear to him. Look at what's happening now."

"I don't know what's happening now. I want to help, but I can't when I don't know anything."

Andy touched her arm. "I wish I could tell you, but I don't know much, either. Tom woke me up and said we needed to leave, that they were coming for the Soul Master."

"They?"

"The authorities . . . they're always trying to bring us down."

"Well, they're instruments of Satan," she said, straight-faced. Hell, to think she'd thought that Sam was crazy. At one point, Jillian had even wondered if she was drugged up in a psychiatric facility, and whether Sam, the island, and her arrest were all taking place in her mind. If not for the gifts she now possessed and knew were real, and her mostly coherent existence, she'd still wonder. "What am *I* doing here?"

"The Soul Master has recognized your special soul, Jillian."

Her special bond with her rich mother, more like.

"Jillian," a gruff voice said. She turned around. Trevor was leaning over the porch railing. "The Soul Master wants to see you."

"I'll get back to the tank." Andy turned toward it.

Her stomach churning, Jillian tromped back to the cabin's front door. Andy wouldn't be of any help. She was on her own, up against two guards with submachine guns, a handful of deluded followers, and a crazy man with a god complex. She had to contact the Fellowship.

Hoping her conversation with Junior would be about Ruth, she entered the cabin. Don, the other guard, tipped his head toward the dining room. Jillian braced herself and strolled into it. Junior, Tom, Jackson, and Maggie sat around the table, drinking coffee and munching on the chips Jillian had bought at the convenience store.

"Ah, Jillian." Junior beckoned to her.

Her skin crawling, Jillian approached him, then fought her revulsion when he took her hand.

"This must be confusing for you," he said. "I wish we'd had more time together before this latest upset."

"I don't understand why we had to leave," she said, pitching her voice higher in an attempt to sound innocent.

"I know. Yet you came with us, without hesitation, without question." He brought her hand to his lips. She struggled to keep the disgust from her face. "This might be difficult for you to understand, but Satan works through those we usually trust. I have to be extremely cautious. The government, the authorities . . . Satan uses them against me, but he doesn't control everyone. Someone loyal to me warned us that I was to be questioned about our finances."

"Why?" Jillian asked, wondering whether there was any truth to it.

"Because Satan whispered in someone's ear."

"I've seen some of the books. There's no reason to investigate us."

Junior nodded. "Exactly. The Lord will prevail, but as you've learned, He expects us to take action, to control our own destiny. So we thought it best to make ourselves difficult to find until our prayers are answered."

"Is there anything I can do?"

He squeezed her hand. "I knew you'd want to do everything you can to help. You must also be worried about your mother."

Adrenaline shot through her. "I don't know whether Andy's told you, but she's not well."

"I know about your difficult situation," he said gently. "I wrestled over bringing you with us, precisely because I didn't want to take you away at such a sensitive time."

Uh-huh.

"Would you like to see your mother?"

Hell, yeah! "I'd like to know that she's all right."

Junior leaned forward; his grip tightened. "If there was a way to see your mother and do a great service for me, for us, would you do it?"

She nodded. "Of course."

"You see, we have food and water, but it will only last us a few weeks. We also might need medical supplies, gas, more clothes . . . but we can't use our credit or debit cards, or touch our bank accounts. They're watching. They'll know. We need cash."

"You want my mother to make another donation. In cash."

"Yes."

"I have money," she said, not wanting to be a complete pushover where Mom was concerned. "I was going to donate it all to the home where Mom will live, but we can use some of it now."

"No. You can't touch your bank accounts or investments. Your mother can."

"What about Satan?" Jillian asked, not wanting to appear too stupid. She giggled to herself at the absurdity of the thought. "What if he influences Mom?"

"It's a chance we'll have to take. Your mother has always been supportive. I believe she may have a natural resistance to Satan's charm."

Sure she did. Apparently Satan blew hot and cold depending on whether Junior wanted to use someone. "What do you want me to do?" she asked, wishing he'd let go of her hand, already.

"I want you to contact her and ask her to meet you in one of the nearby towns." Junior explained how he expected the meeting with Ruth to proceed and what he wanted from it. "We have a few disposable cells. Trevor will drive you to that last town we passed through. Call your mother, then dump the phone."

"I understand." She'd better bring Sam into it now. "My mother doesn't drive. I used to drive her everywhere, so when I decided to enter the program, I arranged for a friend to do it. I gave her the use of my car, in exchange for driving Mom around."

"Do you think she'll cause trouble for us?"

Jillian damn-well hoped so. "No. I hate to say it, but I don't think she'd do anything that would lose her the car."

"I expect you pay her for her time, as well," Jackson said.

She gazed at him. "I haven't been, but driving Mom out here to meet me would certainly earn her a bonus." When everyone chuckled, she seethed inside. If Satan existed, he was in this room. "Should I take Jane with me when I go to call Mom? She could probably use some fresh air."

Junior shook his head. "She stays here. She's on the brink of the abyss. She needs me."

Like hell, she did. Damn. Jillian would have to hope that Junior or Jackson didn't freak out while she wasn't here to protect Jane. "Do you mind if I take her some chips? She hasn't eaten since breakfast."

She tensed when Junior let go of her hand and stood, then wanted to puke when he held out his arms. As she embraced him, she faced away from the others.

"I admire your selflessness," Junior murmured into her ear. "I have plans for you."

They'd better not include more physical contact. When he drew back, she hoped her smile reached her eyes.

"Go see Jane, my little Florence Nightingale," Junior said. "Trevor will be waiting for you."

She filled a bowl with chips and escaped with a sigh of relief. Upstairs, she pushed open one of the bedroom doors and winced at the pathetic figure lying on the bed. "Jane," she whispered. "I've brought you some chips." She set the bowl on the nightstand, knelt, and curled her hand around Jane's arm. She probed. Her stomach roiled. She could heal Jane, cleanse her of the toxins in her body and clear the fog from her eyes. But Junior would only shoot her up again, and it would be better for him to think that he controlled her. "I'm sorry."

Jane turned her head. "Have you seen Amanda?"

A lump rose in Jillian's throat. "No."

"She was just here." Her eyes closed.

"There are chips on the nightstand," Jillian said helplessly. She pushed herself to her feet and stared down at Jane. If she took out Trevor . . . no, it wouldn't work. By the time the Fellowship got here, she and Trevor would have been gone for too long. The team would storm an empty cabin, or discover that it had burned to the ground. She needed to stay with Jane until the cavalry arrived. Assuming she met with Sam and Ruth tomorrow, this would all be over within a day or two.

With a heavy heart, she went downstairs and walked with Trevor to the SUV. A licence plate lay in the dirt near one of its rear wheels; a new one had replaced it. Small towns and rural highways didn't have traffic cameras, but if they had to make a hasty getaway and return to an urban area, they were prepared. Jillian climbed into the passenger seat and looked at her tired reflection in the side view mirror. When she saw Sam and Ruth tomorrow, she'd do her best not to cry.

Chapter Twenty

WHEN RUTH MURMURED, "Turn left at the next road," Sam flicked on the indicator and slowed down. "The store should be on our right."

When Sam turned the corner and the early morning sun hit her full in the face, she flipped down the visor. Even though they'd had to rise at 4:00 a.m., the early morning meeting suited her for the same reason Junior had instructed Jillian to set up the rendezvous for that time. They hadn't passed a single car for at least ten minutes, and the store's parking lot was deserted. Good. Nobody would see Junior's men hit the pavement.

"There are only two guards," Ruth said, as Sam deliberately crawled through the parking lot so she could scope out their surroundings. Neither guard appeared armed. Hidden firearms, then.

"There might be others we can't see."

"Jillian will know."

Sam braked next to a black SUV and shifted her attention to the three people waiting for them. Jillian . . . thank goodness. She'd worried that Junior would consider Jillian expendable after the call to her mother. The plan could have been to grab Ruth and eliminate her chauffeur. *Are you all right?* she said to Jillian.

"I've had better days," Jillian said.

"Is anyone else with you apart from those two?"

"No."

"Okay. We'll take out your guards," Sam said as she unbuckled her seatbelt. *"Get r—"*

"No!" Jillian's voice rang through Sam's mind.

"Why not?"

"Because if I don't return with them, Junior or Jackson will go off the rails and kill Jane, and maybe everyone else, too."

"Jane's with you?" Sam said, to Jillian and aloud. Ruth raised her brows.

"Yes. Give us the money and let us go. I can tell you where we're holed up. We're not going anywhere."

"Plan B," Sam said to Ruth. "Find out as much as you can."

Ruth nodded and opened the passenger door. "Jillian," she said, holding out her arms.

Jillian glanced at her two guards, then came to Ruth and hugged her. Sam rounded the car and hovered nearby, eyeing Jillian's companions. She didn't care if she aroused their suspicions. It would be odd if she wasn't curious about this strange meeting.

When Jillian and Ruth moved closer to the guards, Sam followed them. "This is my mother," Jillian said. "This is Trevor and Don."

"Pleased to meet you," Ruth said, smiling at them. "Now, tell me what's going on, sweetheart."

"Tell me to go away. Then you and Ruth move away from the SUV," Sam said.

"Okay." "You remember the Soul Master?" Jillian said.

Ruth nodded.

"Well . . ." Jillian looked past Ruth. "Sam, would you mind giving us some privacy for a minute? Just for a minute." She grasped Ruth's arm and pulled her a few steps from the SUV.

"Sure, no problem." Sam wandered between the two vehicles, leaned against the sedan's back door, and folded her arms. She peeked at Trevor and Don. Trevor was watching Jillian and Ruth, but Don's eyes were on her. She'd wait for the handover, when neither would resist checking out the money. She only needed a few seconds. *I wish we could take her now.* But she understood why they couldn't and why Jillian hadn't escaped earlier.

Several minutes later, Sam popped open the trunk when Ruth came over to fetch the bag. *"It's worse than we'd thought,"* Ruth said as she lifted the money from the trunk. Sam slammed it shut and watched Ruth return to Jillian and hand her the bag.

Jillian dropped it to the ground, crouched, and unzipped it. Both guards looked down. Sam pressed the tracking device she'd palmed onto the SUV, then quickly leaned against the sedan again, in time to see Don lift his head, and then the bag.

Jillian waved Sam over. "Thank you so much for bringing Mom. I know you probably think this whole thing is strange, but I told you I'd gone on a retreat once, right?"

Sam nodded.

"I'm on another one, and I forgot to bring some stuff with me. Mom wanted to meet early, so you wouldn't be too late for work."

"We'll have you out soon. If not tonight, then tomorrow." "You don't have to explain. I'll probably fall asleep at my desk, but your mother's offer to pay for my gas this week was too generous to turn down."

"Be careful." "I'm glad. It's nice to see you."

"You, too."

"We'd better go, dear. I don't want Sam to lose her job." Ruth gave Jillian another hug and pecked her on the cheek. "If you need anything else, let me know. I'll do what I can to help."

"Thanks, Mom. I knew you'd understand."

"Well, the entire affair is disgusting," Ruth said indignantly. "I don't know why they always go after organizations that are trying to help and ignore corrupt corporations."

Jillian gazed over Ruth's shoulder. "I don't think Sam needs to worry about this."

"You're right." Ruth turned to Sam. "Let's get you to work."

"Bye," Sam said to nobody in particular. Jillian and company didn't move. *"They want us to leave first, so we can't follow them,"* she said to Ruth. They climbed into the sedan and waved as they drove away. Frustration clenched Sam's jaw. She hated leaving Jillian behind. "Do you know how to get to them? I planted the tracker and I assume it's working, but . . ."

"I do. It's a ways away, but a straight line, for the most part."

"You said it's worse than we thought."

Ruth's mouth pinched. "Yes."

Sam listened to Ruth's account of who was with Jillian and how many were armed, the cabin's layout, the explosive materials, Junior's mental state, Jackson's violent streak, Jane's predicament. When she was sure that Jillian's group wasn't tailing them, she pulled onto the side of the single-lane rural road. "We have to get Jillian and Jane out ASAP."

Ruth's brow furrowed. "You mean, now?"

"We know how this is going to end, Ruth. Junior will go out in a blaze of glory, and he'll try to take everyone with him." Sam thumped the steering wheel. "Did she say why they're on the run?"

"Junior thinks the government is coming for him."

"Based on what? Thin air?"

"It's not your fault."

No? She'd sat around while a green Deiform, who happened to be her responsibility, had infiltrated a cult. "You're not helping."

"Trust the Lord."

"I do trust Him!" Sam's voice rose. "Trusting Him doesn't mean everything will work out. Ask the early Israelites. Ask the Christian martyrs. Bad things happen to people who trust Him."

"That's not—"

"I know. It's acceptance of whatever comes and whatever happens. It's peace." She wanted to leap from the car, run through the nearby field, feel the warmth of the sun on her face, and not care, for once. Why did she have to care? "With the types of situations we deal with, I believe He works through us. We can screw up."

"But we didn't this time."

Ruth sounded so sure. "We should have pulled her out the same day she told us about Jane."

"That would have tipped them off. You were right, we had to walk her out at the same time Jackson's residence was searched."

"I should—"

"Sam, we can sit here all day and discuss how we could have done things differently, but that won't help matters. We can't change what's done. The question is, what's next?"

Her chest tight, Sam gulped down some air. "I do trust Him, you know."

"I know you do."

"I just don't think that means I'm never guilty of making a mistake."

"Well, you won't get any argument there," Ruth said, her tone light. "But you take too much responsibility upon yourself. You can't control everything." She rested her hand on Sam's arm. "Trying to control could be construed as a lack of trust," her fingers tightened, "but I'm not saying it is." She lifted her hand. "It will take some time to assemble a team and get it here."

"No team. If Junior were to spot a heavily armed strike force, he'd flip out. It would validate every deluded fear he has. You and I can slip in and find Jillian. Between the three of us, we should be able to get Jane out quietly. We'll do it tonight, after dark. You said there are only ten of them. Jillian's with us, Jane won't be a problem, I doubt Andy is armed, which leaves Junior, the two guards we just met, his entourage, and Jackson's wife. Out of those . . ."

"She said everyone's armed except Jane, Andy, and the wife."

"Then six have weapons. We can take them all."

"Tonight, then?"

Sam nodded and pulled out her phone. Good, the tracker was working. She watched the slowly moving dot. "Let's check out the cabin. I'll go in, see how jittery everyone is and confirm the layout. I'll also tell Jillian that we're coming in tonight." She put the car into drive and pulled back onto the road. She *did* trust the Lord, but He'd called her and given her the gifts so she could act as His agent in the world, the operative word being *act*. Not, "sit on the sidelines and let whatever happens, happen."

I'm sorry. I know that's not what Ruth, or anyone, means. I know I'm to do my best and accept whatever happens. And she could do that—as long as whatever happened wasn't her fault.

AS JILLIAN LISTENED to Junior ask the same questions again, she wondered if she was the only one in the room who recognized that he was paranoid.

"You didn't tell her where we are?" Junior said.

Trevor shook his head. "Jillian said we're staying somewhere safe. That's all."

Junior focused on Jillian. "When she asked why, did she look like she believed you?"

"Yes. Mom would have no reason to think I'm lying, and I wasn't lying. I told her we had to leave town for a while, because people who'd like to see us fail are causing trouble. Mom understands that good deeds don't go unpunished."

He swivelled to Don. "What about the driver?"

"She seemed bored. She didn't ask any questions."

Junior's eyes widened slightly. "Don't you think that's strange?"

"I'm sure Mom answered any questions she had on the way," Jillian said. "It's a long drive."

Junior grunted. "You counted the money?" he said to Trevor.

"Yes. It's all there."

"We'll ask for more in a few days."

"What?" Trevor breathed, at the same time Jackson's brow furrowed and Maggie said, "No."

"Don't question me!" Junior thundered. Jillian exchanged a sidelong glance with Andy.

"With all due respect, Soul Master, five thousand dollars should last us a while," Jackson said. "Assuming we remain here, our expenses will be low. We asked for the money in case we have to leave in a hurry."

"When preparing for war, one can never be too prepared or stockpile too much."

A heavy silence followed Junior's words. Jillian resisted the urge to glance at Andy again. What did he think about all this? Junior was clearly over the edge. Why didn't anyone speak up and tell him enough was enough, that he should stop this game before it got out of hand? Trevor and Don had freaking submachine guns on their shoulders. Junior was armed, but he wouldn't have a chance to reach for his gun. Jillian couldn't stand up to him; she was unarmed and only here because she was supposedly loyal and her mother was their personal bank.

"We need to decide what to do about Jane," Junior said. "She's not responding. I don't know if there's anything more I can do for her."

"I warned you that Satan had taken her," Jackson murmured.

"I had to try."

"Do you want me to—"

Junior lifted his hand. "Let me have one more session with her later. Then I'll make my decision."

Jillian dug her fingernails into her palms. Roberta had said that her priority was survival, but she couldn't stand by and watch Junior give Jane a lethal dose, or Jackson beat her to death. She wouldn't be much use to the Fellowship if she were lugging around a ton of guilt on her back. Overpowering them all wasn't possible—not with her nascent gifts—but she didn't have to make it easy for them. If she could make Trevor or Don collapse and get her hands on a submachine gun, or figure out who had the key to the armoury and relieve them of it . . .

All fantasies. Even if she managed to arm herself with a serious weapon, she wasn't going to kick the cabin door open and mow everyone down, so how would she hold them at bay? How would she search them to make sure they'd surrendered all their weapons, make a phone call, keep an eye on her prisoners until the Fellowship arrived? One distraction, one lapse of concentration, and they'd overwhelm and kill her. She'd be Satan incarnate to this crowd, and deserve to die. If only she wasn't alone in seeing this madness for what it was.

She'd try to get through to Andy again, but she'd have to be careful. He might be soft on her, but his loyalty was to Junior. Sam hadn't said exactly when the Fellowship would move in. How much time would they need to prepare? Would they get here in time to save Jane?

"Lock up the money," Junior said to Jackson. "We need to beef up security. I want two guards around the clock. Tom, pair with Trevor. Maggie, pair with Don. Don and Maggie, go get some rest. You'll take the overnight shift." They went upstairs without a word of protest. Junior pushed back his chair and wandered into the living room. Meeting over.

When Andy headed for the kitchen, Jillian followed him. "Do you want an apple?" he asked, plucking one from the bowl on the counter.

"No, thank you." She moved closer to him. "What will happen to Jane if she doesn't respond during her next session with the Soul Master?"

"He'll have someone drive her into the city and leave her at some type of shelter, I suppose."

"Are you sure? He sounds—" *Sam.* Expecting to see her, Jillian turned, because somehow she knew Sam was here, in this room. Nobody was behind her. *"Sam?"*

"You know I'm here?"

Startled, she sucked in her breath. When she was learning about astral projection, Sam had told her that Deiforms could communicate with those who were projecting, but since they couldn't sense them, the conversation had to be initiated by the projector. *"Yes, I do. When are you moving in?"*

Silence, then, *"Tonight, after dark. I'm scouting out the place."*

"Good, because I don't think Jane has much time."

"Jillian?"

She shook herself and refocused on Andy. "Sorry. I thought I heard something." She cleared her throat. "Jane can lead people to us. That's the last thing the Soul Master would want."

"*Be ready,*" Sam said. Jillian didn't reply; she could sense that Sam had moved on.

"Maybe we'll leave," Andy said.

"Where would we go?"

Andy shrugged and took another bite of his apple.

God, was there any way to kick his brain into gear? "What did you think about the Soul Master wanting more money in a few days, so we can be prepared? What do we have to prepare for?"

He crunched on his mouthful of apple and swallowed it. "Why are you asking so many questions?"

This was hopeless, and if she didn't back off, he'd wonder if she was in Satan's clutches. "I just don't want us to be found. My mother loves me, and she's fond of you. She also supports what we do." She lowered her voice to a whisper. "Yes, she's not well, but even her suspicions will be raised if we ask for thousands of dollars every few days."

"You must trust the Soul Master, Jillian. Our faith is tested during trying times." He put his hand on her shoulder. "For someone who's still relatively new, you're doing well. Trust the Soul Master." His mouth turned up at the corners. "Trust me."

She was on her own. The Fellowship would move in tonight, but Jane might not have that long. Jillian wouldn't let Junior murder her. If she was going to die standing up for Good and doing whatever she could to save Jane's life, so be it.

Chapter Twenty-One

SAM OPENED HER eyes and blinked up at the sun filtering through the trees. She pushed herself to a sitting position.

Ruth lowered a pair of binoculars. "Welcome back. You just missed a pretty hummingbird." She frowned. "What's the matter? You're as white as a sheet."

If it were anyone else, she'd say, "Nothing," but Ruth had taught her, nurtured her, understood her more than most. "Jillian knew I was there."

"You said you were going to let her know—"

Sam shook her head. "No. She knew before I said anything to her." She searched Ruth's face.

"When you were training her, did she ever astral project when you didn't know about it?" Ruth asked.

What did that have to do with anything? "Why?"

"I'm wondering if you can sense her."

"Why?"

Ruth rested the binoculars on her lap. "Have you read about the Deiforms Jerome and Valeria, or Ambrose and Paul?"

"How far back are they?"

Ruth pursed her lips. "Seventh and twelfth centuries, I think."

"I'm up—or rather, back," she said wryly, "to the fourteenth century."

"I believe there are more, but those two pairs belonged to our cell."

"What do they have to do with this?"

"Some Deiforms can sense each other. I'm willing to bet that you'll be able to sense Jillian." Ruth quirked a brow. "That will come in handy, won't it? Now, what did you find out?"

Under different circumstances, Sam would point out the change of subject. "Junior is paranoid, all right, more paranoid than we thought. Did Jillian mention anything about live explosives rigged in the storage and walk-in pantry?"

"No, she only mentioned the materials in the shed."

"That cabin is ready to go up in flames."

"Someone must have rigged them while Jillian met with us. She said she'd projected and had a good look around."

"Well, now she's sitting on a bomb." *Flames licked at her, choking smoke, couldn't breathe, lungs burning . . . the crushing realization that all her training was for naught . . . Lord!* She felt Ruth's hand on her arm.

"It was a different situation," Ruth said quietly.

No, it wasn't. Sam dug her trembling fingers into the dirt. "I don't know who has the detonator. If it's Junior, it's in twitchy hands. I should go in alone."

Ruth's eyes widened. "You can't subdue all of them. All right, you could, but you'd be so drained that you'd be useless afterward. We'll only have about fifteen seconds to disarm everyone."

"If the explosives detonate—"

"Let's not assume the worst-case scenario." Ruth pointed in the direction of the cabin. "Are there guards outside?"

"Two."

"If the same applies tonight, we'll take them out first and make sure they'll stay down for a while. That will leave only six to subdue. Between the two of us and Jillian, we shouldn't have any trouble." Ruth smiled at Sam. "Perhaps we should pray that they're all in the same room. It would make things easier."

"But it wouldn't give us enough time to search everyone for the detonator. We'd barely have enough time to disarm them. So if we have to take everyone at once and I tell you to shift, don't hesitate. Shift." Sam swallowed. "Let's hope most of them are asleep. If we're quiet, we can take them in pairs." She'd observed that most of the bedrooms had double beds.

"You can have another look around before we go in." Using the tree next to her for support, Ruth slowly rose, handed the binoculars to Sam, and brushed dirt and leaves off her pants. "I'd say let's shift and be done with it in ten minutes, but I'm hungry," she said with a sheepish grin. "I don't want my grumbling stomach to give us away, and I wasn't joking when I said we should take the time to pray." She looked down at Sam. "Did you tell Jillian about the explosives?"

"No."

"Why not?"

Sam peered up at her. "For the same reason you didn't tell her about the bodies we found on Jackson's property. What would have been the point of letting her know she's sitting on live explosives when she can't do anything about it?"

"She could leave."

"Not without Jane."

Ruth frowned. "She's supposed to worry about herself, first and foremost. Roberta won't be pleased."

That was Roberta's problem. Sam agreed with Jillian on this one. She accepted Ruth's outstretched hand and stood. "Let's drive back to the town that had the restaurant and church."

"It will be nice to be back on the island, won't it?" Ruth said as they returned to the car. "I don't mind the occasional foray into the world, but this has been a bit too long for my taste. I want to get back to my garden."

"I'm looking forward to it, too." She'd go to the undercroft and look up the Deiforms Ruth had mentioned.

HER MUSCLES ACHING from the tension, Jillian sat next to Andy and watched Junior tenderly stroke Jane's hair. Everyone except Maggie and Don, who stood guard outside, and Jackson's wife, who seemed to be more of an appendage than a spouse and had been shooed upstairs, had formed a cleansing circle around Junior and Jane. They'd pushed the furniture against the walls to make room. As much as Jillian tried, she couldn't stop glancing at the vial, syringe, rubber tourniquet, and latex gloves that sat on the end table near Tom. Where the hell was the Fellowship? She should have asked Sam about the approximate time and how many were coming, but sensing Sam, trying to communicate with her, and actually succeeding had unnerved her, and she'd also had to converse with Andy.

"I'm so sorry," Junior murmured. Her head in his lap, Jane groaned, but her drugged mind was in another room and with other people, including Amanda. "You came back to us too late. Too late." Jesus, were his eyes tearing up? Maybe he actually believed his own bullshit.

Junior lifted his head. "There's nothing more I can do for her. It's up to the Lord now."

Shit.

"I agree. It's time to send her to the Lord," Jackson growled.

Andy shifted. "Send her to the Lord?" he said; Jillian could hear the fear in his voice.

"Don't worry, Andy," Junior intoned. "What I'm about to do is an act of mercy. The Lord will receive and cleanse her. He'll set her free."

Andy gulped. "You mean she might die?"

Junior's face darkened. "It will be an act of mercy," he thundered. "Why are you questioning me?"

Andy's shoulders hunched. "I—I'm not. I'm asking for Jillian, so she understands what might happen." Jillian didn't know if he was serious or thinking on his feet. He was certainly in denial. There was no "might" about Jane dying.

Junior's face smoothed. "Of course. She's still learning." He beckoned for Jillian to approach him. "Look at Jane, Jillian. See the corruption."

Doing her best to appear meek, which didn't come naturally, Jillian stood and shuffled into the circle to check Jane's condition. The only visible blemish was the ugly bruise on her left cheek that marred an otherwise peaceful face. Jane mumbled to herself, blissfully ignorant of the nearby instruments of death, one holding her in his arms, the other sitting on an end table.

"I've done everything I can for Jane," Junior said, with a regretful shake of his head. "She strayed from the true path, and by the time she realized the error of her ways and returned to us, it was too late. I've tried. Lord knows, I've tried. But it's time to let go and release her from her torment."

"Amen," the group murmured.

Junior brightened. "Fortunately my efforts have cleansed her enough that she'll pass from my arms to the Lord's. He'll complete what I've started. I wish she could remain in this world, but the time for that has passed." He looked down and tenderly caressed Jane's cheek. "I do this for you, my sweet."

Jillian's mind raced. Jackson had a pistol tucked down the back of his pants. A submachine gun rested on the floor next to Trevor. She'd bet that everyone else, except Andy, was armed. So . . . she could stand here and watch Junior murder Jane in cold blood, or she could try to keep him talking until the cavalry rode in, and they'd damn-well better be here soon. "I don't understand," she said. "Why do you have to kill her?"

Junior winced. "Kill is such a negative way to put it, especially when I'll actually be giving her life." He looked past her. "Do you understand what I'm about to do, Andy?"

She glanced over her shoulder in time to see Andy nod. Great. "But as long as she's alive, she can be redeemed."

Junior's face reddened and he blinked rapidly. "Listen, you—" He sucked in a deep breath and took a moment to regain control of himself. "She is past the point of redemption in this world," he said, enunciating every word. "To be saved, she must move on to the next. Satan's hold on her is too strong. I've managed to keep him at bay, to prevent him from owning her soul, but the Lord is the only one who can save her now."

Jillian shifted her weight. "But—"

"Have you ever euthanized a sick pet, Jillian?" Tom asked.

"No."

"Do you understand why people take that step? They're not being cruel and heartless. Relieving a pet of pain and suffering is the most loving thing someone can do, especially since it causes them great pain to do so. It's a selfless act, one that takes great strength."

"Sometimes people put down pets because they're inconvenient. That's hardly selfless. It's selfish and pathetic."

When Tom started to push himself up, Junior motioned for him to stay seated. "She speaks the truth." He focused on Jillian. "But that's not what we're doing here. We've done everything we can for Jane. Look at the state she's in. It would be cruel for us to prolong her suffering. It's time to send her home."

Tom handed Junior the latex gloves. Junior pulled one on and flexed his hand, then turned his attention to the other glove.

Forget the Fellowship. Time had just run out. "She's in that state because you put her there." Jillian edged around the circle toward the end table. "You've been shooting her up with god knows what, because you're a sad, deluded man. Don't you see what's happening here?" she said, to stunned faces. "Andy, do you think it's right for the Soul Master to commit cold-blooded murder? What about the rest of you?" she asked rhetorically. Almost there.

Tom sprang to his feet. "Shut your filthy mouth!"

It was now or never. She stopped Tom's heart. Gasps pierced the air as he toppled over. Everyone's eyes were on him. Jillian snatched up the vial, dropped it to the floor, and stomped on it. Pain exploded in the back of her head. She staggered forward, turned—Jackson's fist smashed into her nose. She fell backward; her teeth rattled when her head hit the floor. She stared at the ceiling in confusion. Jackson loomed over her. He pulled out his gun. She reached for her centre through her hazy consciousness, willed herself to shift—

Jackson pitched forward and landed with a thud next to Jillian. Groggy and gritting her teeth, she pushed herself to a sitting position. Everyone was prostrate. Sam and Ruth were . . . tossing weapons . . . Jillian groaned and gingerly felt the back of her head. Stickiness. She wanted to lie down and go to sleep . . .

"Shift! He has the detonator!" Sam roared, shocking Jillian into clarity.

Junior had recovered and held a small box in his hand. *Detonator?*

Ruth shimmered and disappeared. Back on his feet, Tom rushed Sam. Junior raised the detonator. "Let the world know what happened here today," he shouted.

Jillian struggled onto her hands and knees. Blood dripped to the floor. She lifted Jackson's gun, gripped it with both hands, levelled it at Junior's chest—and pulled the trigger. The discharge sounded unusually loud. Junior's eyes widened. His fingers loosened; he fell to his knees. Holding Tom at bay with her pistol, Sam plucked the detonator from Junior's hand as he sank to the floor. Jillian dropped Jackson's gun and swayed, struggling to remain conscious.

A piercing wail made the hairs on the back of her neck stand up. "You killed him!" Andy took Junior into his arms and rocked him. Tears rolling down his cheeks, he looked at Jillian in disbelief. "You killed him."

She sagged onto her side, curled into a ball, and closed her eyes.

Chapter Twenty-Two

Jillian lay still and listened to her surroundings. What was that hum? And why was the floor cushy? She opened her eyes a crack. A face swam before her. "Jane?"

"Oh, you're back with us. Good."

"Where are we?" she asked, not quite ready to sit up and have a look around.

"On a plane."

A plane?

"How do you feel?"

Her head! She probed with her fingers. Dry. "My head's filled with cobwebs, but otherwise, all right." With a groan, she pushed herself upright. "You look great," she blurted. Not a hint of a bruise, and Jane's eyes were clear.

Jane's forehead creased. "Much better than last time you saw me, I'm sure."

"I'm so sorry. I wanted to help you, but—"

Jane shook her head. "I understand why you couldn't."

"Still." Realizing they were aboard the Fellowship's plane, she looked for Sam and Ruth. Sam was fast asleep across the aisle. "What happened?" she asked as she continued searching for Ruth.

"You'll have to ask them when they wake up."

"I'm awake," a voice piped up from behind them. Rustling, then Ruth sank into the seat next to Jane. She tipped her head toward Sam. "She took care of Jane, the brunt of the healing. Your head and nose weren't as challenging."

Jillian touched her nose.

"It was broken."

"Really? I don't remember feeling much pain, but I wasn't thinking straight." She scrunched up her face. "Was there a detonator?"

Ruth nodded. "Unfortunately, we didn't have enough time to find it before Junior regained consciousness."

Her breath caught in her throat. "Oh my god, I killed him." She gazed at Ruth in horror. "I killed Junior."

"You stopped him from blowing everyone to smithereens."

But she'd killed someone. She'd taken another life.

"You didn't have a choice," Ruth said.

She didn't have to pull the trigger.

Ruth's eyes bored into Jillian. "Would it have been better to spare his life so he could take it himself, along with everyone else's?"

It would have been better if none of it had happened at all, but . . . "I suppose not." That didn't mean she'd let herself off the hook, though. Could she have handled it differently? Should she have volunteered to inject Jane and then dropped the vial? Should she have spoken so harshly and honestly to a group that was too deluded to reach? Why the hell had she shot to kill? She should have thought it through. Maybe she should have shot his hand or arm.

"Don't do that," Ruth said.

"What?"

"That. It's done."

Not for her, but she appreciated Jane's supportive nod of agreement. "What happened after I passed out?"

"With their leader dead, the rest were primarily concerned with saving their own skins. We let them go."

Her jaw dropped. "You let them go?"

Ruth raised her hand. "For now. Our goal was to extract you and Jane. Now that you're safe, we'll figure out what to do about everyone else."

"They must be confused. I don't think anyone expected my mother to crash the party."

"I spun them some yarn about Sam convincing me to get you out of the soul healers as soon as possible. I said she had some counselling experience and our meeting with you that morning had made her suspicious."

"You mean, you made her out to be some sort of deprogrammer?"

"Something like that." Ruth's mouth turned up at the corners.

"Nobody saw *me* with a gun, and I'd shifted back in so quickly that nobody noticed I was gone."

"How did you explain them all passing out?"

Ruth shrugged. "They didn't ask. They had more pressing problems on their minds. Once they accepted that we weren't after them, we came to an agreement." A smile played on her lips. "They helped carry you and Jane to the car."

"You're kidding."

"No."

"I shot Junior." They should have been out for her blood, not sliding her into a backseat and waving her on her way.

"Only Andy saw it happen. Tom's attention was on Sam, and everyone else was still out."

"But Junior's obviously dead. Once the police interview Andy . . . What agreement did you reach?"

"Never mind that for now." She patted Jillian's knee. "Relax. After a rest and a good meal, we'll meet and discuss our next move. I feel like a cup of tea. Anyone want one?"

"No, thank you," Jane said. Jillian shook her head.

Ruth rose and sidled down the aisle. Jane crossed her legs. "I've never been to the island. Is it nice?"

A lump rose in Jillian's throat. "It's beautiful."

EVEN THOUGH SHE was safe on the island, Jillian dreaded hearing that the police were interested in talking to a Jillian Harwick in connection with the shooting death of Junior. They'd have a description and address, and they would have spoken to Andy, Jackson, Tom, anyone else who'd had contact with her. It was time to face the music.

Refreshed and alert after a good sleep, long shower, and decent meal, she strode into the conference room and self-consciously settled into a chair. "You look much better," Roberta said from her habitual spot in front of the control panel.

"I feel better," Jillian said, admiring Roberta's tact and restraint. She'd freaking shot Junior and must have the authorities nipping at her heels. Her disappointment with herself, her mixed emotions over pulling the trigger, the mess the Fellowship would have to clean up . . . not a good showing on her first serious case, and she was wearing her acute sense of failure on her face. Sam and Ruth were seated across from her; she couldn't bring herself to meet their eyes. "I imagine the police are looking for me." Might as well put it out there and take it on the chin.

Roberta blinked at her. "No, they're not."

What?

"Here's a news report from earlier this morning," Roberta said, turning on the monitor.

Jillian leaned back and watched the report, which raised more questions than it answered: "And now an update on the shocking find we first told you about last night. Acting on a tip, police have taken Jackson Peters into custody for questioning in relation to what authorities have confirmed is a triple-homicide investigation. Peters owns the property where police found the remains of the three murdered women. Sandy Rodriguez is standing by outside the Peters home. Sandy . . ."

"Good morning, Jean." The woman touched her earpiece. "I'm standing outside Peters' home, located in an upscale, gated community, and today, a shocked community. Late last night, police discovered several bodies on the grounds of the Peters home, which explains the presence of the coroner," Rodriguez said, as the camera zoomed in on the coroner's van. "Peters belongs to the Association of the Sacred Souls, commonly known as the soul healers. We don't know yet whether the police will extend their investigation to the organization. All they're saying right now is that Peters is a person of interest."

"So he's not a suspect?" the anchor asked.

"Well, they're being careful not to say he's a suspect, but you'd have to think he's on their list."

"That was from a few hours ago. Here's a later one." Roberta pushed a button on the control panel. Rodriguez again: "Police just updated us on their investigation. We can now report that Anthony Lancaster Jr. is wanted for the murder of three women."

"What?" Jillian shrieked.

"Lancaster Jr. is the leader of the soul healers, and police are worried that he's used the cult's financial resources to leave the country. According to those close to him, including Peters, Lancaster Jr. hasn't been seen for several days and had been acting strangely for the past couple of months."

"Stop, stop," Jillian said, reeling. "How can they think Junior's skipped the country? He's dead."

"The authorities don't know he's dead." Roberta turned off the monitor. "We didn't send them to the cabin. We tipped them to Jackson's location after they'd left the cabin and were on the move."

Jillian's stomach flip-flopped. "So Junior's rotting on the cabin's living room floor?"

"No, he's in the graveyard," Sam said. "We buried him this morning."

"They don't have a body," Ruth added, "and since Jackson murdered the poor girls buried on his property, he's more than happy to implicate Junior, especially since he knows Junior's never going to resurface and contradict his story. Nobody else will, either. They want the authorities to spin their wheels searching for Junior."

Oh my god, Junior's body had been on the plane. "What about Andy? He saw me shoot Junior."

Roberta shook her head. "You and Andy ran off together, remember? Everyone at the learning centre knows that."

"Where is he?" Jillian asked, afraid of the answer.

"He's with someone experienced in gently re-acquainting cult members with their former selves."

"Once he's himself again, he'll go to the police."

"Everyone will contradict his story. He wasn't even at the cabin. Neither were you." Roberta raised her brows. "They won't squeal on you, and you won't tell the police what Junior intended to do to Jane, while they all watched. We also believe it likely that Andy will accept our offer to become a Supporter. He won't turn you in."

"We're bringing him into the Fellowship?"

"It's the best way to keep him quiet, and his faith was misplaced, not insincere."

Jillian couldn't quibble with that.

"Jillian . . ." Roberta's voice softened. "Pat, the woman you told us about. She was one of the women found on Jackson's property. In fact, we believe her murder might have been what set off Junior. The other women were cult members for years. Their families had given up on them. But Pat was relatively new, and her parents were still trying to get her out. Junior knew it was only a matter of time before they went to the authorities and reported her missing."

Jillian swallowed. Poor Pat. Would it be any consolation to Pat's family that her murder had acted as the catalyst for Junior's flight, and led to his death and likely the destruction of the cult? Probably not. "I didn't know her well, but . . ." Life sucked. "We can't let that son of a bitch Jackson get away with it."

Roberta nodded. "We don't intend to. I've asked Brian to rectify the situation."

Jillian didn't give a damn what Roberta meant by that. Jackson deserved whatever was coming his way. "The rest of them were complicit, too."

"We're not sure about that. We know Junior and Jackson were thick as thieves, but we don't have any reason to believe that the others knew about the murders. They were cult members who followed Junior, no questions asked."

And sat by while Jackson beat women. What did they think had happened to those they never saw again? Did they even notice? "They all knew that Junior was going to give Jane a lethal overdose. Maggie wasn't there, but she must have suspected."

"You're right, but we'll have to look the other way as far as they go." Roberta paused. "We want them to keep quiet about what happened at the cabin."

Jillian wanted the floor to swallow her up.

"All of it, Jillian. Not just your part."

Jillian gave Roberta a grateful nod and finally looked across the table at Ruth and Sam. "Thank you for getting me out of there." She had more questions, particularly for Sam. But first she'd digest what she'd just heard, and hope that she'd stop seeing Junior's eyes widening in shock at the fatal wound in his chest. She'd killed him. Jesus, she'd killed him. "Where's Jane?"

"She's working in my garden," Ruth said with a smile. "It's very therapeutic. In fact, if there's nothing else, I'd like to go and join her."

"That's all for now," Roberta said. "We'll touch base later." Everyone except Roberta pushed back their chairs. "Jillian, would you stay for a moment, please."

Jillian lowered herself back down.

Roberta waited until Ruth had pulled the door shut. "You were supposed to save yourself."

"I know, but when Andy came for me, I didn't know what was going on. I didn't know that Junior had decided to run and we were going to hole up in some cabin. I didn't know that Jane would be along, Jackson would be beating the shit out of her, and Junior was trying to cleanse her by shooting her up. You didn't really expect me to walk away, knowing that Jane wouldn't stand a chance?" Her voice rose. "I know I screwed up by shooting Junior. I accept responsibility for that. But there's no way I'm going to apologize for sticking around to protect Jane." Her chest heaving, she stared at Roberta, but couldn't read her face.

The silence stretched on. Jillian clasped her hands so she wouldn't fidget, then jumped when Roberta rolled back her chair and stood. "I'll have something for you and Sam soon. Why don't you get some practice in on your guitar? I'd like to hear you play sometime."

Jesus. The thought of performing for Roberta terrified her. Why the hell did Roberta want to hear her pluck away on her guitar? And was that it? She turned her head when Roberta patted her shoulder, and watched her move to the door and open it. "When you . . . recruited me, I told you I wouldn't be a good fit," Jillian said, not sure whether she'd disappointed Roberta, or what.

Roberta rested her hand on the door handle and turned toward her. "On the contrary, you're an excellent fit." She turned and left.

Confused, Jillian surveyed the empty conference room and decided to tell Sam about the short conversation. Maybe she could shed some light, help Jillian deduce if she'd just received an A or an F. But after checking the study, the library, the kitchen, and knocking on Sam's bedroom door, she concluded that Sam had left the house. She was probably in the chapel, maybe praying to be freed from her annoying green sidekick. Jillian chuckled, but then she saw Junior's eyes widening and heard Andy's wail.

SAM DESCENDED THE steps to the undercroft and went straight to the display case that held the record of the cell's twelfth century Deiforms. She raised the lid, lifted out the English translation someone had produced in the nineteenth century, and carefully placed it on the table. Ambrose and Paul, Ruth had said. On the second page, the scribe had thoughtfully written an alphabetical list of names. Alexander,

Ambrose and Paul, Augusta, Bernice . . . why were Ambrose and Paul listed together? A quick scan of the list indicated that they were the only pair.

She carefully turned the pages until she reached their entry. The spidery script and older English were challenging, but she understood enough to make her jaw clench. Only the tempering effect of her dismay prevented her from throwing the precious book across the room. *Why are You doing this to me?* What about Jerome and Valeria? Hoping and dreading at the same time, Sam found the twentieth century translation of the seventh century record and sank back into the chair. She almost couldn't bear to read it. Jerome and Valeria . . . her dismay deepened to despair. *Why?* Tears prickled at her eyelids. No. No, no, no. The dam held.

Why? I've done everything You've called me to do. For half her life, she'd faithfully served, done whatever Roberta asked of her, willed her way through the dark periods of doubt and resentment. She'd stopped envying people clustered at bus stops, drinking and chatting on cafe patios, walking their dogs, strolling arm in arm, stopped wondering what it was like to have a normal life, because she didn't know anymore. She'd accepted her purpose, given her all to every investigation, found contentment in her books, music—and solitude. She'd made peace with her lot in this life, had embraced the wonder and privilege of her role, and let go of the rest. Then Roberta had called about the older than usual reluctant Fledgling.

Did Roberta know? Had she always known? Sam returned the books to their cases and marched back to the house, hoping she wouldn't run into Jillian. It wasn't her fault. She'd likely be just as horrified when she found out. Sam stopped short on the front steps. Maybe she was jumping the gun. So Jillian had sensed her? So what? One incident? It could have been a fluke. And *had* Jillian sensed her? Maybe she'd tried to communicate periodically, hoping her fellow Deiforms had followed her back to the cabin. She hadn't known Sam was there; she'd simply pushed out a thought at the right moment and mistaken luck for certainty. Sam thought back to their short conversation. *"You know I'm here?"* she'd asked. *"Yes, I do,"* Jillian had replied. Well, of course she'd known at that point; Sam had spoken to her. Still, it wouldn't hurt to feel out Roberta.

Sam found her in the library, her nose in a theology book. "Do you think Jillian's ready to work on her own yet?" she asked, knowing that Roberta wanted her to work with Jillian on a few more cases, regardless of whether Jillian was ready to go solo.

Roberta lifted her head. "What do you think?"

"I think you're not telling me something." Sam folded her arms. "What aren't you telling me?"

"You'll have to be more specific." Roberta tucked a bookmark into the book and set it on the round table next to her. "I don't tell you a lot of things."

"Why do you want us to work together?"

"I've already explained that to you," Roberta said calmly. "We lost Jim. I don't want to lose Jillian. I'll feel more comfortable if she works with you for a bit. From what you described, she almost got herself killed at the cabin."

Sam shook her head. "When Jackson pulled out his gun, I could see that she was about to shift. She would have survived."

"And then what?"

"And then, we don't know. Junior might not have flipped out if Ruth and I hadn't burst in. Under the circumstances, Jillian did everything right."

Roberta's eyes danced. "You mean, she did what you would have done, including staying to protect Jane. Well, I suppose you trained her."

"Why did you ask me to train her?" Sam said levelly.

"Why don't you sit down?"

"No. I'm fine."

Roberta frowned up at her. "Tell me what this is about. If you're looking for an answer, the quickest way to get it will be to ask the question."

It would also be the swiftest way to shatter Sam's denial, but she'd rather have ample warning than wonder what was happening at the worst moment. She didn't want to repeat the terror and confusion she'd experienced when she was nineteen and involuntarily shifted. "Something happened at the cabin."

"What happened?"

Sam sank into a chair. "I was projecting, scoping out the place. Jillian didn't know Ruth and I had followed her back. She wasn't expecting us to be there." She flexed her clammy hands.

"And?" Roberta prompted.

Sam swallowed. "She sensed me. She spoke to me, before I spoke to her."

Roberta's expression didn't change. No surprise, no nod, nothing to indicate whether she was hearing something unexpected.

"Ruth told me to look up Jerome and Valeria, and Ambrose and Paul." She studied Roberta's face, but couldn't glean anything.

"I'm a little surprised that you've come to me with this so soon," Roberta finally said. "I thought you'd chew on it more."

"You knew, then." Normally Sam liked to be right, but not this time.

"I had an inkling. I wasn't sure. I'm still not sure. Jillian sensing you could be the joint gifts stirring, or it could have been . . ."

"A fluke?"

"Perhaps."

"That's what I'm hoping for."

Roberta leaned forward. "Why?"

"Because I like to work alone."

"We'll have to see what happens. The two of you were going to work together for a while anyway. Time will tell us whether that arrangement will be temporary or permanent. I expect you to tell me if more joint gifts surface."

"Until today, I didn't even know about the joint gifts."

Roberta waved a dismissive hand. "There was no reason to know about them. You can't train in them. Unless the Lord bestows them, and He rarely does, you can't use them. You have to admit, if it turns out you have them, they will be of tremendous help."

She'd rather work alone. "What about Jillian? I don't think we should say anything until we know for sure."

"Sam!" Roberta's exasperation came through loud and clear. "How can we not tell her?"

"I don't want her growing . . . dependent on me for no reason. We're not sure, right? If another gift surfaces, I'll tell her. I promise."

Roberta's eyes narrowed. "It could be frightening for her."

Sam thought about a couple of the joint gifts she'd just learned about. "It'll be frightening, even if she knows. As you said, we can't train them. They're like boons in that sense."

"I suppose so." Roberta tapped her lower lip as she studied Sam.

"All right, keep it to yourself for now, but if either of you experiences a joint gift, don't keep her in the dark." She wagged a finger. "Do you understand?"

"I won't." She rose. "I'm going to the chapel." The Lord sometimes answered prayers. She rarely knelt and begged Him for something, but today, she'd make an exception.

HER GUITAR RESTING across her lap, Jillian gazed out at the water. It was difficult to play when she couldn't get Junior's death out of her mind. She forced herself to think about the news report she'd watched before finally grabbing her guitar and heading outside. The soul healers were in a shambles, much to the delight of families who'd desperately missed their loved ones. The cameras had captured the happy reunions—well, happy for those whose eyes were alive. She hadn't required captions to tell her who the former cult members were. They were the ones stiffening when they were hugged, their dull eyes staring at nothing. Counsellors and cult experts were on hand to help ease everyone's transition into the real world, but how many minds would remain imprisoned? Would Christine return to university? At least she wouldn't need rescuing from the cult, but she wouldn't have joined if Jillian hadn't stood by and watched. Would she come away from every investigation burdened with guilt? Was it the nature of the beast?

"Can I talk to you for a minute?"

She didn't have to turn around to identify the speaker; she'd grown familiar with Sam's resonant voice. "Sure." She moved her guitar off her lap and waited until Sam had lowered herself onto the rock, then said, "I thought you'd be sick of me by now."

Sam hugged her legs to her chest. "I remember how I felt the first time I killed someone. I thought I'd see how you're doing."

"Does it ever get easier?"

"No."

Despite herself, Jillian chuckled. "You don't need to be gentle with me. Just give it to me straight."

"Would you want it to get easier?" Sam snapped.

Her amusement died. "No, I wouldn't. It would be nice to be able to stop thinking about it, though."

"Give it time." Sam turned to her. "You have nothing to feel guilty about. You shot him in self-defence."

"I didn't have to kill him."

"If you hadn't, he would have blown the place to kingdom come."

Jillian slowly exhaled. "We don't know that for sure."

"Come on, you know it's a pretty safe bet. Another second and the cabin would have been an inferno."

"*You* didn't shoot him," Jillian pointed out.

"I had someone charging at me."

Fair enough, but Jillian realized what had nagged her about those few seconds. "You didn't shift, either. You told us to shift. Why didn't you?"

"Someone had to stop him."

"But why you? Why tell us to shift and go after him by yourself? If he'd pressed the button . . ."

Sam chewed her lip. "You and Ruth would have been safe—if you'd shifted."

"I heard you, but I was confused, and then I saw Jackson's gun right there," she said as she pondered Sam's response. She had trouble believing that Sam had risked herself to save those in the cabin. Jane, maybe, but the rest . . . Andy was a gray area. The Fellowship had offered him a new life because he'd witnessed the shooting. How many other Supporters would take such secrets to their graves? "I don't know if I would have been able to shift. I wanted to shift when Jackson pointed his gun at me. It wasn't as easy . . . If you hadn't arrived, I probably would have managed it, but I don't know." Her head had felt fuzzier than a baby blanket, making it difficult to reach her centre.

"As your gifts grow stronger, you'll be able to cut through pain and confusion." Sam scratched her nose and abruptly changed the subject. "Can I ask you something about the cabin?"

"What?"

"When you called out to me, when I was projecting, had you figured that we'd followed you and you were trying to make contact?"

Jillian thought back. "No. I wasn't thinking about you at all. I was trying to get through to Andy. Then I suddenly sensed you were there. It was a bit of a shock, to be honest. I actually turned around expecting to see you." She snorted. "You said we can't sense each other projecting."

Sam's face tightened. "That's what I was taught."

"You've never sensed someone else?"

"I've never tried."

Jillian gave her a sidelong glance. Should she suggest that sometimes it was just a matter of trying, that testing the boundaries was sometimes all it took? No, she wouldn't, because she'd always played by the rules, so lecturing Sam would be a bit rich. Jillian had taken most of what she'd been taught at face value, rarely questioned, rarely pushed. How long had she gone to church and mouthed the words? Hell, as she'd told Sam, she hadn't been trying to make contact, so she couldn't take credit for conducting a bold experiment. "I wasn't trying, either," she said again.

They sat in silence for a minute. "I know you want to work alone, but Roberta still thinks we should work together for now," Sam said, staring out at the water.

"Now you're doing a different sort of projecting," Jillian said with amusement. "I'm not the one chomping at the bit to be a solo act." Which was weird. When she'd worked for the agency, she'd avoided meaningful attachments. She'd known that her friendships would last only as long as her current assignment, and she'd been perfectly okay with that. When she was home between operations, she'd told herself that having friends wouldn't be practical. Her numbness had spared her from feeling lonely. But now . . .

She'd be lying to herself if she didn't admit that she'd grown attached to Sam. Maybe it was because she'd lost everyone else, or that Sam had seen her at her most vulnerable, or that she didn't feel the need to wear her "I'm the most confident and self-assured woman in the world" mask and protect herself with Sam. From day one, she'd risked being honest with her, and it had only become easier to be herself. She enjoyed the freedom. At this point, to see Sam only in passing when they both happened to be on the island didn't appeal to her at all. "Don't worry. I'm determined to show that I'm capable of working on my own," she said, forcing a light tone to cover her mixed feelings about it. "Though I'm not sure Roberta was impressed by my performance. She reminded me that I was supposed to save myself and didn't say much beyond that. I couldn't tell how she thought I did. What do you think? Do you think I did okay?"

Sam gave her a puzzled look. "Why do you always want a score?"

"I don't know, I guess I'm used to receiving performance reviews."

"In that case, you'll be pleased to know that everything you've done will be taken into consideration during the only performance review that will count."

Jillian bit her tongue. "I was hoping for a hint in the here and now." And apparently she wasn't going to get one, she concluded when Sam remained silent. Nobody had read her the riot act and Roberta had said she'd have something for them to work on soon. Based on that, Jillian would assume that she hadn't completely screwed up. "Has Ruth talked to Jane about Amanda yet?"

"They had a conversation about it over Ruth's tomatoes."

Jillian smiled. "What did she tell her?"

"The truth. That we know Andy delivered the drugs to Junior, and that Junior was alone in the room with Amanda. But we don't know if Junior killed Amanda, or if she committed suicide or accidentally overdosed."

"Given what happened at the cabin, I'm pretty sure Junior killed her."

"But we don't know for sure." Sam paused. "I wasn't sure we should mention the suicide possibility, but Ruth wanted to tell her everything."

"I hope Jane and Andy never work together."

"She sees him as a victim." Sam met Jillian's eyes. "She sees Amanda as a victim. Even if she committed suicide, the soul healers provided the means and probably drove her to it. But I'm with you. I don't think she did."

"I'm glad Jane's here. She needs a rest." The bruises and all traces of Junior's poison were gone, but physical wounds often healed quicker than emotional ones—especially when a Deiform was involved.

"Me too." Sam stood. "You did well, getting the information from Andy. It's given Jane some peace. As for everything that happened at the cabin . . ." She squinted down at Jillian. "You'd pass a performance review." She walked away.

Jillian leaped to her feet and whirled. "Sam!"

Sam turned.

"Do you want to go for a walk or something?

Sam stared at her, then jerked her thumb over her shoulder. "I'm in the middle of a book."

Jillian shoved her hands into her pockets. "See you . . . later, then." She turned back to the water and let out a heartfelt sigh.

BREAKING NEWS: Police announced new developments today in the soul healers triple murder investigation. Jackson Peters, a high-ranking member of the now defunct cult and the owner of the property where the three bodies were discovered, was found dead today of an apparent suicide. Police spokesman Constable Davies said that drug paraphernalia was found near Peters' body, but police won't know the cause of death until they receive toxicology results from the coroner.

According to sources within the police department, Peters left behind a suicide note in which he confessed to the murders of the three women. While police would still like to speak with Anthony Lancaster Jr., the former leader of the cult, they no longer consider him a suspect.

Other titles by Sarah Ettritch

Threaded Through Time
The Salbine Sisters
The Rymellan Series
The Missing Comatose Woman

If you'd like to be notified when the next Deiform Fellowship book is released, sign up for the notification list at Sarah's website: www.sarahettritch.com.

Thanks for reading!

www.ingramcontent.com/pod-product-compliance
Lightning Source LLC
Chambersburg PA
CBHW031232210726

48287CB00003B/751